Northern Darks

Kevin H. Hilton

To Simon

CONTENTS

Misguided   7

The Bunker   60

Beyond Belief   102

Beware of the Postie   134

Trying   212

Shark Bait   257

Misguided

Eddie was sitting on his sofa, distracted again by events, when he was snapped back to the real world as the door-bell of his fourteenth floor apartment rang.

'Bollocks!' he cursed himself for half watching the TV instead of getting prepared.

He immediately grabbed two empty glasses from the coffee table next to a note pad and pen, and went into the kitchen with them. His eyes scanned the room as he went. It was now a practiced routine.

From the kitchen he went straight to the corridor pulling a door closed and locking it, by which time the door-bell rang a second time. Coming back into the lounge and looking the lounge over once again he crossed to the door and opened it.

'Hi Guv,' the younger man greeted him eagerly even before the door was fully open.

'Hi Gavin…Come on in.' Watching his new employee step through, Eddie followed up with something work related. 'How did the delivery go? You're back from Carlisle sooner than I expected.'

Eddie closed the door, but Gavin stopped to answer rather than go all the way into the lounge. 'Oh fine. The 69 was pretty clear and…Rodney was it…? His lads were there to help unload.

'Good.'

'So what's up Guv?'

'Are you in a rush to be elsewhere?'

'Nope…What is it, an urgent pick-up?'

'No…I wanted to have a chat about something.'

'Oh a *chat*,' his shoulders seemed to sag. 'You're not letting us go already are you?'

'No, no. Take a seat.'

Gavin took a seat on the sofa, and looked around the room. He had never been invited in before. It seemed nice enough, but he had somehow imagined something different.

Eddie didn't feel comfortable watching someone look his place over and blurted. 'Do you like Australia?'

'Australia? Bit of a trek for furniture isn't it?'

'No, I mean the Nicole Kidman film,' he said pointing at the TV as he joined Gavin on the sofa.

'Oh…Huh, sorry…I ur…To be honest…I'm not into historical films much.'

'Oh.' Eddie wondered what to say next, not wanting to rush things.

But after a pause to watch a bit of the film Gavin said 'Too much history of my own like.'

'Right,' Eddie said with a nod.

'That's why I'm so grateful to you for giving me this job at your store and all. I'll quite literally do anything to return the favour.'

'No problem.'

'My record didn't bother you, did it?'

'Not overly, no.'

'It made it difficult for me to get work elsewhere you know.' When Eddie had no response to that, Gavin continued, 'I Guess folk think I'm going to need watching.'

'Well, to be honest, I *have* been watching you, through the week.'

'Oh…'

'As I would any employee…' he rushed to add, 'and all things considered I think you could be the right man for the job.'

'That's great, because I really enjoy the work.'

'Good…Glad I've helped you back on the straight and narrow.'

'Aye,' Gavin smiled.

As Eddie continued to watch Gavin he could see he wasn't engaging with the film because his eyes began to wander round the room again. 'So what films *do* you like then Gavin?'

'Films? Oh um Into the Blue.

'Porn.'

'Porn? No, well maybe, but no. Into the Blue is a diving film. I like old stuff like that. The Deep. You know.'

'So you must have liked Jaws then.'

'Actually I had nightmares and found it difficult taking a bath for some weeks after that one.'

'Ha…I guess you must like those undersea documentaries though.'

'Aye, fascinating.'

'Done any diving yourself?'

'No.'

'Well I guess it can be a bit expensive as a regular hobby.'

'Aye, but more importantly you've got to be able to swim.'

'Can you not swim? I thought everyone could swim these days.'

'Not me like,' Gavin's embarrassment was evident in his fidgeting.

'Didn't you have to do it at school?'

'Well I would've if I hadn't been such a truant like.'

'Oh...Well I wasn't too keen on school either. I suppose I just couldn't think what to do with myself in Stevenage if I'd bunked off though.'

'I lost out on quite a few things, me like, thinking I was cool and didn't need to know stuff off others. You know what I mean...If only I could go back in time and make things right.'

'Well why don't you go to the college in the evenings?'

'Oh I cannot be doing with that like, at my age?'

'*Your* age? You're only thirty-something.'

'Aye...But...the college...will be full of kids.'

'So? It would be a great way for you to meet other people too.'

'I just don't think I've the bottle to do that.'

'Nonsense, you had the confidence to come and ask me for a job.'

'That's different. I was desperate.'

'Hmm...Did you get any lessons or workshops when you were inside?'

'Aye, cookery,' he broke into a smile.

'That's useful and you probably enjoyed it.'

Gavin nodded, 'also woodwork, and printmaking.'

'Like screen-printing?'

'Aye. I *really* enjoyed that like, but I cannot afford to buy that sort of kit for a hobby, never mind a business. I don't think I'd get a loan with my record.'

'But surely they'd have the facilities at the college.'

'No! I don't want to be going there. It'll…I might fall back into my old ways.'

'But why would you?'

'I don't deal well with failure or criticism.'

'I tell you what I think would help you build confidence is going to the baths and learning to swim. Once you've got that sorted I bet you'd feel a whole lot better about yourself.'

'I'd be embarrassed.'

'What's a bit of embarrassment for a lifetime of fun eh? You could start dive training then. There's plenty of clubs in the North East.'

'Suppose.'

'You know I'm right.'

'No offence Guv but if I can't afford screen printing kit I don't stand a chance of affording diving gear like, which you said yourself was expensive. And diving would be my only reason to learn to swim.'

'Hang on though, there're cheap flights to the Med, and diving lessons and rental along the coast. Or… you could just swim about with a mask and snorkel. Don't be so quick to talk yourself out of an opportunity.'

'Mmm. But I wouldn't want to go on my own like.'

'Right…Yeah, you said at your interview, you don't have anyone close.'

'No. No family and not much good with the girls…in that way.'

'You need to build up that confidence, like I said. People find a bit of confidence attractive, and of course, being found attractive then boosts your confidence,' explained Eddie, drawing a circle in the air.

'If you say so…You know, once, a girl chucked me only ten minutes into a date. When I asked her why, she said I was 'Just too *dumpable*.'

'Yeah well, some girls are mean, even to confident people like me. Of course you really need to know *who* to ask.'

'Seems I just don't have the first idea about what women want.'

'You've just got to watch'em and listen. Start by working out whether they are fighters or quitters.'

'Fighters? What like kick boxing?'

'No, no. Fighters are the ones who're prepared to work to make it fun. While the quitters are just looking to say it's over at the first wrong step, because they lack confidence themselves.'

'I thought you meant girls who get a bit aggressive like.'

'No…And I'm not just talking women here, I'm talking people. It's more about personality, and the consequences of behaviours, see.'

'Uh huh,' he didn't sound sure. It was all a little too academic for Gavin.

'Quitters cause people to lie, or at least hide things, and encourage you to tell them what they want to hear, just to make things work. Lots of people get by that way.'

'Right.'

'But invariably it doesn't work well. And sadly, by far the majority of people are quitters.'

'You a fighter then Guv?'

'I've tried to be. But you've also got to know when to let go. I've spent a number of years trying to find the right woman.'

'And have you found her?'

'I tried speed dating for a while.'

'I wouldn't be up for that like.'

'Sometimes there're groups of lasses, from the same workplace, just looking to compete against one another's cards for the number of matches the organiser reports back. For a laugh, you know. No real intention of going out with a lad.'

'Oh.'

'Then the others I met were clearly just looking for one night stands, and that's not me.'

'But better than nothing eh Guv?'

'Depends what you're looking for. And I dare say it works for a lot of people or else you couldn't make a business out of speed dating. However, I was after a partner to share life's experiences, not just date. Caring for one another, and doing stuff together. You know.'

'Right…Like diving with dolphins?'

'Well, whatever floats your boat…Anyway, I got to looking on the Internet at dating sights, but frankly I found them a waste of effort. They can take an age to fill in with all the bloody questions at the front end, only to provide you with next to no real matches.'

'You'd have thought, with all the people on the Internet, it would be easy to find a good match.'

'Absolutely…And with all that social networking being as popular as it is, but hell, relationships are still bloody difficult to arrange. I did wonder whether I was being too picky…Then I started to find all this other stuff on Russian wives and the like.'

'Russian wives?'

'Yeah, a number of countries have taken to promoting women.'

'Promoting?'

'Well…Selling more often than not.'

'Selling?...You're not thinking of buying yourself a wife! Is that what this chat's about?' Gavin returned to wondering why he had been asked round, and felt uncomfortable again.

'No.' Eddie could see he needed to put him at ease. 'What I'm saying is…whatever you want, it *is* out there. The Internet has opened it all up…but you do have to be careful, obviously.'

'Right,' he still couldn't see where this was leading.

'There are some sites out there that focus on getting your details, promising to fulfil your dreams, asking all these questions about your perfect partner, promising to act as a more successful introduction agency.'

'Right.'

'They know that some people will see this as a service worth paying over the odds for. And once the person gets to the end of the detailed description process their fantasy partner seems real and as good as found. That's when the site asks for payment.'

'How much like?'

'Steep…Yet many people do pay it.'

'What happens then?'

'Nothing.'

'Nothing?'

'No Gavin, nothing. It's a bogus site. You'd wait and wait, and hope and hope, but you'd hear nothing, your money gone, with no idea how to get it back, or who to complain to. Writing to the contact email address it just bounces. And most people wouldn't want to own up to having been suckered like that anyway.'

'A neat scam.'

'Then there're others which do match you up, but it's always a foreign woman, and one of many they're looking to get into our country.'

'How do you know about all this? Did it happen to you Guv?'

'Uh, yeah...The no reply scam...I had to change my account in case they cleaned me out.'

'Shit.'

'But it taught me a lesson.'

'I'll bet.'

'Do you want a drink?'

'Yeah sure.'

'Old Speckled Hen?'

'Ur.'

'Or a Carlsberg maybe. We have other options.'

'We?'

'Mm?'

'You said *we*. I thought you lived on your own Guv.'

'Oh...I... actually live with...Liridona.'

'Liridona?'

Eddie's slip had opened the can of worms earlier than he'd intended, but now it was done it seemed best to get on with it. 'Yeah.'

'Ffff.'

'What?' Eddie didn't understand what seemed so amusing.

'Sorry Guv. I've never heard that name before. Sounds like Liridona's parents were a bit new-age like, for not settling with a simple Donna.'

'Actually, her parents...are...not good folk.'

'Oh?'

'I took her in off the street.'

'What, she's a whore like?'

'No, no...But she could easily have ended up one.'

'So a homeless person then?

'Not exactly…She came from Albania.'

'Oh an American?'

'No…Albanian.'

'Sorry, I was never too good at geography.'

'Albania's over near Greece.'

'Okay...' Gavin didn't look any the wiser. 'Does she keep in touch with her folks?'

'Hell no…She's not to talk to anyone...For her own safety you understand.'

'What? Is she a runaway like, with people after her and that?'

'Yeah, that's one way of putting it.'

'So one of them illegal immigrants?'

'Yeah.'

'Whatever are you doing with someone like that Guv?'

'She needed somewhere decent to live.'

'Why didn't she just move somewhere else in Albania, instead of coming here? I know I wouldn't run off to be with a bunch of foreigners if I got into trouble here.'

'Of course you wouldn't…But you see Albania's one of those countries that's in a bit of a mess. She had to get away to survive, but then got caught up with traffickers.'

'So you met her when you were…buying drugs?'

'Not exactly, no,' he shook his head. 'Do you want that drink?'

'Uh, yeah.'

'Which?'

'Oh urr…the Carlsberg, please.'

Eddie went to the kitchen and returned with two opened cans of beer. Handing Gavin one he turned the TV off before sitting back down again. 'They were on offer at the supermarket, twelve for the price of eighteen.'

'Bargain.'

'I mean eighteen for the price of twelve.'

'Even better.'

'Mind you, the price they charge for stuff these days, their idea of an offer is more like *not ripping you off but wanting you to thank them for it.*'

'Aye, it is,' Gavin had no argument with that.

'Like all that loyalty card racket. They're just charging you extra on everything and giving you a bit of that back as a reward for being a chump.'

'Is that right?'

'Sure. As far as they are concerned it's good business. Like making shopping at their store more convenient than their competitors, like the corner shops, by offering free parking, wider choice, and bargains.'

'Aye, it does make it much easier, unless you have a very good corner shop like.'

'Well there're none left near here now.'

'No.'

'I don't like the way these business millionaires are all out for themselves, just legal gangsters, with their henchmen managers, trying to make out that they have your interests at heart, whilst slowly pulling the carpet out from under you. The bastards…They seem to be untouchable though, taking whatever liberties they choose.'

'Aye…My Dad was a supermarket manager.'

'Oh…right…What is he now?'

'Dead…Took a shock off a freezer unit, which threw him into one of those shelf packer trollies. His head got caught in a strap on it and it broke his neck… Just like *that* they said,' he clicked his fingers for emphasis. 'The packer close by said it was a bit unnatural like…like a scene out of a Final Destination film.'

'I'm sorry Gavin, I didn't…'

'No, no. At least it got into the local papers. Shop Shock Gallows, it read…But it was sort of fitting…he really *was* a bastard.'

'Where I used to live, there was this old git across the road, real snooty sort. He was in our neighbourhood watch…and some kind of big-firm high-flyer before he retired and started putting more of his time into the church.'

'I fucking hate church-goers like. Yelling from the Monument, like any of us wants to listen to how we're all doomed…Fuck.'

Gavin's burst of negativity surprised Eddie. '*Oh dear*, and this chat was to see if you'd come to bible class.'

'What?!'

'Just messing with you.'

'Thank God.'

'Anyway…So I got possessed of this need to test this old git's holier than thou attitude.'

'Why?'

'Well, at one of the neighbourhood watch meetings, he started spouting off what should be done about criminals, without any consideration of why they might have ended up like that.'

'Like those posters about youths I've seen around that say Don't Demonise, Realise.'

'Yeah I guess…So I got this urge to see whether he would ever do anything criminal himself.

'So what did you do like? Slip an *e* into his tea?'

'No I pinched his little sports car off his driveway one night and hid it at the back of my garage.'

'Ha ha…but…how did that test him?'

'Well, I waited till he had claimed on the insurance and got his replacement. Then I put it back.'

'Oh mmm,' he nodded. '…I don't get it.'

'I wanted to see if he'd report it, or keep it.'

'Why shouldn't he keep it? It *was* his.'

'Because he'd got another on insurance, and you're supposed to notify them if the stolen vehicle is found.'

'Ffff.'

'Now, the replacement he'd gotten didn't look as good, so I reckon he was a bit short-changed by the insurers…They're all after easy money, never keen on holding up their side of the deal…So he must have felt justified in the eyes of his god.'

'So what did he do?'

'I watched him drive it away, before anyone saw it. I did think he might drive it to the police. But a week later it was back, a different colour. And he'd changed the number plate.'

'How do you know it was the same one like?'

'It had the same little dent on the right of the front bumper.'

'Maybe he just got the bumper switched.'

'Ur no...I don't think he would have done that.' Eddie frowned at the suggestion.

'I'd have sold it, and gone on holiday.'

'Well I just wanted to see if I could turn him.'

'What would you have done if you'd been caught?'

'I was going to claim I was testing our neighbourhood watch out, if I was spotted taking it. Not so sure what I was going to say if I was caught putting it back though.'

'Tricky.'

'Well sometimes we do things before we've thought through all the consequences...Mind you, by then there was quite a bit of bad feeling in the neighbourhood watch, as no one had seen the car get taken. He'd made such a fuss about the lack of vigilance, and pointlessness of the group, that I don't think people felt so inclined to keep an eye on his property after that.'

'How did you know how to take a car anyways?'

'What is this, twenty questions?' Eddie sounded a little prickly.

'Sorry Guv. Just inquisitive like.'

'No worries. I used to do a bit of joyriding in Stevenage when I was a lad.'

Gavin nodded. 'I used to shop lift.'

'So…I'll have to start checking your pockets for furniture then.'

'No Guv, you can trust me now like.'

'I'm joking.'

'Oh…right,' he frowned, he couldn't tell when Eddie was being serious.

'Was it about the thrill for you too?'

Gavin nodded, 'But mainly for pocket money like. I used to sell stuff to mates.'

'And I'm guessing it got out of hand.'

'Aye, straight out of my hand and into someone else's,' he attempted a joke.

'Ha.' Eddie appreciated it.

'I started break-ins with this other lad who was doing it for drugs money. And I got this job serving in a bar when I was nineteen, which proved a good way of finding new buyers for my lifted goods.'

'Didn't you ever worry that someone might turn you in? Or you'd find out an interested buyer was actually police?'

'Sometimes, but it was a risk I continued to take.'

'So exactly how did you end up doing time?'

'I made a mistake.'

'No,' Eddie said in mock surprise.

'Aye. I do make mistakes…There was this lass…

'Oh here we go.'

'No, no. Not a girlfriend like…I used to hang around the university and college campuses, looking for students carrying laptop cases like. To follow them home. See where they lived, and then when they were out I'd go in and take what I could.

'You wouldn't believe the way these kids make no attempt to hide stuff like. Leaving it all over, in the open, ready for the taking, you know what I mean.'

'Did you never feel guilty about stealing from individuals, rather than say businesses?'

'Not often no. They had more than me.'

'What if that was all they had?'

'Don't know. Never bothered thinking about that like.'

'So this girl…?'

'Aye…So I staked out her flat on the next evening I had off from the bar like, and waited for her to leave. I thought she'd gone out, as I saw a few of them go off down the pub. Flat mates and friends I guess. Anyhow the lights were off, so I went in round the back. Used a wheelie bin to jump over the wall into the yard, then jimmied a window open and was in. But this lass, she'd stayed home, it turns out…with a migraine.

'Oh dear.'

'I started by rooting through the downstairs rooms. Always went for the easy stuff first. Then I headed upstairs, and was at the top when she came at me like some ninja, kicked me to the wall, then up the side of my head. I fair cart wheeled down those stairs. It's a wonder I didn't break my neck.

'I remember sitting in the police cell after my interview, thanking my lucky stars she'd been sick with that fucking migraine, or I'd probably have been dead.'

'Quite a story.'

'Aye and there's more. I then found she was trying to get me done for stalking and attempted rape, because it turned out she'd spotted me a couple of times as I'd followed her home.'

'Bad luck. You were out of your league with that one.'

'Aye she was a smart lass, that's a fact…There was no evidence of intent to rape, and as I'd come clean about that burglary, and others, I got off with a lesser sentence they told me.

'But that whole issue of rape stuck with me. I'd never thought about women thinking that, you know what I mean.'

'Was she good looking?'

'Aye, she was gorgeous. Shame I couldn't have met on different terms like. Though I don't know what she'd have seen in me.'

'Don't put yourself down.'

Gavin didn't know what more to say and there followed an end of conversation silence that began to get awkward, before he prompted, 'this woman from Alabama then…?'

'Mm? Oh, Liridona…From Albania.'

'Aye. Is she here…now like?'

'Yes.' Eddie started to look uncomfortable, but pressed on, 'I will introduce you…but before I do, I think I need to explain a few things.'

Gavin shifted his position on the couch. This was promising to get more interesting.

'When people mention slavery, what comes to mind?'

'Black people in America, farming, I guess.'

'Right, but what a lot of people don't appreciate is that people are still being taken and sold across the world as slaves in the twenty-first century.'

'No…To do what?'

'Mainly sex.'

'Like on Taken?'

'Yes, and domestic servitude.'

'I haven't seen that one.'

'No I'm referring to being a house servant.

'Oh.'

'Some are even taken for organ harvesting.'

'Like selling their kidneys?'

'Worse. Like having *all* their organs removed and sold.'

'But they'd…'

'Die yes…According to the human trafficking websites and the like, these slaves, women mainly, tend to get recruited from countries with very poor living conditions, like certain parts of Eastern Europe, Africa, India, and China.'

'What, they just go and ask if they want to be slaves? That cannot be right.'

'No…Usually they are falsely offered work that will be in a factory or office, to get them away. Then they end up captive.'

'Then what?'

'It depends on the abusers needs.'

'You mean sexual needs like?'

'Or sadistic needs…If people have the money and the place to hide someone they can get up to anything, and many of these people are never seen again.'

'Shit…Like the West's?'

'Could be, yeah. Then there are other cases where a network is used, mainly among brothels, so these slaves get passed around.'

'No.'

'Yeah. When girls aren't so popular any more they move them on, or arrange a swap.'

'Shit. For real like?'

'Oh yes…I swear on my mother's ashes. And while there are people with needs like that, prepared to pay, then the recruiters and transporters will continue to supply. It's significant money, worth the risk for some, when they don't value human life as anything more than a roll of notes.'

'Aye, but not many'll get through UK customs though surely?'

'They do if the paperwork's correct. Sometimes it's very good forgeries, but mostly it is authentic papers, just to get them in. Then they get *disappeared* later.

'Disappeared?'

'All part of a plan of course. But usually they rendezvous, with or without a trafficker, in a city centre meeting place like a square or monument, to be picked up by their abusers. You can see them if you watch often enough.'

'But do they not have any idea what's going to happen to them like?'

'A few do.'

'Why do it then?'

'They are desperate for something better. But even if it turns out worse, and they manage to get away, they won't go to the police.'

'Understandable.'

'Many have been told that the police will torture and kill them, so that it ensures they don't even think about going to them. And if the police do manage to intercept them, the system tends to send them back to their own country, where it can start all over again'

'Why don't they just come and get a bar job or something manual?'

'Many do try I guess, and may believe it's been arranged, but it is difficult if you don't have the right papers for working, unless the landlord is a bit dodgy, and in that case such employment could lead to manipulation.'

'Fucking buggered both ways then.'

'Like I said…desperate situations…People who do get work, working in groups, in factory units or farms, work horrendous hours for next to no pay. Just so that we will get better prices on our supermarket products. The thing is you don't know whether or not the salad you eat or the microwave you use has involved such people in their making. We are distanced from it all because we don't know how to question, or don't want to know.'

'I'm not sure *I'd* want to question Guv.'

'That's my point. *We* want to be okay. *We* don't want to find out the things we buy are the product of some *other person's* misery.'

'But what are we supposed to do Guv?'

'Raise our awareness, and report things that don't add up, even if it might turn out we're wrong. There are books about this stuff, like Chinese Whispers, which cover a number of cases, like what happened at Morecombe Bay.'

'What, those people years ago who drowned picking cockles?'

'That's the ones…Mismanaged, often by people from their own country, looking to make as much money as they can out of them. Sometimes the brothels turn slaves into recruiters. Buying them good clothes and jewellery, and sending them back home to tell stories about how easy it is to make money and gain respect as business women. Their families

26

wouldn't want them back if they knew they'd been forced into prostitution…No desire to understand and forgive you see.'

'Why? These lasses have been forced...They didn't choose that work.'

'I know. But some cultures don't value life the same. They see it as more important to manipulate people through social shame which is stronger than family bonding even.'

'Unbelievable.'

'In some African countries they also use religion to manipulate the slaves. And some mothers are used to farm new human stock, and the slaves are told that it's God's work, and if they disobey or run away then their families will be cursed or killed by the hand of God.'

'And they believe that?'

'Yeah…Religion and the fear of God can be very powerful in those communities.'

'Not like here then.'

'No. Not like here.'

Both of them took another mouthful of beer.

'So you saved Liridona from her intended abuse,' Gavin wanted to hear more.

'She had no idea what was going to happen to her. When I picked her up, she was scared. I could tell she was, as I sat across the way, pretending to read a paper. She and her transporter were waiting around for some time. She wasn't the sort I had been considering abducting from these traffickers, but in her case, oh I don't know, I felt I *just* had to do something.'

'So it wasn't total impulse then? You were there planning to abduct someone? To kidnap them like?'

'You make it sound bad Gavin. I saw abduction as rescue under these circumstances, to give someone a chance of a good home.'

'But why didn't you report them, like you said?'

'I was naïve then. I thought if I could save someone in trouble she'd be more likely to love me for it.'

'So, did you go and hit the bastard and run off with her?'

'No. He looked like a real piece of trouble. The abuser was clearly late for the pickup, and maybe the transporter went to check, but I saw him tell Liridona to stay where she was, and he walked off towards Hippy Green.'

'And you took your chance.'

'Yeah I did. I walked straight up to her, confidently like, not in a rush, and said *you're coming with me*, and took her by the arm, firm but not rough, and led her off down Grey Street. I was actually shaking like a leaf, with the adrenalin.'

'And nobody saw you?'

'Well, there *were* lots of people around the Monument that day, but incredibly no one said a thing, and I've never had anyone question me in the street or come for a word in the two years since.'

'Two years?!...But, does that mean she's not been out of here in two years?'

'That's right. But it's been for her own good. She *does* understand that you know.'

'But...but that's like...Being *inside*.'

'I'd rather think it is better than that.'

'Still…House arrest for years could drive a person crazy like, if they don't know how long it will go on for.'

'Well, she *has* had her moments, but I've helped her through them.'

Gavin took a deep breath, as though he was going to say something, but said nothing.

'Probably the worst time for us both was not long after I brought her here, when she got a fever. I thought she was going to die. I was convinced she just needed antibiotics, but doctors are not keen on giving them to people at the best of times.'

'Ffff.'

'So I couldn't even try and get them for myself, to then give her. I couldn't call a health helpline for advice in case I aroused suspicion. I couldn't call in a doctor or health-worker, because I was sure I'd be in deep trouble. The authorities wouldn't care about the good I was doing.

'I was so angry with how things were turning out, as if we hadn't enough to worry about. I mean, how on Earth do you catch a bug like that staying home? I started to wonder if she'd sneaked out of the flat when I was at work. But I thought that unlikely as she has no shoes, coat, or money…'

'No shoes or coat Guv?'

'No need to buy her shoes or a coat when she stays inside. She's got tights and stuff that we get off Amazon, and some thermal socks.'

'But what about what she came in?'

'I threw those shoes and coat away.'

'Why?'

'I suppose I was worried she might run away before she had time to realise what I was doing for her. She was in quite a state for a while.'

'I'll bet.'

'I hadn't been prepared for how she would behave. I had to do a lot around here to ease the situation. And it didn't help that her English was so bad… You know they pick slaves with bad English when coming to the UK to make it more difficult for them to ask for help.'

'Shit…So I'm guessing you have the only phone…on you like…to stop her phoning other Albanians.'

'Well yeah. To remove temptation of course...And our computer is password protected.'

'So how does Liridona feel about that like?'

'At first, before the fever, it wasn't an issue. She was miserable but submissive. She did as she was told. She cried a lot in her room. But soon, I guess because I didn't beat her, she gained confidence and then the arguments began. Well ranting really, what with the language barrier.'

'Had she start refusing to do as she was told?'

'No it wasn't that, the trafficker had told her she was going to work as a cleaner in some factory in Sunderland.'

'Ffff, a narrow escape there then like.'

'She'd expected to be sharing a flat with other women from the factory. So she soon realised I was not the person she was supposed to have been passed onto. She was concerned about her family, because the factory job was supposed to send money back to them to live on. She was in tears telling me her father would beat her mother as a result of her disappearance.'

'Why…was it her mother's idea like?'

Eddie nodded, 'She had heard about work in the UK from people in her town and encouraged Liridona to go for a while to earn money till times got better at home. But Liridona didn't need encouragement to leave. She told me her father had been raping her for some years, when he was drunk, and her mother had found this acceptable, apparently.'

'Why didn't she get a place of her own once she was old enough?'

'With what?'

'Whatever she was earning?'

'The only earnings she made were when her father prostituted her with his friends.'

'Sounds like she really is better off here then…So how did you deal with that fever?'

'Oh, I kept giving her cold baths till she stopped jabbering in Albanian. But all the time I kept thinking, if I caught the virus we could both wind up dead.

'I also started thinking I might have to dispose of her body if she didn't recover. And with the virus it was like she was becoming some resident evil. I didn't feel safe in my own flat.' Eddie seemed to gaze blankly into the past for a few moments. 'But when she did recover, things seemed better between us. The sickness seemed to bond us somehow, and she stopped seeing me as her kidnapper.'

'So is this how it's going to be…forever like?'

'It feels that way sometimes…Till a better solution presents itself.' He paused again as he tried to make a decision. 'I think maybe it's time I introduce her to you.'

Eddie got up from the sofa and went down the corridor, leaving Gavin on the sofa running a hand through his greasy hair, before picking at the skin at the sides of his nails, uncomfortable and unsure how to deal with the developing situation. Eddie could be heard heading back towards the lounge with Liridona but she sounded reluctant to meet anyone.

Still out of sight. She pleaded with him in hushed tones. 'No Eddie I'm scared. Maybe make mistake…Like before.'

'It's fine. You will like Gavin. He *works* for me.'

Gavin stared at the still empty doorway listening with deepening concern, fingers now rubbing lips nervously. Then Eddie entered with Liridona in hand, dressed in jeans and T-shirt.

Gavin got to his feet almost an involuntary reaction. 'Oh my God Guv…How old is she?'

'Fourteen.'

'Fourteen?!' Gavin's body language suggested he wanted to run for it, while Eddie and Liridona stood there looking tense.

'It's okay. *Both* of you!' Eddie tried to keep control of the situation.

'Okay?!' Gavin's voice was almost strangled.

'Yes.'

'Huh. How can it be okay Guv? If anyone finds out they'll say you're a paedo.'

'Rubbish. It's more like being a foster parent.'

'I don't see how like.'

'Think about what I've been telling you. I didn't set out looking for a child. I was after someone to share with, not to have responsibility for. I've had to put all of my own needs on hold because I took pity on Liridona's distressing situation.'

'But haven't you gotten yourselves trapped now. She can't go out, and you can't find a partner.'

'I wouldn't say that. It's not totally impossible that I can find a good woman who understands what I'm doing here, and can help.'

'For the rest of Liridona's life?'

'No!' Liridona protested, looking at Eddie for reassurance.

'No, no. Once she is old enough, the plan is to find a way for her to be free…Somehow.'

'I want to be free now. Like other girls. Like on telly.'

Eddie turned to her, 'We've been through this *so many times*. You know I worry you'll just get picked up and sent home and then I can't help you.'

'I'd look after myself. Like those telly girls.'

'But that is not *real life*. It's sugar coated to make it watchable.'

'East Enders is not sugar coated.'

'Well no, maybe not. Some programmes have a bit of a rough edge…But it doesn't make them real. I let you watch TV to help you cope and learn, but you haven't convinced me you could manage not to get in trouble. Your English still hasn't improved enough. I had thought the TV would be a great way to learn.'

'*It is*. I speak English clearer than you're thinking.'

'No.' Eddie shook his head. 'I'm thinking more clearly than you're speaking English.'

'You're thinking not so good when you put hand down my knickers.'

'That was a mistake!...and I apologised.'

'Fuck...' Gavin's discomfort was going through the roof. 'I think I better be going now, Guv.'

'No!...No, stay. I want you to understand.'

'Oh I do. I do. It's all very difficult like.'

'In the first year, after the fever, she came to me in tears. At first I thought she was having another bad period, but it turned out she was bemoaning not having a boyfriend. She wanted to go clubbing and dating like she'd seen on TV. Then she kissed me and started coming on to me, and it all went wrong, and for a moment I lost control.'

'Then that Christmas you say we had to go bed together.'

'Fucking hell!' It was all too much for Gavin.

'Liridona!' Eddie barked. 'You know why we had to do that...There was that power cut. No light. No heating. No way to make a hot water bottle. I needed you to stay well. Not get sick again.'

'Guv. I'm sure you're a good man like. But I'm not sure how to deal with this right now...I really had best be off.'

'Don't go Gavin.' This time it was Liridona reaching out to him. 'I would like to talk some more.'

'Maybe another time pet.'

'Please Mr Gavin.'

'I...' His concern for the girl urged him not to leave her like this.

'I get you more beer yeah?'

'Urm...'

Liridona dashed to the kitchen. Eddie watched her go, wondering how to deal with this situation.

'Look Gavin. It just takes time to adjust to the idea. It'll be okay. But you do have to give it time. In the first year of this I explained it all to a mate of mine I used to meet at the pub. I tried to get his support but he didn't give it a chance. Liridona and I worried for weeks that he'd go to the police, but nothing happened, and I never saw him again.'

Gavin's stance relaxed a little conceding to stay a little longer, then he sat on the arm of the sofa, at which point Liridona returned to the room with two cans of Carlsberg for Gavin and Eddie and a bottle of Evian for herself, then sat where Gavin had been sitting. Eddie did not move from where he stood feeling he now had the higher ground to push his argument forward, but before he could continue Liridona actually started to defend him.

'Eddie treats me okay Gavin. But says I'm a teenager from hell. So I don't get to drink alcohol.'

'What's to stop you drinking what's in the fridge when Eddie's at work?'

'She has done a couple of times, unfortunately.' Eddie admitted. 'I found the empties, but whenever she misbehaves she knows I will punish her.'

'You hurt her?

'No Gavin, I don't want her comparing me to her father.'

'He grounds me,' she says.

'Eh?' For a second Gavin wasn't sure whether that involved hurling her to the floor, since you surely couldn't be more grounded than house arrest.

'I lock her in her room with no TV, or other electronic entertainment,' Eddie explained.

'Her door has a *lock* on it?'

'Yes. It has been a necessity.'

'I hate the sound of it locking,' said Liridona. 'Sometimes I can't breathe as I panic.'

'I sealed over her windows. It looks like the curtains are drawn to anyone looking up from below. A good job.'

'No windows?!' Gavin was appalled.

'I hate it so much,' Liridona agreed with his response, 'I try so hard to be a good girl.'

'I'm sure you do pet. You're only human. This isn't right Guv.'

Liridona continued, 'I love to spend my time here in the lounge, with the big window on the world,' she pointed. 'I enjoy watching weather from up this high, and sometimes watch the police helicopter from behind the sofa, searching, scary. But sometimes, when the sun shines, I think it would be a fine day to step out of the window.'

'Onto the balcony?' Gavin questioned.

'What is…Balcony?'

'Liridona!; Eddie barked. 'She's just joking.'

'No joke Eddie. You know I'm not good with jokes.'

'But you don't mean you think of *jumping*?'

'I mean this some days.'

'Now now, we all get dark thoughts at times. It's natural.'

'I guess…Sometimes, when father raped me and mother knew, but did nothing, I hoped he kill me.'

'Sure…And sometimes I think if I got knocked down by a bus I wouldn't have to deal with this anymore.'

'I don't think that is the same thing Eddie…If bus hits you…What happens to me, then?'

'Oh I…Well…It won't happen.'

'What if it does, and you don't return?' she asked anxious now.

'Oh…You could shout for help and someone would come.' Gavin tried to help.

'No one has come when I've screamed with anger.'

'That's because I soundproofed your room.' Eddie explained.

Gavin turned to Eddie with further shock. 'You haven't?'

'Yeah. It cost a fortune too. But I had to, to deal with her incessant crying.'

'But even when I screamed in here,' Liridona pointed out, 'When you were working, no one came for me.'

'You shouldn't have done that!' Eddie said crossly. 'When was this?'

'First year. You can trust me now…I think.' To prove the point she owned up to something else. 'I also wrote note and threw as a dart out of the window.'

'Damn it! What did it say?'

'I used your address off the post, and wrote 'Help child here'.'

'Shit Liridona! You shouldn't have done that, either.'

'No worries Eddie. To my sadness it went into a chimney across way. Then I started to think this is my fate. I'm meant to be trapped.

Maybe I am a bad girl, and deserve this. I didn't do it again.'

'Imagine if it were you Guv…' Gavin tried to reason, 'unable to get out.'

'I do at times. But it just makes me think it's actually me who's worse off, with all the worry of this. I'd love to be the one at home, not having to be out bringing in the money and keeping us secure. Oh to be kept. There's plenty to do, keeping the house clean, and watching the TV...I give her tasks and entertainment so she doesn't get bored, or to feel too much like a…a prisoner.'

'People don't really appreciate what it can be like inside Guv. They think it's an easy life. Roof over your head, food, bed, telly…and for some that maybe true, but for most it's a loss of control, choice, and freedom.

'You promise yourself you'll never let it happen again. You've learned your lesson. Certain things stick with you as reminders. Sometimes it's memories of what happened to others.' Gavin paused as if getting his facts straight, his lips almost muttering. 'There was this one time when my cell mate Big Ted was in tears after visiting time. His wife had told him how she'd found their young lass talking to a wall she had made out of Lego bricks. And when she got closer she'd noticed there was a hole in the wall with bars in it. Their lass explained it was pretend, so that she could talk to her dad any time, and tell him she still loved him.'

'What was Big Ted in for?' Eddie was curious.

'Hit and run. Some old lady had collapsed into the road just as he passed. They reckon it was brain haemorrhage and she might have been dead before he hit her, but the problem was he hadn't stopped because the car was stolen.'

'Sounds like a bad man to me.' Liridona decided.

'One of many people who've lost their way pet…It wasn't planned.'

'My town, in the mountains,' said Liridona, 'do not waste time with prison. Police give *justice*, and sort things quickly.'

'What sort of justice?'

'Beating. Maybe break a leg. This one woman kept stealing bread, she got her hand broke with a hammer my mother said.'

'Maybe that was just to scare you.'

'I don't think so. Sometimes mother asked *me* to steal for us. Lots of desperate people are stealing food, and money, and people are sick of this.'

'Which is why,' Eddie jumped in, 'we need to make sure you don't get sent back.'

Liridona nodded then the three of them fell silent.

'What music do you like Gavin?' Liridona enquired.

'Oh…Urm…I like girl bands mainly.'

'Old girl bands, like Tatu?'

'I haven't heard anything of them in years. I prefer bands that are in the charts.'

'I like rap.'

'I tell her rap is not proper singing,' says Eddie 'and that's why it is spelled with a silent C.'

Gavin turned back to Liridona. 'Were there no uncles you could have gone to live with back home, in a different town or city?'

'The men in our family are not good. They enjoy beating people too much, especially women and children. Way of life. Men only considered proper men if rough. I think it's different here.'

'Possibly. But still there *are* some bad men *and* women here.'

'No.' Liridona couldn't accept that. 'English people are good people.'

'Not all of us Liridona.'

'If we were all good people,' Eddie pointed out, 'it would be safe to let you out of here.'

'If we were all good people, you wouldn't even be here.' Gavin added.

'Well you are a good person Gavin.'

'I haven't been.'

'Why?'

'I've been in prison for stealing.'

'Stealing? Why did you steal? English people have everything.'

'Not all of us. Not as much as we want, and some of us just want what isn't ours.'

'I'm surprised.'

'Well I guess I got into it out of resentment for my father. He didn't used to give me any pocket money like other kids got. He used to spend all his money on beer and tabs.'

'Tabs?'

'Cigarettes,' Gavin explained the northern expression.

'Oh, I see.'

'And he used to beat me a lot. He said it was because child services kept reporting that I had not been going to school. But then he would hit me for almost anything.'

Liridona nodded. 'Maybe most fathers are like this.'

'I don't think so.'

'What's your mother like?'

She died an alcoholic. I always felt I was an accident. She'd rather see Jack Daniels than me.'

'Was Jack her true love?'

'Ha, yeah. You could say that.' Gavin looked at her, not sure if she even knew she'd made a joke. 'So how did you get to the UK?'

'My mother made arrangements with another villager. He knows a man who finds work. She paid for passport then this man came and took me away. It seemed okay, but soon he passed me on to other man in the city. I see the villager is given money for me. This next man he *very* bad. He takes me on very long journey in the back of a van. In the dark, I get travel sick. He beats me, and rapes me a number of times.'

Eddie interrupted to add some background. 'It is common for these girls to be raped during transportation to break them and keep them submissive, so that when they are put to work, here or elsewhere, they'll do exactly what they're told. Submissive girls get a higher price. It's believed to be happening to some of our own missing children.'

'Shit!'

'So I change mind,' Liridona continued, 'I want to go back, but this man not listen. He tells me of a girl he killed for not being a good girl. He broke her arms and legs and buried her *alive*.'

41

'What?!'

'Not good Transporter. Not like Jason Statham.'

'Probably just a scare tactic.' Eddie suggested. 'Losing the *goods* is a last resort. Though, according to the websites some traffickers have been known to throw their *goods* from cars or over the side of boats if chased by the authorities, to slow the pursuers down, so they can get away.'

'Bastards.'

'There's worse. In some countries, children, mostly boys, are disposed of at the end of a season's fishing. Simply chucked into the sea, far from shore, to save paying them what they were promised.'

'Bastards!' Clenching his fists Gavin was not sure he wanted to hear anymore.

'Makes you think twice about eating foreign fish and shellfish.' Eddie remarked.

'So I learned to be thankful to live another day.' Liridona explained. 'A good day is a day when not beaten or raped.'

'Hell,' Gavin moaned, 'and I think I'm having a shit day when there's no good looking lasses to watch on the telly.'

'Oh yes,' Liridona's eyes lit up, 'Eddie makes me a star.'

'A star?'

'Not exactly...' Eddie tried to give a better explanation, but Liridona raised her voice with excitement over him.

'He puts me on the Internet.'

'We *have* made some video's where Liridona tells girls like herself the truth about slavery, and warns them not to come. Not to be tricked.'

'In some he ties me up. But in all I'm disguised with tape.'

'Will people believe it?' Gavin questioned. 'Will they not think it's just set up?'

'No I'm good with makeup,' said Liridona proudly, 'I know what my cuts and bruises looked like as well as how to cover them up. Eddie says I look great.'

'Maybe some viewers do see it as false.' Eddie admitted. 'They'll believe what they want to believe, like *it won't happen to them*. There is what they call the 'Pretty Woman' syndrome, where girls believe it will start out bad but all turn out right in the end. But at the end of the day, if these videos can stop even one getting taken in, then it's been worth it.'

'I suppose.' Gavin didn't really sound convinced.

'Eddie is a very clever man.' Liridona added her support.

'So you're happy with this?' Gavin looked for the truth in Liridona's deep brown eyes.

'Happy…no. But maybe if I'm good, it *will* come right for me.'

'But you *are* good.' Eddie urged her to believe it. 'It's the situation that is bad.'

'But our situation is because of me,' she reasoned, then seemed to have an idea and turned away. 'I need to go to my room, to get something.'

'Get what?' Eddie called after her.

Gavin watched him tensing up. 'I don't know how you deal with this in your life…and come to work seeming just like…anyone else.'

Without turning his nervous eye from the doorway, Eddie replied, 'I expect lots of people have secrets Gavin. People and things you wouldn't believe. Like the underage sex offenders, the slave labourers, appearing to be respectable people, someone's neighbours, and someone's friends. The problem is worse when people see something is wrong and choose not to believe it. Turn a blind eye, or decide it's acceptable because it involves someone they don't know. It's worldwide Gavin. It's happening *as we speak*. Somewhere at this very moment a child is in trouble.'

After a moment's silence Gavin got to the crux of the matter. 'Why *have* you told me all of this, Guv…Gotten me involved?

'Because Gavin…we need help. I realise that now. Someone we can trust.'

'But *me* like?'

'Sure. You wouldn't risk losing your job, now would you?'

'You'd sack me?'

'If this all goes belly up, it could destroy my reputation, I could lose my business.'

'What would you do then?'

'I expect I'd end up inside, unless I was able to make a run for it. I have made plans for running, with or without Liridona, but I'm not sharing those plans with anyone.'

'But have you really thought everything through?'

'The best I can Gavin, yes. But I'm facing an unexpected challenge now.'

'But I don't see how I can help like.'

'For a start you could help with some of the shopping and stuff.'

'Stuff?'

'Watching my back.'

44

'What do you mean?'

'You know. Keep me right. Like today with your questions. Making sure I don't take a wrong turn again.'

'I don't follow.'

'The thing is…The thing is…Liridona is almost a woman…And I'm starting to have fantasies about her, since the big mistake.'

'No man…She's still a bairn.'

'I know…Sorry…I hate the thought that I might change into what I'm trying to protect her from, but she's becoming so attractive…'

'No…'

'And what with her own sexual needs and frustrations I fear she's becoming irresistible. This all started because of my need for female companionship, and that doesn't go away just because I end up having to play dad.'

'So it seems, but…'

'I find myself thinking, she's not a blood relative, and in a few years' time I might be able to introduce her as someone I fell for abroad. There're plenty of men with young women like that. And as she becomes more…needy, I don't think she will have a problem with it.'

'Oh but Guv…It's just…Wrong.'

'I do know it's wrong. That's why I need to find a good woman…an understanding woman.'

'Very understanding.'

'So, what I'm thinking is…The reason I called you round…Is maybe we could go down the town a couple of nights a week and see about getting fixed up.'

'Urr…'

'Or…Okay, the real deal is I'll need you to be my Minder…Need you to babysit Liridona, while I get myself sorted.

'Mmm?'

'You would likely need to sleep over, if I'm sleeping with someone. I mean I wouldn't be able to bring a woman back here until I got her really keen and trusting me. Liridona might react badly to another woman here at first. But I can see that having you here is different. She's enjoying your company.'

'I don't know Guv.'

'I'd pay you extra of course, for what would mostly be just sitting and watch TV.'

'What if someone calls round?'

'Liridona knows the drill. Only I answer my door.'

'Can I think about it Guv?'

'Sure.'

Finally Liridona returned to the lounge. She had changed into an iridescent sequin dress and black tights, and had applied makeup as if expecting to go out. The inappropriateness caused Gavin to feel even more uncomfortable.

'Liridona!' Eddie barked at her angrily. 'Take that off immediately.'

'Yes Eddie,' her hands went slowly to the fastening at the back of her halterneck.

'Not here! Go to your room!'

'But I want Gavin to like me.'

'He likes you fine. Just not like that. Go and change.'

Gavin found himself wondering where this behaviour had come from.

'No! I like to look classy,' she rebelled. 'If I went back to my village with this, they would think I landed a good job.'

'But that would be a lie.'

'Half-truth. I do your house work…servitude.'

'It's not like that.'

'Is so. I do work here, so you buy me food and nice dresses, and let me wear them when I want…*except now.*'

'I give you tasks to keep you occupied and buy you things to keep you happy. That is not work.'

'Ach. You say potato and I say tomato.'

'Go on. Go and change…You're making Gavin uncomfortable.'

Instead Liridona sat back on the sofa next to Gavin and put a hand on his thigh. 'I don't discomfort you do I Gavin.'

'A little pet…Aye'

'Don't you like my beautiful dress?!'

'Liridona!' Eddie barked again, but all her attention was on Gavin.

'No, no. It's nice pet.'

'See Eddie. It's all good. Gavin likes it.'

'Gavin is just trying to be polite.'

'Gavin is polite yes, but also a little shy, I know how to deal with shy boys,' she starts to stroke his thigh. He stands up and steps towards the front door.

'Liridona! Go to your room immediately!' Eddie commands with little effect.

Liridona simply stands up. 'Sorry! You frustrate me! You don't act like real men in my country.'

'You mean we don't act like the men you were brought up by.' Eddie corrected. 'Look I'm trying to teach you there are other ways, Liridona.'

'You make it too…complicated.'

'She's not wrong there like. I really think I better head off.' Gavin took another step towards the door.

'No please,' Liridona pleaded again. 'I'll cook a snack.'

'No, no. Don't put yourself out pet.'

'Stay for one more beer then.' Eddie urged, realising he still hadn't achieved what he wanted from the evening. 'Liridona will behave herself.'

'Yes Gavin. Please.'

'I uh…Okay. But I need to use your loo.'

Eddie nodded. 'It's the first on your left.'

When Gavin was out of earshot Liridona turned to Eddie. 'Can we can trust him then, Eddie?'

'I hope so.'

'What if you're wrong?'

'Then we could be in big trouble.'

'I still don't understand Why you take the chance?...Are you sick of *just us*?

'No…I love you. We need help to get through this. It has been too difficult doing this alone. We have been lucky, so far.'

'I don't feel so lucky.'

'What? Would you rather I never took you?'

'Maybe by now I would be a cleaning supervisor.'

'You know that is not true!'

'What if Internet stories are not true.'

'What would anyone gain by putting false stories of slavery on the Internet?'

'Keep poor people away from work, stop them getting food and good clothes.'

'That's illogical. If you can get someone else to work for you who will accept little pay, it makes more sense to employ them, and earn off managing them, than to try and keep doing the work yourself.'

'So everything on Internet true? I don't think so. Our movies are made up.'

'They are *simulations*.'

'Good lies?'

'Sort of.'

'Why did you never *save* a second girl, and give me company?'

'Are you kidding? I couldn't cope with *two* of you!'

'Sure you could. Making plenty of money on those Internet scams.'

'I mean it would be too difficult trying to deal with two girls. I need the help of a woman around here.'

'There are plenty of nice older women in my country.'

'Too complicated. I need someone British. I can't risk doing anything like this again.'

'Are you saying I am a burden?'

'Sort of. No. You are good company. Most of the time. But we need more help with the situation than I can give you.'

'You sorry you took me?'

'No, don't say that…But I'm sorry I wasn't able to make it *all right* straight away.'

Gavin returned to the lounge, but just stood at the door listening, not knowing what to say.

'Maybe you make it right by sorting boyfriend,' Liridona suggested next.

'You know I can't do that. We've been through this before. It's too soon…When you are older you will meet someone, maybe.'

'Why not now?!'

'Too young.'

'I'm fourteen. Girls have boyfriend at ten.'

'No! You will get found out and taken away.'

'Not if the boy is a slave.'

'What *are* you suggesting?'

'You save boy. Boy love me loving him. I'll be good with that. Make both of us happy. Be less of a burden.'

'That's a dreadful suggestion.'

'No. It's good…You just not want me to be happy. Just your *slave*.'

'That's not true!'

Gavin chipped in, 'Eddie was telling me earlier that it takes a fighter to make a relationship work. What if the boy's a quitter and runs away?'

'No. Eddie's smart. He'd find a good boy. Then I make the boy love me. Work out just fine.'

'But life's not like that, pet. You cannot *make* someone love you.'

'But I'll be *very good* to him. Better than *other* girls.'

'That still doesn't guarantee love, or love that stays…And what would you do if you did get found out?'

'I'd tell the police that I'm a good girl, Eddie's a good man, and I just want a job so I can be English…And just hope they don't kill me.'

'But the authorities wouldn't think I was a good person once they found how I have been keeping you. You probably wouldn't see me

50

again. Probably you'd get sent back to Albania…to your parents.'

'No. England home now.'

'The authorities won't see it that way.'

'So how will this ever work out Eddie?'

'I've found someone to create false papers for us. New names, birth certificates, N.I. numbers, all that sort of stuff…When the time is right I'll…'

'Like agent?' she romanticised.

'Yeah, okay. Like agent…We'll have to learn to be other people.'

'Like Alias.'

'What worries me, is the risk of blowing it now because your English is still not good enough after two years of TV. You're not a convincing English girl.'

'Now I know I must be an agent, I will work harder.'

'But you won't *be* an agent. You'll always be an illegal immigrant, living in fear of being found out some day.'

Liridona looked about to cry.

'Hey Guv, I'm not sure that's helping.' Gavin stepped forward.

'If you can be a convincing English girl, in two years' time…'

'Two more?!' Liridona was horrified by the prospect.

'Yes. Then I'll see about arrangements.'

'If my English is not good enough for you after I try hard for two months, I'll go…balcony.'

Eddie growled with frustration and went into the kitchen to get more beer.

'I think you need to be patient for the Guv,' suggested Gavin, 'if you don't want to go back to your family. You've gotten into a terrible situation. You have to be honest with yourself. Is this really better than home?

'There's things…Eddie not so good about.'

'Sorry?' Gavin leaned closer.

'Eddie is a crook.'

'What?'

'He made an Internet site, like for finding love, but not find, just take money.'

'What?'

'But he's nothing to worry about. My country makes really bad crooks. World famous,' she claimed with some pride.

'Right.'

Eddie returned with another can each, but nothing more for Liridona who still had half a bottle of water.

'My parents make money any way they can. Father carjacks tourists on mountain roads, leaving them stranded, and sells cars and belongings. When he works with my uncle, they beat the men unconscious, scare the women then rape them. Father enjoys a woman's fear.'

'Do the police never catch them?'

'My uncle has friends in the police.'

Eddie explained further, 'many police forces round the world do not get paid like the British police, and that makes them much easier to bribe and corrupt.'

'Mother says djall send tourists to feed us.' Liridona wanted Gavin's attention back on her.

'Djall?'

'Urr… Devil.'

'Why would the Devil feed you tourists?'

'Continue our suffering of course.'

'Can't your village grow enough food?'

'The weather has become unpredictable these days. Crops fail. Animals get sick. Can't afford medicine. People starve. Not tourists though…They drive by in 4x4s showing off riches. Children run to beg, but they ignore them, mostly. Some take photos.'

'What about work in the cities?'

'Many jobs have gone.'

Eddie butted in to explain again. 'As soon as a country looks as if it is going unstable, a lot of investors pull out, and businesses close. If too many people quit, a tipping point comes where it all starts to collapse.'

'I'd hate to be caught up in something like that. But it won't happen here,' Gavin said confidently.

'Don't be so sure.'

'What do you mean?'

'We're all connected and dependent upon other countries nowadays. Think where our oil comes from, and how many of our factories are now foreign owned companies.'

'Yeah but that's because we are stable right?'

'We weren't so stable when Iceland was mismanaged.'

'Aye. Though I didn't really understand all that. It started with Iceland, but they are still there. It's Woolworths that disappeared.'

Gavin's mobile bleeped, and he took it from his pocket to read the message and text back immediately. He explained, 'someone I haven't seen in a while wants to know if I'm about this evening. I've said I'll text him later.'

'Take me along,' Liridona begged. 'You could say that I'm a relative.'

'No.' Eddie forbade it. 'That's a really bad idea…Without shoes or a coat you'd look suspicious.'

'Aye, no shoes would look a bit odd,' Gavin agreed. 'She could put a few pairs of socks on. They might pass as soft boots like.'

'Gavin! Don't encourage her.'

'Sorry Guv. I just thought maybe if she got out for a bit, and we were careful like, it might help her cope with being inside, you know what I mean.'

'Or make her all the worse.'

'Please Eddie.' Liridona took his hand. 'Just once? Promise I'll be good. Come back first sign of trouble…Maybe you come too.'

'No…That could be more dangerous. If they see me with you, they could track you down. People may know where I live. Presently there is no connection between the two of us, and that may be what has kept you safe for two years.'

'Safe is a poor word. I feel like I wait in a cave, while the djall waits outside.'

'I'm sorry Liridona. It's for the best…For now.'

'But I want to see some of the city, and not from a window…Not go far, just till the screaming in my heart goes.'

'Look. Why don't I pop out and get a couple of DVDs we can watch. Mm?...I could get…What was it?…Into the Blue,' Eddie tried to think of other diving films Gavin would stay to watch with Liridona, 'or ur Sanctum was it?'

'Mmm, I don't think she'll like the last one Guv, what with feeling trapped and all.'

'Oh, right.'

'Pretty Woman.' Liridona suggested.

'We have that here, and you've seen it dozens of times.'

'But I *like* it. It gives me hope.'

'Okay we'll stay in and watch Pretty Woman.'

'I'd rather not watch a chick-flick if you don't mind Guv. Wouldn't you like to watch a diving film Liridona?'

'Well…Maybe.'

'Okay. That's settled,' Eddie decided, 'I'll go and get us some DVDs and maybe some popcorn and we'll pretend we're at the cinema.'

'Okay,' she sighed.

'I'll be twenty minutes, half an hour max.' Eddie promised.

'Okay Guv.'

As soon as the front door clicked shut behind Eddie, Liridona turned to Gavin, 'Would you like me to slip into something *sexier*?'

'What? No. Please don't start that again!'

'Eddie buys me plenty lovely clothes.'

Gavin shifts over to the window, looking down to the street, growing nervous. 'Tell you what pet, let's see you in those jeans again. And do you have a jumper?'

'Sure. But too warm.'

'Well *you* suggested you'd like to show me your clothes. I'm just asking to see you in a jumper like.'

'Oh. Okay,' she frowned wondering where he was going with this one.

As Liridona went to her room Gavin looked down to the street for Eddie, got out his mobile and began to text. Just as he pressed send Liridona returned and gave a twirl. 'Ta da.'

'Smashing. Now remember what I said about wearing three pairs of socks, to look like soft boots?'

'Yeah?'

'Well howay then, let's see how that looks?'

'What's going on Gavin? Do boots and jeans turn you on?'

'What? No…Look, not everything's about sex pet.'

'But quite a bit eh?'

'Is this how your people talk back home?'

'No. They don't talk about sex and feelings. Family values are most important to us.'

'Family values?' he scoffed.

'Yes. Respect your elders. Children serve parent's needs.'

'So why do you behave like this now?'

'I learn these ways since I left home.'

'Did the Guv…Eddie…Has he ever forced himself on you?'

'Not…Exactly…'

'What do you mean?'

'In the first year, with difficult times, my illness, then Eddie's friend who wouldn't help, Eddie got to drinking himself to sleep a lot. Then one time, when I helped him to his room, I…took advantage of him.'

'*Took advantage*? What do you mean? Took his keys and left?'

'No. I had sex with him.'

'Why would you *think* to do that?'

'Eddie's not my father, but won't love me. I thought while he's drunk, give him what he needs, and then I can change his mind about me.'

'How?'

'Make him feel good, to take me out. Like girls on telly. But it just made things worse.'

'You're too young pet. And the telly's not for real. You need *help*.'

'You help me then?'

'I'll try.'

'Thank you...So we have sex now while Eddie gone, and then I look forward to your babysitting every day.'

'No Liridona! It won't be like that. I may be a wrong'n in some people's eyes, but I know when someone isn't being treated right.'

'I don't get it...What *do* you plan we do?'

'We don't have much time. I want to take you to see a friend before Eddie gets back.'

'But Eddie'll be back soon, there's no time for any visit,' she looked at him as if he had gone mad.

'It won't be a visit Liridona.'

'But you said...'

'We won't be coming back.'

'You'll run away with me?'

'Not far. I know someone through the probation service who I think can help you.'

'Who?'

'She works for a group who support troubled people...It's called Cyrenians. I texted her when I went to the bathroom.' Gavin waggled his mobile.

'Cyrenians? What sort of support?'

'They run hostels...homes for vulnerable women. She will know what's best.'

'Like Tracy Beaker?'

'Urr...Possibly...She texted to say she will take us to see someone from SCARPA.'

'What will they do?'

'I'm not sure. I've never heard of them before.'

'What if they are police and they kill me.'

'No I don't think they'll be police. And they're *not* going to kill you.'

'But what *will* they do? Why *would* they help me?'

'We'll have to see.'

'I'm not sure I want this. It would be simpler if you did what Eddie wants.'

'Simpler isn't always right pet. I've learned that.'

'What about Eddie?'

'I don't know.'

'I think Eddie will be angry. He hasn't told you everything yet.'

'C'mon pet get those socks on.'

'I'm not sure I can do this….I'm scared to leave.'

'Look…I'm scared doing this to…I'm going to lose my job. Quick, before I change my mind.'

'Will you stay with me Gavin?'

'I won't be able to pet. I'll take you there in the truck. It's just down on the street. But then I'll have to get off.'

'You'll leave us?...And go home?'

'No I won't be able to go home. The Guv would find me, but I can't leave the city, I'm on probation, so I'll have to lay low. But I don't think the Guv will stay around long if you've gone. He'll do a runner if he can't find you.'

'So everyone will just leave me?!'

'You've been saying you want out of this…To escape like…I'm offering you the chance…There *are* people who *will* help you…Properly.'

'I do want out of this, but I'm always scared that djall is waiting.'

'Sometimes we have to face our demons. You know what I mean pet.'

'I know what you mean like, Gavin…I put my trust in you.'

'Right then. C'mon.'

But instead of going to her room first, Liridona went to the coffee table.

'What you doing?'

'Just writing a note for Eddie to say *thanks for saving me.*' Liridona kneels at the coffee table and writes her note. Gavin moves from the window to the door to wait.

Liridona finished her quick note, and rushed to her room. 'I'll get my...' She returned with her socks on, and a big bag bursting with clothes.

'What's all this?'

'I need these things if I'm leaving.'

'Right. Let's go.'

'Would you carry them?' Liridona handed Gavin the bag without waiting for agreement and rushed back to her room again.

'What now?' Gavin turned opening the door to check the coast was clear then turned back inside as Liridona returned with another bundle in her arms. 'And what's *that*?'

In a lowered voice Liridona said 'Baby Freddie.'

In stunned silence Gavin almost stumbled backwards through the door, bag in hand, as Liridona followed with Freddie closing the door behind them.

The Bunker

Sand sprayed into the air and the three men standing on the grass of Ryton Golf Link twisted to turn their backs to it. 'Stannnn! We've told you! That's not how to get out of a bunker.'

The only response from Stan was another spray of sand.

'You're useless! Let me show you,' Dave jumped in before Stan could take another swing.

'You'd have thought after what…five years, Stan would have it sussed by now,' said Bill.

'Maybe,' suggested Mike, 'he doesn't have it in him.'

'Oh shut up,' Stan snapped. 'It just so happens I have a knack of getting into the worst places.'

'Ha yeah,' Dave smirked, taking the iron off Stan. 'So how's it going with that small-holding you got at auction?'

'I should be getting confirmation of ownership any day now.'

'And you still feel confident about the size of the renovation project?'

'Sure. The only thing that's challenging me presently is at the corner of my far field.'

'What's that then?' Mike quipped, 'A bunker?'

'Ha ha. No. It's one of those underground reservoir humps. Only it's not on the deeds, or any map. I phoned the water board and they denied any knowledge of it. I asked them what it could be, and they said some land owners had their own reservoirs. I told them it was not on the deeds. They said it was not their problem, like I was boring them.'

'You…Boring?' said Mike.

'Hey,' defended Dave, 'get off his back Mike, or he might just stop entertaining us with his blunders.'

Finding a letter of confirmation from the solicitors on the hallway floor when he arrived home in Prudhoe, Stan decided he could wait no longer and drove out to the small-holding.

By the time he got there, however, his stomach was rumbling, and he realised he should have thought to bring some food out with him. Parking in the barn he checked his glove box for a snickers bar he thought he might have left there, but he must have eaten it already.

Too excited to go and get food, he decided to check out the anomaly at the far side of his property first before checking the present condition of the farmhouse. He had viewed the house some months ago, but there had been some heavy rain of late and there might be leaks he needed to attend to.

Donning his wellingtons at the tailgate of his 4x4 he took his walking stick with him and marched down through the first field to the gate. Climbing over it rather than unlatching it he headed across to the hump, hidden under long grass.

He told himself it was clearly more than a natural hump in the ground because it was flat on top with angled sides. Attempting to reason what it was again he discounted it being a cesspit as it was too far away from the house, but would the same not apply to a reservoir tank? And wouldn't a cesspit or other tank need some form of maintenance hatch?

The ground was quite boggy near the hump, which was why Stan had come prepared with wellington boots. He trudged around the sides of the hump prodding the metal tip of the stick into the ground.

All of the sides had a relatively even six inches of soil below which felt like stone or concrete. He moved across the top in a sweeping pattern finding more solid structure below. He was about to give in, but as he reached the far edge the stick tip struck what sounded like metal.

More focused prodding determined there was some sort of square hatch just a few inches below the surface. Stan used the tip of the stick to dig away at the turf, then grasping a handful of the tall grass. Getting his hand under the turf he began to rip it up.

It was hard going at first, but as the rip was widened it became easier, until the square hatch was exposed. Dusting the hatch off and pulling the turf clear of the sides Stan located a box with a hinged lid. Pulling the lid back he discovered that the hatch was not padlocked as he had expected but was simply a four digit code lock.

He remembered how he had once opened an abandoned bike lock in under half an hour and thought he would give it a go. He tested it first. It was locked. Then he zeroed it and tested it again, locked, then moved it on to 0001 and tested it again, locked. He began moving up through the numbers, locked, locked, locked, knowing it was unlikely to be within the first hundred.

The figure turned out to be 7734. It was a shame he had not understood any significance to the number, seeing it only the right way up.

By the time he had the hatch open the light was failing. He had had the forethought to bring a small but bright LED torch. Clicking it on Stan shone the beam down the hole and saw a ladder that descended a couple of metres or so.

It *was* a tank full of water and yet the steps led to some sort of gantry. Maybe the gantry was for maintenance, he wasn't sure. Leaving his stick outside he decided to take a quick look inside before heading back. Gripping the torch between his teeth he stepped backwards down to the gantry.

There was no telling how deep the water was, he could not see the bottom, but he did notice another hatch at the other end of the gantry. This hatch was above a large tube that descended into the water, but instead of another code lock this hatch had a wheel, like he had seen on submarine movies.

As he began to turn it he wondered whether it was actually just a valve to control water flow and that he was only imagining it was yet another hatch. Nevertheless, when he fully turned the wheel there was a slight hiss. He lifted the hatch and looked inside and saw it contained yet another ladder which went down further than the beam of the torch penetrated. Again he decided to just quickly check this out before heading back. He just wanted to know what he was dealing with.

Torch still gripped between his teeth he descended rung by rung, occasionally stopping to tilt his head and look down but could not see the bottom.

Shortly, when he thought to look up, he could not see the top either but decided to press on downwards with a faster rhythm. It was not long after his increase in speed that the ladder rungs suddenly ran out and he slipped. His body weight jerked his fingers loose of the ladder and he fell.

His natural reaction was to put his hands out to grab the sides of the ladder and elbows out to the sides of the tube, but this did not slow him much, just hurt his fingers on the ladder fixings behind. He came to a sudden halt with an echoing clang that jolted the torch from his mouth and made him bite his tongue.

Picking himself up he scrabbled after his torch which had rolled away from him and realised he had badly twisted his ankle.

Retrieving the torch and looking around he appeared to be in a short corridor with metal walls and slots in the sides. He wasn't sure whether they were supposed to be viewing slots or vents. He shone his light into a couple and decided the latter. There was a door at the far end but it had no handle. He limped his way to it and pushed but it did not budge.

This was as far as he could go. What was more to the point was when he returned to the bottom of the tube and looked up he saw that the ladder was well out of anyone's reach, this was as far as he was going *anywhere*.

He took his mobile from his jacket, but as he feared, there was no signal.

'Fucking useless phone services!' Stan spluttered his annoyance.

He slumped to the floor, considered how long it would be before someone came looking for him, and his stomach rumbled loudly as if making its own protest, echoing around his metal cell. He searched his pockets for anything to eat, but the closest he found was a piece of previously chewed gum wrapped back up in its foil.

'You are such an idiot Stan.' He considered shouting up the tube, but even if any sound carried up as far as the surface, who would be there to hear it at the bottom of the field?

The closest to a good idea he had was to tear all his clothes into strips to make a rope and try to throw it up to the last rung of the ladder. But what, he wondered, would hook it in place? And with his clothes shredded he would surely slip into hyperthermia all the quicker. He decided he had no good ideas at all.

Somewhat less rationally he then decided to punch himself hard in the side of the head. His ears were filled with a rushing sound, not quite the ringing he would have expected. It sounded more like a gas leak. As the noise continued he started to cough and feel dizzy. It didn't just *sound* like gas, it *was* gas.

He stumbled to stand under the tube with the ladder to holler for help, took a deep breath and slid into unconsciousness.

Stan was surprised and relieved to wake up in a different situation. However, he was somewhat less relieved to find himself not tucked up in bed but bound to a chair in the dark with his wellingtons still on but not his jacket.

'Hello?' he called tentatively into the pitch blackness. He could tell from the sound his voice made he was no longer in the same room that he had passed out in. This was a smaller space.

'Hello?!'

As he listened he thought he could hear movement, but not in the room with him, then he was startled by a loud voice over a speaker which was not unlike a railway public announcement system for its profound lack of clarity.

'Ooo are you ma friend?' The voice sounded slightly South African, but that could have been the poor PA. 'Ooo are you?!' the voice repeated louder, creating feedback and making Stan wince.

'Stan Gillespie. Who are you?'

'Are masking dur questions ear ma friend.'

'Sorry?' It was less an apology, more a request for clarity.

'Har dew git ear ma friend?'

'Someone brought me here, after I fell down a hole. I don't know.'

'Ooo brought you ear? Oo?'

'If it wasn't you it was one of your people I guess. I saw nothing after the room at the bottom of the long ladder.'

'Doan chew plea funny bug-us whit me ma friend. Are masking har you farn displace?'

Stan had to conclude he was still down the hole, but why was there someone down here? 'You know, I'd understand you a lot better if you just came in here and talked to me.'

'Oh you'd lark debt wooden chew booee.'

'Maybe if you put someone else on…With less of an *accent*?' Stan wondered whether there was only this strange subterranean hermit.

'Watch oo sane?' There followed the sound of a muffled discussion and some angry shuffling then a new voice came over the speaker.

'Or rate pawl.' It sounded like a dreadful approximation of Scottish. 'Wee jess want tee know, how yee foon us doon here?'

'I was investigating an unmarked underground reservoir on my land and fell in.'

'Oh *your* land yee say laddie?'

'Yes I'm the new land owner.'

'Well forgive me if your story soons a bit hearty believe, but if it *were* unmarked howdy jew know we was here?'

'I didn't know *you* were here. All I knew was there was something at the bottom of my land which was not on the deeds and the water board denied knowledge of it.'

'Is that so?'

'Yes…Look can you just untie me I need the toilet.'

There followed some further muffled discussion. 'Or rate. Wheel send in the *old guy* to untie yee but no funny business or there'll be trouble further both o'yee.'

'I don't want any more trouble.'

'Well you came tudor wrong plays ear ma friend,' the South African put in.

Stan sighed and waited.

Eventually he heard the sound of a door opening. No light came through the door but he heard raspy breathing and the tapping of a stick, then he felt fumbling fingers touching his hands then his knees. The old man groaned as he knelt down and started to unbind Stan. It felt like he had been bound to the chair by bandages and safety pins.

'Who are you?' Stan asked.

'The last one,' the old man answered somewhat cryptically in a low voice as if not to be heard.

Stan lowered his own voice. 'What do you mean *the last one*?'

'The last one to come down.'

'Down here? You came down like me, and you've been here ever since?'

'Be careful what you say.'

'What is this place?'

'A secret bunker.'

'A secret bunker?!'

'Shh.'

'What's the bunker for?' Stan returned to whispering.

'Survival.'

'Why did no one come and get you out?'

'No one knew I was here.'

'I have friends who will come looking for me.'

'But the grass will have been replaced over the hatch by now and your friends probably won't think to look under the turf. Will they?'

Stan sighed. He feared that the old man was right. 'So who *were* you before this?'

The old man did not reply at first, as if wondering whether he should say more. He released Stan's arms and then got to his feet with some effort. 'Wait there till they turn the lights on for you.'

'Okay.' Stan heard the old man go to the door and stop.

'I am the previous land owner.' He closed the door after him.

Stan had understood that the previous owner had died of a stroke about eighteen months ago with no known living relatives, with the proceeds of the auction going to obesity research. At the auction however he heard a rumour that the previous owner had taken on the small-holding when his brother, the original owner, had suddenly disappeared.

The lights came on to reveal what looked like a police cell. It was clean. In fact it looked as if it had never been used before. Stan limped over to the toilet and relieved himself, at which point he noticed that his belt had been removed. Then as he made an attempt at freshening himself up at the sink he saw that the towel provided was the size of a hand flannel and took this as another precaution against prisoners hanging themselves, or using them as weapons.

'I'm hungry!' he called out.

This time the voice on the PA system sounded like some old Baroness. 'Food is being prepared young man. Dooo be patient! We were not expecting this intrusion!'

'Who are you people?'

There was no answer. Stan went to the door to see if it would open, but just as he suspected it was locked. He tried to push aside the cover over the view slot in the door but that would not budge either.

He sighed and turned his attention to the cell bunk where he saw the bandages he had been bound to the chair with. Going across and sitting down he decided to strap up his swollen ankle. Removing the wellington and sock he saw the ankle bone was almost hidden under the black and blue swelling.

'Now young man, just keep sitting on the bunk. The gentleman who attended you earlier will be back in with some food and drink for you in due course. Then after you have eaten we will talk again.'

'Fine…Thank you,' he added.

As he waited, Stan considered making a run for it as soon as the door was opened, but he didn't know which way to go or how many people were out there, and as he had said, he didn't want any trouble. He hoped the follow-up discussion would resolve this, though he wasn't sure quite how. He didn't want anything like this going on at the bottom of his property.

As if their metre had suddenly run out of coins the lights went out without warning. Stan sat still and heard some fumbling outside of the cell door before it opened. Then he heard a tray being picked up and the old man doddering in with it.

'Where are you?' the old man whispered.

'I'm over here on the bed.' Stan said softly. He heard the man shuffling towards him. 'Why didn't they leave the lights on for you?'

'Doesn't bother me.'

'Doesn't it?'

'No,' the old man said, pressing the edge of the tray against Stan's chest for him to take it. 'I'm blind.'

'Is that why you are stuck down here?'

'What?'

'Why you never tried to get away?' Stan asked in more of a whisper.

'I did once.' He whispered back.

'What happened?'

'*They* blinded me.'

'Bloody hell,' Stan exclaimed in less than a hushed tone.

'I must go,' the old man said nervously.

'Tell me more about this place…Please.'

'I mustn't stay. Maybe I will be able to say more later on.'

'But…' It was no good, the old man was off. Stan let him go and as the door sealed him into his pitch black cell he wondered if he was now expected to eat in the dark, but just as he was about to voice his complaints the lights came on again.

The food smelled good, but looking at it Stan wondered if that was only because he was starving. The plate contained what he could only guess were some sort of military rations. What passed for meat by taste had the texture of Quorn which he had tried once. There was some sort of synthetic mashed potato and gravy with it. At least there was enough there to satisfy his empty stomach.

Emptying his glass of water Stan put the tray onto the chair. 'Okay I'm finished.'

His announcement was met with silence.

'I'm ready to talk now!'

Still the speakers remained off. In fact he could hear no more movement nearby. 'I just want to go home!' he yelled with frustration, then for good measure added 'Please.'

He waited and he waited. He found the whole experience tiring, so lay down on his bunk, and was soon asleep, thanks to the strong sedative in the food.

When Stan woke up he felt a bit dizzy, and it was dark again. He made to lift a hand to his face but then realised he was restrained to his bunk, although it felt like a harder surface than it had when he lay down. He struggled to get up which confirmed that not only were his wrists and ankles secured, so was his neck.

'Hey! Let me go!' he roared. 'I've had *enough* of this.'

'Debt remains to be seen ma friend,' said the voice all too close to his ear.

'Shit.' Stan cursed with exasperation.

'Sars you know what to expect if you doan tell us dur truth, arm gunner give you a bit offer taster ma friend.'

Stan was just thinking how the PA system wasn't fully to blame for the dreadful South African's accent when he felt a towel get draped over his face. He tried to turn his head. 'What the f…?'

He didn't finish his words as water was poured over his head, leaving him coughing and spluttering as it filled his mouth, ran up his nose and down the back of his throat. It reminded him a bit of the Kamikaze slide at Wet'n'Wild, except that that was over in a few seconds and this seemed to be going on and on. Running out of air he tried to hold his breath, but the water in his throat was causing a choke response and then his lungs overrode his breath holding and he inhaled water. He was being drowned.

The towel was removed and Stan vomited water from his nose and mouth tried to gulp air in and then was raked by coughing with the water in his lungs. He needed to sit up but couldn't.

'Are weak leer ma friend?'

'What?' Stan gurgled in disbelief through his coughing.

'Are weak leer? Tell dur truth. Or you'll be gittin more lark debt.'

'No please. You've almost drowned me.'

'Doan beer little baby booee. Debt was jester splish.'

'Just talk to me.'

'Are you whit the essay yes?'

'Sorry?'

'D'dew come whit the essay yes?!'

'I haven't brought any bloody essay with me no!' Stan sobbed, this was all madness.

'Doan miss smear bart you dumb fucka!'

'I don't understand what you are talking about!'

'Are mappy to plea thistle day ma friend.'

Stan felt the wet cloth being draped over his face again and screamed 'NO!!' The cloth remained there as he listened to a bucket being filled under a tap. 'Please STOP!!'

The man returned, but the bucket was placed on the floor besides him, and the towel removed. Stan tried to control his breathing, and realised this whole thing was about control, and telling the man what he wanted to hear. The big question was *what* did he want to hear?

'Maybe if you rephrase your question I will understand better.'

'Did Sikhs poo chew in ear?'

'I don't know any Sikhs.'

'Farve?'

'I don't know one Sikh never mind five of them.'

Stan realised that honesty wasn't working for him as the towel was returned to his face, immediately followed with the pouring water. At the moment the towel went on Stan drew a deep breath before the water hit him.

He did his best to seal off the back of his nose and throat with what he guessed was the back of his tongue then it was down to how long he could hold his breath.

As the water poured over his face he started to feel he could probably hold his breath till the bucket was emptied, that was until the man stopped when the bucket was only half empty and punched Stan hard in the stomach. His air seemed to blast from him, leaving him winded as the pouring water resumed, and he was drowning again.

Stan was convinced he was going to die even as the bucket ran empty. He vomited water under the towel. His nose and throat burned as he tried to drag bubbling mouthfuls of air through the sodden towel. Then he heard the bucket being refilled. He had no idea what was expected of him. He just wanted it to be over.

'Get the Baroness!' he gurgled.

'Baroness? Who's debt?' The man stopped, putting the bucket down beside Stan's head and removing the towel.

'The woman!' he spluttered.

'Which woman's debt booee?'

'The one I said I'd be happy to talk to.'

'I doan noah bart debt.'

'She spoke to me before.'

'Just tell me what are need to know.'

'For fucks sake, I don't know what you want to know! You're not making any sense!' he almost cried.

'Ooo nose we're ear?'

'No one knows you are here. *I* didn't know you were here. I don't even know what this place is.' He wasn't about to mention anything the old man had mentioned.

'It's a survival bunker for preppers.'

'To survive what?'

'Terrorism.'

'That's ironic then.'

'What dew mean booee?'

'It seems to me you've become what you fear.'

'Har dew mean? *This* is jester sick-uri-tea precaution.'

'And when will you be satisfied you are secure?'

'Ha…When you are dead ma friend, when you are dead.'

The waterboarding continued.

When Stan came round his hair and top were damp but he was no longer restrained. He jumped off the bunk and threw his hands out in front of himself in the dark then span around, knocking the fingers of his right hand into the chair in his cell. His fingers were still sore from the ladder fixings and he cried out, pulling his hand in to nurse it in the dark. He crumpled to the floor. How could he escape this hell?

After some time sitting on the hard floor with no inspired thoughts he heard the door opening. He got up and feeling for the bunk sat on the mattress. He could smell food again, and assumed it was the same old man.

'What is your name?' he asked softly as the man entered.

'Larry…Here is some more food.'

'Thank you Larry.' He had heard somewhere that in a hostage situation you should try to make friends. Then in even more of a whisper, when their heads were closer for the passing of the tray, Stan suggested, 'Why don't we help one another escape?'

'Oh I couldn't help you.'

'I appreciate you are blind, but you must know your way around some of this bunker.'

'Yes.'

'And the way out?'

'Yes.'

'Then why not work with me?'

'I want to live.'

'How many of them are there?'

'I have to go.'

'Wait…How many?'

'Too many.' Larry sealed the cell behind him, and after a few minutes wait they turned the lights back on.

Stan wondered why they waited before the lights were switched on, and then when he looked at the contents of his tray he wondered why the same food? Was this all they had? Was this all they could synthesise in this survival bunker? He considered a few other questions as he ate his meal, the last question being why he felt so tired again so soon after waking. Had the waterboarding ordeal exhausted him that much? He never wanted to go through that again.

This time when Stan awoke the light was still on, and this time he was not alone.

'I'm glad you've decided to join us again Mr Gillespie,' said the figure with the voice of an old Baroness. 'You said you wanted to talk freely with me.'

Stan didn't know what to say now that he was presented with the opportunity because he was too surprised by the sight of the woman sitting in the chair wearing a hazmat suit. He was even more surprised by the sight of a rather threatening looking flask placed on the toilet lid.

'What is that?' he pointed at the flask.

'A rather tiresome little bug from Africa I believe, which I hope you understand is why *I'm* wearing this,' she said pointing at her hazmat suit with its mirrored visor.

'Why have you brought it in here?'

'It is so that you understand the importance of being honest with us.'

'I do, I do. I have been.'

'I do hope so. I understand that after it initially makes you pass out you come round to sickness and diarrhoea before it makes you go blind.'

'I don't want to be blind I'll tell you what I know. Just don't open the flask.'

'Okay then young man…Why did you come down here?'

Stan sighed. 'As I've said, I came to find out what this water reservoir was.'

'Forgive me but that hardly makes sense. If you knew it was a reservoir, why would you need to investigate it?'

'It was on my land, and there was no record of it.'

'And was it causing you a problem?'

'Until now, no.'

'Then I ask again. Why did you come down here?'

'Curiosity I guess.'

'And we know what curiosity did…So what has your curiosity taught you?'

'Not to go down hatches you don't know.'

'Quite so. But what have you learned since your time with us?'

'Nothing.'

The figure rose from the chair and went to the flask.

'No!' It was clear that was not the correct response. 'I ur…I've learned…that you are all very concerned about being discovered down here.'

'Because…?' she probed.

'It's your survival bunker.'

'And what is the best way for us to keep it secret Mr Gillespie?'

'I continue to keep the secret.'

'Are you good at keeping things secret?'

'Oh yes very,' Stan tried to reassure her.

'Even under *duress*?'

'Oh yes your secret is safe with me.'

'So if you were tortured you would never give us up?'

'Absolutely not.'

'Well young man you know what that means don't you?'

'I'm free to go?' Stan asked hopefully.

'No. It means that you may not have been open with us during your waterboarding.'

'No no! I was…I was.'

'But I hope you appreciate the conundrum you have presented us with. You just said you would not crack under torture.'

'You just have to trust me.'

'Trust is such a challenging little word don't you think Mr *Gillespie*.'

'Well I…'

'Is Gillespie not just your code name?'

'*Code name*?'

'Yes an ironic code name. Giles Spy. Giles Fordham the Director of MI5 sent you, didn't he?'

'Director…Giles…That's not ironic, that's absurd. I'm just the new landowner. Why can't you believe that?'

'Yes…I wonder why.' A gloved hand released the top of the flask.

'NO!!' Stan ran to reseal the flask but the Baroness seemed ready for his reaction and punched Stan hard in the stomach.

By the time Stan had recovered from the blow and picked himself up from the floor the Baroness had managed to knock on the door pause a moment then push on the door and leave. Stan resealed the flask, but he knew it would be far too late.

Stan sat in the dark facing the wash basin with his backside on the toilet, feeling so washed out, from the diarrhoea and vomiting and wondering how long it would be till his sight was gone. He would never know if the lighting was not put back on again. He tried again to think of a way out of this mess, and wept.

'Or rate there pawl?' the Scottish voice asked over the PA system, sounding inappropriately cheerful.

'Of course I'm not fucking alright, you bastard!'

'Well noo, I half it on good authority that we do half a serum for that bug of yours.'

'What?'

'Yes, yes, an antidote. Yee just have to tell us who you're working for. But don't go leaving it too long.'

'It's Giles Fordham. Director of MI5. He sent me to find out what you are up to down here. I'm supposed to tell him that you are a bunker full of preppers, but I'm going to report that I found nothing but a water reservoir.'

'Is that so?'

'Yes. Absolutely.'

'Well…I don't believe you.'

'Damn it! Why not?'

'There is no *Giles Fordham.*'

'But the Baroness said…'

'Who?'

'The Baroness! The woman! The fucking woman with the bugs!!'

'I'll check in again later maybe, when you've head tame tee calm doon. And see if you're ready for your serum then.'

'I need it now y'bastard!!'

Stan found himself on the cell floor where he had collapsed away from the basin and toilet. He was shivering and exhausted. He didn't know how much more of this he could take.

His head span as he tried to stand and pull his pants up. He saw stars before his eyes in the darkness, and hoped that meant he was not yet blind.

He went and lay down on the bunk, pulling the single blanket over him. At least he didn't feel like he was going to need the toilet or basin any time soon. He had to be empty by now. His guts were sore from start to finish.

As weak as he was now he knew he had to get out of the bunker somehow, and as hungry as he was he was pretty sure that the meals he was being fed were putting him to sleep as a prelude to torture. He might not survive eating again. If he didn't make a break for it the very next chance he got he doubted he'd ever make it out.

Escape was all too complex a problem for Stan and he doubted anyone in his position would have been much better prepared. He desperately needed the antidote to what he had been infected with, but not only would he not know what it was or where to find it, he had no idea how to get away once he had taken it.

If he could evade capture by these people, who may well come after him, he would need to get straight to the hospital in Newcastle and hope they would believe his story and work out what the infection was.

The situation felt hopeless. He remembered hearing somewhere that in desperate situations it was down to making the best of what options were available, taking it a step at a time, and holding on to any hope that something helpful would turn up.

The sound at the door told Stan it was feeding time at the zoo again. He considered whether to dash at blind old Larry as soon as the door was opened, but that might be expected, and anyway he really needed to get a bit more rest. He left Larry come in with the tray without attempting to engage him in conversation, playing the full extent of his exhaustion card, to hopefully put him off guard on his return.

Soon the light came on and Stan's eyes welled up. He wasn't blind, yet. He looked at the contents of the tray. It was another torture in its own right. He was desperately hungry but knew he must not eat even a mouthful of it, nor drink the water. He wondered whether the water in the tap could be contaminated too. He decided to use his thirst and hunger as his drive to escape, and held on to the thought of eating when he was free, even if it happened to be hospital food.

Leaving the tray of food where it had been placed as usual on the chair, Stan wondered if Larry knew the food was intended to knock him out, and whether he knew what was being done to him. Had he gone through the same ordeal and survived?

Stan held to the idea that it was possible to survive, but after the waterboarding and biological warfare, he wondered what they intended to do to him next, and at what point had they stopped torturing Larry? What had Larry done to make them stop?

Stan lay on his bunk waiting for Larry to return. He had no idea whether he was being watched, but guessed his refusal to eat would soon prompt a reaction if he was, but then what response would that get from them? Force feeding?

No comment was forthcoming over the PA however, and after sufficient time for him to eat and then fall asleep, the light went off again.

There was no immediate opening of the door and Stan became jumpy as he lay there rehearsing his only plan. He would wait for the sound of the tray being lifted, bolt up and get out the door. He intended to pull the door shut and lock Larry in, in the hope they would not be so hard on him for not giving chase. Then once in what he presumed would be a corridor he would feel the walls for a light switch, and wait for the people to come as surely they would.

He fully expected Larry to raise the alarm. Then it was all down to how much fight he had left in him and how much luck was on his side.

Stan had once paid for training in Pan-Go-Lin. The sensei had made it sound more interesting than the more common martial arts, though the name sounded to Stan more like some musical instrument and less like a way of fighting.

The latter concern certainly turned out to be the case as when he reached green belt without any need for a grading, at a cost of a thousand pounds of tuition, he found out a pangolin was an animal.

All the fake sensei had taught him and the other two gullible people was how to flail his arms about while cartwheeling erratically, which he *had* told them quite correctly was enough to put most people off.

Finally the door opened. Stan held his breath till it was time to move then was up. He took the blanket with him in case it was of any use, but pulling the door shut the trailing blanket got caught.

'Shit!' He pushed the door ajar to pull the rest of the blanket through.

'Don't lock me in!' Larry cried.

'It's for your own good Larry. Sorry.' Stan tried to explain as his searching hands found the handle. He felt Larry pulling at the door frame. 'Mind your fingers.'

'Please don't!' he pleaded.

'I'll be back with help.'

'You'll never get away,' was his warning as Stan found the lock latch and slid it home.

Putting the blanket over one shoulder he was straight onto the next part of his plan, the hunt for the light switch.

If he could find one surely he would find the others more easily, and light would be an advantage if he could find a switch before other people came. Nevertheless, rather than the hoped for switch, Stan found a neighbouring door. He was about to open it when he reasoned that this was where the South African, the Scot, and the Baroness might be, and so limped along with a hand on the wall doing sweeps at around standard switch height. But as he did so still unchecked he began to wonder why he was not being chased. They must surely have heard his escape. Maybe they were watching to see what he did, as yet another test.

The wall ran out. This was either a bend in the corridor, or a junction, so with hands outstretched he found the other side of the corridor and then tracking along first one way then the other determined that it was indeed a junction. Which way should he go?

He decided on going left. This was a long corridor, with no doors on the right-hand wall that he was still sweeping for switches.

Exercise seemed to be easing the pain in his ankle so he picked up pace. Unfortunately this brought on déjà vu, as the wall continued but the floor didn't and he found himself crashing down a flight of stair and hitting his head at the bottom, where he lay still for some time.

Stan thought he was on his bunk. He tried to pull the blanket over him better. However, the mattress was cold and hard. He picked himself up off the floor. Had he knocked himself out? He wasn't sure, but the one thing he was certain of as he rubbed his head was that nobody had come to get him.

Where were they all? What were they doing? He wished they had not taken his jacket. He could have used his phone on torch mode to make better progress. He stumbled against the wall to his left and began sweeping for switches again and almost immediately came to a door.

He tried the handle expecting it to be locked but it opened. Feeling around the wall just inside, he found his first light switch and flicked it up. He was greeted with the scene of a large kitchen. It was a canteen kitchen with a wide serving bay looking out onto an unlit eating area which looked like it could seat fifty plus people.

Getting his wits about him the first thing Stan did was arm himself with a carving knife. Then he investigated the cupboards and fridges.

The cupboards were filled with containers of powder, labelled as potato substitute, various flavour gravies, salt, sugar, and custard. The fridges were empty, all but one, which had a couple of re-sealable containers containing the Quorn type stodge. He tried some of it cold and thought better of it. He turned to look for an oven and spotted a microwave.

Everything in the kitchen looked so antiquated to him, but as long as it worked. His next try of the Quorn was better but clearly needed some of the flavouring and he soon found himself making the same meal he had been fed this last couple of days.

While it cooked he went through a door at the end of the serving bay into the eating area and at the far end, leading back onto the corridor, he found another light switch.

This was more than a canteen; it also served as a recreational area. There was a dart board and a bulky old CRT TV in one corner near some sofas. One of which had a cushion stained from a possible food related accident. At a beep from his microwave he went and served himself his meal. Bringing it back to the sofas he turned the TV on but all it received was static. He tried to find a channel and checked that the aerial was actually in to no avail, so switched it off and ate in silence.

He thought how ironic it would be if he managed to knock himself out with his cooking. Maybe the food in the fridge was all pre-treated. He was so hungry and with no one appearing to be after him he was past caring.

With the meal finished, he left the dishes in the sink next to a rubbish chute and continued his exploration.

Across the corridor from the canteen he found a meeting room and then next to that what he guessed was a communications or security room, with screens and what looked like a radio but there were no phones to be seen. On investigation the radio appeared to have been broken, on purpose.

Very disappointed he continued looking around the room. Searching draws and cupboards Stan acquired a torch, a bunch of keys and a hand gun. He had never fired a gun before or even handled one but knew that the rounds were usually kept up the grip. Also you couldn't shoot with the safety on, and recoil could cause you to fire above the target.

He worked out how to unclip the magazine and it appeared to be full so he clicked it back home and placed the gun in his trouser pocket. The weight of it pulled his trousers down a little but he was glad he didn't need his belt to keep his trousers from falling round his ankles.

Leaving the room he came to a small library next, which seemed to hold many more fiction than non-fiction books. Examining a number of more modern looking titles and checking the print dates Stan found nothing older than 2001.

Further down the corridor he came to a stair well and believing that up would be the way out started his climb, still listening out for sounds of other people. It only went up two levels, where he found two sets of double doors. One door opened up onto a large sounding room and turning the lights on Stan revealed that it was a massive concrete garage, which could have accommodated a jumbo jet if it wasn't for the regular support pillars.

Instead it contained a variety of diggers, bulldozers and farming equipment. At a quickening limp he looked frantically for the garage door and freedom.

'Madness!' There was no sign of a door. 'How the hell did all this get in here?!'

Exasperated, Stan continued his search, crossing the stairwell to the other double door and found this was a storeroom full of grains and fertilisers on pallets. He had no idea where they expected to grow crops down here.

He descended to the level below and found that it was full of dormitories. Here he needed to use the keys he had taken. Disturbingly the few rooms that he could be bothered to find the right keys for all looked lived in at one time but now smelled old and dusty. There were pictures of loved ones on bedside tables, and collections of personal belongings on shelves, but no occupants.

Stan returned to the stairwell and this time limped all the way to the bottom. There he found a generator room. There was no sign of fuel and he was no engineer but he didn't think it was nuclear powered, though could hear the sound of what he thought might be a turbine and wondered if the generator might be geothermal.

Next door to that he found a storeroom with electronic and mechanical parts. Back to the stairwell and up he came to what looked like a lab at first but on closer inspection seemed to be intended for food production. He noticed one unit was actively culturing what he assumed to be more of the Quorn stuff, but there was nobody attending to the lab.

The next level up Stan found what he guessed was a sick-bay, with a pharmacy and a whole load of empty beds. This led to a cold room which gave Stan an uneasy feeling as it put him in mind of a morgue. This was confirmed as he slid out a draw and revealed a skeleton. He slammed it back into the wall with a shiver, and opened another, then another.

The morgue seemed to be full of dead bodies. He would have expected to find maybe one dead person with flesh in place covered with a sheet, not dozens of bare skeletons in named draws. Many of them appeared to have been married couples.

Fear began to well up inside as he had visions of a flesh-eating bug that he may well now have picked up, and as if that was not scary enough he almost jumped out of his own skin when his ears were filled by a deafening klaxon.

He stood looking around with his hands to ears. He didn't think he had triggered an alarm, but he couldn't be sure. This was bound to bring the remaining people out of the woodwork he thought. Stan decided to get back to Larry. He tried to remember his way, disoriented in part because of the noise. Using a cross between a limp and a skip he quickly made it up to the canteen level then up the flight of stairs and along to the cells.

Opening his cell door he expected to be accosted by Larry, but he lay on the bunk apparently asleep. The watch on his wrist was flashing and possibly buzzing but could not be heard over the klaxon. Stan nudged him and then shook him vigorously.

'What?' Larry mouthed confused as he turned towards Stan.

It struck Stan that Larry was no old man, he may have been in his sixties but not old to Stan's mind, though he was blind. He looked as if he had had his eyes gouged out some years ago, and his left cheek held the angry scars from what may have been three fingernails. It certainly didn't look like the ravages of any disease.

Larry's gaunt expression changed from one of confusion through realisation to horror. He shoved Stan aside causing him to lose grip of his torch where he held it to the side of his head while protecting his ears. As it skittered across the floor Larry dashed for the door. Stan tried to grab him so as not to get locked back in his cell but Larry had no interest in pausing to shut the door.

Turning back to pick up the torch Stan limped after Larry who he saw stumble right at the junction, down the section of corridor Stan had not yet investigated. It was difficult to keep up with Larry who clearly knew his way around and shortly vanished into an unlocked room. Stan close behind, followed him in turning the lights on to see the man punching a code into a keypad, which turned the klaxon off.

Stan watched as Larry sank to the floor, looking quite scared.

'I think you have some explaining to do.' Stan demanded.

'Sshh!!' The man waved a hand for silence, listening intently.

After a long pause Stan spoke again. 'I hear nothing.'

'My hearing improved after I lost my sight.'

'So what are you listening for?'

'I'm not sure.'

'What do you mean?'

'They never told us what would happen if it wasn't switched off in time.'

'They?'

'The ones in charge.'

'And did they tell you to pretend to be an old man?'

'Sorry yes. They thought it safer for me.' He shook his head. 'How long was that klaxon sounding?'

'Five minutes I guess.'

'Not ten?'

'I don't think it was that long.'

'Are you sure?'

'Pretty sure…So what do you think might happen if the klaxon is not shut off?'

'I think the bunker is meant to self-destruct.'

'Why on earth would it do that?'

'To stop it being used by the enemy.'

'What enemy?'

'Al-Qaeda.'

'Al-Qaeda?' Stan almost laughed. 'Not Islamic State then?'

'Who?'

'How long have you been down here?'

'Since 2001…In the 80's I was approached by a group of people who proposed to use old mine-workings under my land to create a nuclear survival bunker. They said not only would they pay me for the land use and my secrecy they would offer me a place in the event the bunker needed to be used.

It only took them ten years to complete the project and soon enough all the signs of their workings were covered by new growth and it came to look like nothing more than an underground reservoir tank.

'When the 9/11 attack on the World Trade Centre happened the people suddenly came from miles around, by bus and then on foot the last few miles, looking like I was about to host a northern version of Glastonbury.

They all descended the ladder tube one by one, their rucksacks being lowered down on ropes. I was told that it was time for me to join them. I argued that I couldn't just drop things. They told me I had to come with them there and then because of the 9/11 event.

I tried to reason with them. After all, that was in America, not the UK. The truth was they just didn't want to risk having anyone on the surface who knew they were down below, but I didn't appreciate that at the time. I refused to join them, so they drugged me and brought me down here.

'Outnumbered I decided to go along with the plan, but after a while I could see the plan was failing. The geothermal energy was proving insufficient to power the whole bunker comfortably. Then we were told that something had happened on the surface which was why communications were lost with the surface and the other bunkers.'

'Other bunkers?'

'Yes. This is not the only one…So there was no more television or radio entertainment down here, or more importantly any news. The last we had heard was of the 7/7 bombings in London.

We only had recordings we had brought with us for entertainment after that. Even though we lent tapes and CDs out we grew bored. Someone tried to get a radio to work from the garage but they mysteriously fell down the stairwell.

It was then that stories began to spread that it was a news blackout to keep people under control and underground. Some people went to leave but found the ladder up to the surface had been removed, and with news of that major unrest broke out.

The leaders told us all we must settle down to our new lives underground, as it was believed the loss of communication with the surface was due to nuclear terrorism. However, a group of people didn't believe this because they wanted evidence and decided to blow their way out rather than stay down here. I offered to help.'

'Blow your way out?' Stan queried.

'Yes. The way this place was built was through a large deep tunnel which led to the cavern, at the back of which was the garage and beyond that the bunker. Once everything was delivered the concrete protective wall sealed the garage off. Then the concrete ceiling sealed the cavern and then the tunnel was back-filled to the surface.

When our future generations agreed the radiation levels above would likely be tolerable for life again the cavern ceiling and garage wall were to be explosively demolished with the charges built into them.

Then the digging equipment would tunnel the back-fill aside into the cavern until the surface was reached. No fast escape route. It would take a number of people a few days.'

'So what happened?'

'Word got out as we tried to make our way to the garage and an almighty riot broke out, with people fearing our escape was just going to kill everyone. That was when I lost my eyes.'

'I'm sorry.'

Stan and Larry fell silent. As much as there was to take in, Stan knew there was more to this.

'So how come the morgue is full of skeletons?'

'You found them did you?' Larry sounded disappointed.

'Yes.'

'This bunker was designed to be fully sustainable for hundreds of years. In that time nothing was to be wasted. Food, water, toilet waste, everything was, *is*, part of a cycle.'

'Oh my God…cannibalism?'

'Not quite. All the flesh that is stripped from the dead is put into food processing but actually goes to feed the fungal-meat substitute we have been eating, as does the toilet waste.'

'Urrgh.' Stan started to gag.

'After a while you don't think about it, you just accept it.'

'But how come so many people are now dead. This attempt at survival failed.'

'Yes it did.'

'So where are the other survivors?'

'Hiding I guess.'

'But why hide when they outnumber us?'

'I don't know, maybe they are planning how to finish us off.'

'You said you knew the way out...Let's get out of here.'

'First would you tell me what it's like up there? Is it all destroyed? And who are the Islamic State you mentioned?'

'It is not all destroyed up there, no. There's not been any third world war. But many countries *have* suffered levels of economic collapse and social breakdown. Some are at war with themselves, and often these more recent wars have been encouraged by Islamic State.

IS fighters are often young people who have been brought to believe that the only way for world peace to work is if everyone becomes worshippers of an extreme form of Islam, and if every last infidel, unbeliever, is killed.

However, there are many people who have now defected from IS because their common sense has made them realise that these are not the teachings of the true Islam.

Nevertheless, it is believed that IS now have nuclear capability, thanks to weapons sold by or removed from the collapsed Soviet states. As is the case with many radical movements, the people who drive these groups are themselves driven by anger and hatred. They've developed a twisted need to continue seeing pain and death. It is pure and simple a human sickness.'

'So you are saying it *isn't* safe up there?'

'It is nicer up there than here, but nowhere is ever safe. The bodies in your morgue tell me that here the road to hell, as they say, was paved by good intentions. If there is anything I have learned in my life, Larry, it is that we all have our differences and need to show tolerance. However, there are four evils that turn those differences into sources of misery and death.'

'What are they then?'

'Religion, disease, big business, and politics…In that order.'

'I'm not sure I'm ready to return, Stan.'

'I will see you get help…Come on, show me the way out.' Stan helped Larry to his feet. 'You don't happen to know where they put my jacket do you?'

'No, sorry.'

'Or what it was that the Baroness infected me with? I need the antidote.'

'You don't sound sick to me Stan.'

'Actually, I am feeling a lot better than I was.'

'I think Lydia was just messing with your head. Probably put something in your food. They will have been trying to scare you into telling them the truth.'

'But I have been. When did they stop messing with *your* head?'

'I'm not sure they ever did stop,' Stan said, leading the way out of the room.

Stan followed close behind. 'But I take it that when you survived the failed attempt to escape through the garage they forgave you and came to trust you.'

'Not fully, no.'

'How many others survived that attempt?'

'None.'

'Oh,' he hadn't expected that.

Larry turned right and headed further down the corridor which Stan had not yet explored. He continued to explain, 'I guess they thought a blind man would not be much of a threat, so they let me live. Though they did blame me each time someone had an accident and died. But they never had any evidence.'

Shortly Larry opened a door and led Stan inside. Putting the lights on Stan saw what looked like a general storage room, not a way out. In the middle was what might have been a cold storage unit, with lots of odds and ends propped up against it, including a folding ladder.

It was clear that their previous conversation had been stirring Larry's bitterness about his experience there, and he continued as if there had been no break in his storytelling. 'They just disliked having me here, but couldn't let me go you see.'

'But you weren't killing them were you?'

'What, a blind man?' Larry chuckled at the craziness of the suggestion, as he opened up a locker and reached inside.

'Larry?' A worrying thought occurred to Stan, his hands sliding into his pockets.

'Yes?'

'Why didn't one of the others turn the self-destruct system off?'

Larry turned away from the locker holding a machine gun.

'Stan, ma friend, you do realise arm gunner need to shoo chew.'

'Larry no!' Stan stared wide eyed at the madman with the machine gun, almost stumbling backwards with the shock, hands coming back out of his pockets for balance. Even if Larry was blind Stan knew that weapon would find its target with one or more of its rounds.

'Yes ma friend. Are cannot lit chew go git the police darn ear. Are keeled every last one of dem you see. Are locked most of dem in dare rooms till day starved to death.'

Unseen Stan aimed his gun, remembering to point it low on the torso, but he didn't want to pull the trigger. Right now this man before him needed help, but at the same time Stan didn't want to die trying to reason with him, so fired first.

Larry dropped his weapon with a yelp, clutching his hands between his legs and crumpled to his knees screaming, 'You've gore nan shot ma bloody bollocks off Stan!!'

Returning the safety to his weapon and replacing it in his pocket, Stan watched as Larry fell forwards and smacked his head off the floor. Stepping forward Stan kicked the machine gun aside and turned Larry over.

'Sorry Larry, you made me do that. Let's get you to the sick-bay.'

'No young man,' said Lydia, blood gushing out between clenched fingers. 'There's no pleasure to be had for *me* down *here* any longer.'

Stan knelt beside him.

'Am bleedin oot pawl. Get yousel in there,' Larry jerked his head towards the storage unit doors, 'Take those ladders.'

'But…'

'If you ever see my brother, tell him I'm glad it will be you on my farm not him.'

'I think you'll be seeing him before I do Larry.' Stan said, at a loss what he could do to save him, never mind think what he was saying.

'What makes you so sure?'

'He died eighteen months ago.'

'Wha…?' Larry's question, half cry half gurgle, died on his lips.

Stan stepped away from the widening pool of blood, and wondered if this really meant it was all over.

He opened the doors of the storage unit to reveal not a cold room but an airlock with security controls on the walls and another door at the far side, opening that he found the room with the ladder tube. Returning to the store room and taking the collapsible ladders he soon had them opened out and then connected up inside the tube. He was finally about to make his getaway when he decided instead to go and find his jacket.

Pint in hand, at Ryton Golf Club bar, Stan was being ribbed by Mike as usual.

'I'm surprised your injuries made no noticeable difference to you handicap, Stan.'

'Oh shut up.'

'Only you could have bought land at auction that turned out to be riddled with sink holes.'

'It's a wonder the surveyors never picked anything up,' said Dave.

'I guess the cavities were very deep down.' Stan had no intention of telling them the real story.

'So tell us again, what happened?' Bill asked, sensing that Stan was holding back on something more entertaining.

'As I said, I tripped going through the front door, twisted my ankle and banged my head on the tiles. When I came round I was worried about concussion so drove straight to the RVI.'

'You might have crashed,' said Dave.

'I'm surprised he didn't,' quipped Mike.

'The RVI said I checked out fine, anyway....When I went back out the next day, three deep sink holes had appeared, like there had been an earthquake. You hear about these things mysteriously appearing, but you never think it will happen to you. There's a big one in my main field about twenty metres deep, that unmarked water tank is now a five metre sink hole, and sadly my farmhouse and all its out buildings now rubble somewhere down around fifteen metres.'

'Lucky you weren't there at the time,' said Bill.

'And that it didn't happen after you had completed all the renovation work,' said Dave.

'So what are you going to do now Stan?' asked Mike.

'Well if I get the insurance money that I'm hoping for I'm going to invest in a new plot of land, a *long* way from Northumberland.'

'Where's that then Stan? The Maldives?' Mike joked, with topical news reference to the effects of rising sea levels.

'Ha ha, no. Further still, *and* with mining rights.'

'Australia?' Bill sounded jealous.

'Nope…Mars.'

People's heads turned towards the bar and the source of the raucous laughter.

Beyond Belief

It was a Thursday and for Sara Turner that meant getting the week's shopping straight after her shift at Aldi's then coming home to the housework.

At one time it had also meant cooking the dinner for the three of them as soon as she got in, but since her husband Paul was laid off, things had changed.

He would be down the pub by the time she got back, most evenings, and would not be back till after closing time. Lucy, her fourteen year old, now ate at McDonalds on the way back from school so it usually left Sara eating alone. She tended to snack between evening chores nowadays.

Sara ate her main meal at mid-day, which she felt contributed to her weight loss over the last couple of years, that and of course her worries about Paul.

He was no longer the man he used to be. When Sara had met Paul he was a dashingly handsome thirty-three year old. Paul had reminded her of Aidan Turner the lead actor in the old 2015-19 series of Poldark. However, the only thing they really had in common was their surname.

Nowadays Paul sported a beer-belly which was as attractive as his language. It would seem that gone were the days with talk of love, replaced by criticism and at times emotional and physical abuse.

The blows had only happened a few times when Paul had lost control of his temper, over silly things like Sara not being a mind-reader. The bruises had disappeared over time and thankfully had been easy to hide under her clothing.

Whilst she did not forget she did forgive him each time in memory of the love they had once shared. She blamed the bad management at his workplace for losing him and other colleagues their jobs at the factory. *They* had lost most of their contracts to China and India, leaving Paul and others feeling worthless having been unable to find any work since. Nevertheless, deep down she knew it was no excuse for the violence.

She stood in front of the ironing board watching the new Ian Tennant chat show while she ironed their bedding and clothes. The host of the show was talking to a few stars partners about what it was like living with famous people.

Tracy Headley, wife of Newcastle United footballer Max Headley, recounted how at first it was like some amazing dream date then as the relationship developed there was the need to learn tolerance. Stars were in the limelight through their commitment to the job and this often put a strain on their relationships.

The wives and girlfriends, at times, had to see themselves as being in a support role for it to work well. This could feel like their star was being very selfish and somewhat uncaring. Part of the problem was the way they were managed, developing characteristics which might keep them in the public eye. Being seen places, saying the right things, sometimes the wrong things, and getting it all tweeted. It was all part of competing with the other celebrities.

In summary Tennant concluded that celebrities also needed to be supportive of their partners and realise how much their partners needed time with them alone, not to have to share them forever.

As the show finished so did the pile of Sara's ironing. The news followed with headlines about the governments new directives to deal with the growing threats of nuclear terrorism. Sara didn't want to hear about this again, turning the iron off and lifting the neatly stacked laundry, Sara went upstairs to put it in the airing cupboard.

As she passed her daughter's room she thought she could hear crying.

Lucy spent little time downstairs these days. She had taken to living in her room watching videos on her laptop, or Skyping friends. Sara doubted that she was upset about the terrorism report, if she even watched the news. It seemed more likely she had got upset with someone on Skype, or had been trolled again. She knocked on the door.

'I'm fine,' she responded and the crying stopped.

Sara walked in with the laundry, to see her daughter drying her eyes, knees close to her chest, back up against the wall. Placing the laundry at the end of the bed Sara sat next to Lucy and drew her close.

'What's happened darling?'

'Nothing, I told you, I'm fine.'

'I don't think you'd be crying over nothing. What is it? Is it more trolling?'

There was a long pause before Lucy tried to begin, 'Last night…' but she couldn't bring herself to say it.

'What about last night?'

'Last night…when Dad came back from the pub…'

Sara knew then this wasn't about trolling. She was about to apologise for Paul's previous night's shouting but let Lucy say what was on her mind.

'He came to my room, after the shouting, while you did the dishes, and he took me in his arms…'

'Well I'm sure he's sorry for how he behaves, and just wants you to know he loves you.'

'*Loves me*?! I wish he would leave us!'

'But darling…'

'He didn't just cuddle me, Mum, he began stroking my chest…'

'No, I…'

'He *did* Mum and started telling me how I was becoming a big girl. Then…holding me tight so I could barely struggle, he moved his hand down here,' she slid her hand between her legs, the tears welling back up.

'No Lucy…'

'It's *true*…I knew you wouldn't believe me!'

'It's just…'

'It's not the first time either…He has done this a number of times over the last few months. Coming home drunk…'

'I'm sorry darling, I didn't know…'

They both turned to the door, surprised by the figure standing there. Paul was home early from the pub and was propping himself up in

105

the doorframe. 'What's she been saying?!' he demanded.

'We are just worried about you dear.'

'Worried about me? If you had any fucking concern about me woman, you'd have had my supper on.'

'But you are home early.'

'Don't make excuses. You're as bad as that no-good fucker behind the bar.'

'Well if I'm no good for you Paul maybe you'd manage living here without me!'

'Too fucking right I would. Why don't you get out of my house right now!'

'No don't leave me Mum!' screamed Lucy.

'Shut up you little trouble-maker!' Paul dashed threateningly at his daughter who curled up tighter.

Sara stood up to come between them, but Paul knocked her aside. She stumbled against the pile of washing and ended up with it on the floor, landing hard on her hip.

Paul took Lucy by the collar of her blouse lifting her towards him, tearing the blouse open.

'No Dad, please!' Lucy pleaded but all she got was a hard slap across the face.

Sara got to her feet and came up behind Paul grabbing him by the left shoulder. 'No Paul, let her be!'

'You both need a good seeing to.'

'Listen to yourself Paul!'

Paul thrust Lucy back onto her bed by her throat, leaving her to gag, then span towards Sara his face red with rage and alcohol, and before she could say anymore he slammed his right first hard into Sara's left eye, knocking her backwards.

Tripping over her feet she fell, hitting her head on the doorframe. The fall seemed to happen in slow motion, with Lucy's screaming filling Sara's ears.

When Sara opened her eyes again she was in bed. She turned over and the way the covers resisted her movement told her Paul was next to her, rather than on the sofa where she sometimes found him after a bad night.

She had the distinct sensation that something had happened but she couldn't remember what, she felt dazed and confused.

She noticed her face was aching and her left eye was not opening properly it confirmed something had indeed happened. Then it came flooding back to her, Paul hitting her in Lucy's room, but she had no memory to fill the gap between then and now.

Sara made to get out of bed but her hip made her wince. Biting back the pain she swung her legs out and tried to sit up. The back of her head throbbed and she lifted a hand to feel a lump there.

'How are you feeling love?' The voice next to Sara scared her more than the state of her body, not because of her fear of Paul, but because this was not the voice of Paul.

Sara turned blinking in the early morning light as she stared at the man next to her. She had to be imagining things. There, lying next to her, now propping his head up with one arm was the lead actor from Poldark, Aidan Turner.

'Oh darling I'm so sorry.' He looked gutted about the state of her. 'It was so stupid of me leaving that rake there in the shed like that... Careless... Unforgivable... Your poor face.' He sat up extending his arms.

But Sara backed away, having difficulty handling this. It sounded like an excuse Paul would come out with, but what concerned her more was how this actor had got in bed with her, and was treating her as *his*.

'I ur have work to...' was all she could think of saying.

'Huh, I don't think so. Not in your condition,' he said with his brow clearly wrinkling in the dim light. 'The kids can do the washing up before they head to school.'

'The kids?'

'Yes. They have done it before. Are you feeling okay?' he asked again. 'The doctor at the hospital said you had a mild concussion from the paving after you fell from the shed.'

'Shed?'

'Yes. Oh darling, you *are* in a bad way.' He took her in his arms and held her close. It felt good, her tension melted somewhat. This was not Paul.

'Aldi's,' she muttered, wondering whether she was going to have to call in sick.

'I'll pick up the shopping on my way back from university.'

'University?' She couldn't make sense of any of this. She pinched her sore buttock hard. 'Owch.'

'Sorry, I didn't mean to hug you so tight. I think you need to stay in bed for the day. I'll see to Lucy and Lenny.'

'Lenny?'

'Just rest.'

108

Sara lay back down and watched as Aidan got up and went to the bathroom. Turning to look at the bedside table she saw what looked like a wedding photo of the two of them, looking maybe twenty years younger. It was like the photo she used to have of Paul and her till she put it away in a cupboard.

This was madness. She shook her head but achieved little more than a pain down her neck. The blow to her face must have done something.

As she remained lying there listening to the strange morning noises, her heart began to race as she heard Lucy and Lenny talking.

Lucy's voice was different. She waited for them to leave so that she could get up and investigate what was going on. Lenny was the name she intended for the son she had always wanted but never had. Paul had somehow become sterile after Lucy was born.

What she was experiencing now though was beyond belief. It was as if she was imagining what life might have been like had she married Aidan and yet it all felt wrong. As attracted as she was to Aidan, she didn't know him, and certainly did not love him, as she once had loved Paul. It was as if her brain was asking her to accept what she was seeing and yet not giving her the means to do so.

With everyone out of the house she got out of bed, put on her bathrobe and went to the bathroom. Most of her things were there in the racks, but there was nothing she recognised of

Lucy's or Paul's. This was all a mix of Aidan, Lenny and new Lucy.

Sara caught sight of herself in the mirror. Her black-eye looked horrific. Could a rake really do that? She and Paul didn't even have a shed never mind a rake. She had always wanted to sort the garden but never seemed to have the time.

She walked downstairs wincing with the pain from her hip. Looking out from the kitchen she saw a wonderful garden, not the wilderness she was used to. It was as if some garden-makeover programme had visited overnight. And there was the shed, where the wheelie bins normally sat.

She filled the kettle and switched it on for a cup of Douwe Egberts coffee. Opening the cupboard she found it full of lots of other things she would not normally be able to afford.

She found herself wondering why Aidan Turner was working at a university when he was a famous actor. Adding sugar and stirring her coffee she decided to go and look at her Being Human and Poldark DVD box sets.

She found them where she left them in the cupboard under the smart TV, but the covers were different. The lead role was played by someone called Peter Maynard, who she had never heard of, though he did look a little like Aidan. This didn't make sense.

She switched on the Smart TV and searched IMDb for Aidan Turner, but turned up nothing. She started wondering had she ended up in a reality where she had somehow changed Aidan Turner's career path?

Thinking of careers Sara thought she should call her line manager at Aldi's.

'Is that you Mary?'

'Yes.'

'It's Sara, I...'

'Sara who?' there was no sound of recognition in her voice.

'Sara, Sara Turner.'

'I'm sorry I don't know a Sara Turner.'

'This *is* Mary Trent?'

'Yes.'

'But...Never mind.' Sara hung up, disturbed that her line manager had not recognised her.

She wondered around the house, cup of coffee in hand, looking at its familiar but mostly unfamiliar contents. Lenny's room was what she imagined a boy's room would look like, but Lucy's room looked different to what her Lucy had had.

It wasn't just that she was able to afford better things it was that there was clearly a different personality to this Lucy. The room was nowhere near as tidy. Sara looked at pictures of her but it was not the Lucy she knew and loved.

Both Lucy and Lenny were a mix of Sara's and Aidan's features, but Sara realised she felt no connection with these children other than that. She broke down and cried, and over her crying she could hear her Lucy's scream like an echo, *'No don't leave me Mum!'* Sara was sure she was going out of her mind.

Sara felt uncomfortable staying in the house. Finding some large sunglasses to help hide her black-eye, she headed out of their Jesmond home for a walk down into the dene. Her hip ached but she decided that further exercise might ease it.

Away from the house it was as if the strangeness of the morning faded away, but not fully. The dene looked like it always did. There was nothing out of the ordinary to see out there, but inside her head was a different matter. She knew that she and her Lucy had been victims of Paul's domestic violence. However, she couldn't explain how someone could get from that situation to being married to Aidan Turner. It just didn't make any sense, yet it did not feel like any dream she had ever had before.

She could hear the birds in the branches and the babbling of the stream; feel the bark of the trees and the hardness of the bench she sat on. Maybe just maybe when she got home she would find everything as it should be. But then it shouldn't be like that; Paul shouldn't be like that. She had to help Lucy.

Back at the house she found it as she had left it, Aidan and Sara's home. She turned the TV on and flicked through the channels half expecting to see other differences in casting, as if she was now in a world where people were married to celebrities and there were unknowns in their place on the screen, but everything looked normal.

She rang her doctor's surgery to make an appointment, but there were none available till Tuesday, and she found herself agreeing to an early Tuesday morning appointment.

Turning the TV off, Sara went out into the garden. It looked just how she would have liked it. It actually looked loved, but loved by whom?

Sara had no memory of doing any of this. How could she, she hadn't. The thought struck her, what had become of the Sara she had replaced, or was it further madness to be thinking such thoughts?

Back inside she went to the TV and started looking up amnesia on Google which took her to Wikipedia. *A deficit in memory caused by brain damage* it said. It went on to suggest that she might have retrograde as opposed to anterograde amnesia, since she believed she was remembering everything fine since she had woken up.

It said the amnesia could be brought on by head trauma or certain drugs. Had she taken any drugs? Maybe Paul drugged her after she had fallen. The thought sent a shiver down her back and tears to her eyes again. She wiped her eyes and winced. The black-eye was *so* sore.

The Wikipedia page mentioned nothing of *alternative* memories, but she did spot the link to *false* memory at the bottom of the page. As she read the new page it described false memories as being specific to an event, possibly involving a traumatic experience. She had certainly had one of those, but it offered no explanations for remembering a whole other life of memories, or experiencing an alternative life in the present.

Her eyes fixed on a line that read *'false memory can be declared a syndrome when recall of a false or inaccurate memory takes great effect on your life. This false memory can completely alter the orientation of your personality and lifestyle.'* Sara certainly felt disoriented, with the now, the present, still feeling unreal.

She needed someone to talk to about this *syndrome*, and considered phoning the Samaritans, but worried that they might think her a prank caller once she tried to explain what she was experiencing.

The day did not feel like it had flown but at the sound of the front door Sara looked at the clock on the mantelpiece and it was 4:00. She hadn't even eaten.

Lenny came into the lounge. 'Hi Mum.'

'Hello dear,' she replied, hurriedly closing off the webpage.

'How are you doing?'

'Oh a bit sore, you know.'

Lenny came and gave Sara a hug, 'You look like you've been in a punch-up. Either that or poorly planned slap-stick…get it?' he tried to cheer her up with reference to the rake.

Sara pulled away to arms-length looking at the boy she had never had. It felt like she was looking at some long lost relative, and she was conscious of the fact that she would have to act more motherly if she was not going to arouse suspicion of her condition.

'What do you want for tea?'

'Pizza.'

'Okay.'

'Really?' he looked at her as if she was joking.

'Sure.'

'But we had pizza last night, don't you remember.'

'Oh yes, well I'll just…' she headed for the kitchen to see what was in the fridge-freezer.

114

'But I don't mind having pizza again.'

'No I think we'll have that another day.'

'Right.'

'How about chicken pie?'

'Fine.'

'How about Lucy?'

'Ha, you're kidding right?' he frowned, unsure and oddly unable to read his mother.

'Urr…'

'She's vegetarian.'

'What?' Her Lucy wasn't vegetarian. She had to get her wits about her. 'Doesn't a battery hen count as a vegetable?'

'Ha, you crack me up.'

Sara smiled at him smiling back. He did appear to be the son she always wanted. He looked about twelve, and had more of a look of Aidan in real life than Lenny did in his photos.

'I'm just going to go get my homework out of the way,' he said pointing at the ceiling before turning and grabbing his school bag.

Sara had no idea when the other two would turn up, but knew she was going to have to say something to Aidan. Maybe that was the key to this delusion. Burst the bubble and get back to dealing with reality.

By five o'clock she had prepared veg, located the Quorn for new Lucy, and decided to sit on the sofa and watch some TV.

Aidan returned just as she was trying to figure out the rules to Make'em Pay which she had heard of but never watched before.

'Hello darling. I thought you were going to rest up today.' Aiden came in and gave her a kiss, kneeling in front of her.

'I *had* to get up and do *something*.'

115

'Just like you.' He examined the bruising. 'I'm so cross with myself. Your beautiful face bruised because of me not putting the rake away properly when that hail came down the other day.'

'Don't blame yourself Aidan. I should have been looking where I was treading.'

'But it was too dark. And it should have been me who went out to look for the WD40 for that bathroom cabinet door.'

'What's done is done.'

'You are so forgiving. I don't deserve you.' He kissed her again.

It made Sara's heart race, but then she felt confused, like she was cheating on Paul. She had to sort this out. She had to burst the bubble, but maybe *after* they had eaten.

'Did Lucy say when she would be back?' she asked.

'Not to me…' he said with a shake of his head. 'But she's usually back before six on a Friday, isn't she.'

Sara wondered if she was giving her amnesia away too soon. What if it became obvious during talk at the dinner table? She felt anxious again.

'Are you okay?' he asked.

'Yes. I'll be fine.'

'Let me do the cooking tonight.'

'You've been working.'

'*If* you can call supervising some very talented drama groups *work*… Anyway, it will make a change. You just put your feet up and watch…Oh you're not watching this, surely…' he said looking at the TV. 'You hate this.'

'I was changing channels when you came in,' she bluffed.

'It's not like you to give rubbish TV a second chance. Let me get the Amazon remote for you.'

'Thanks…I've prepared the veg and I thought we'd have chicken pies tonight, and there's Quorn pieces and veg gravy for Lucy.'

The dinner was relatively quiet. Sara was not looking to say anything that might give things away. She spent her time watching her new family and listening to Lenny and Lucy describe things that happened at school. From what Lucy said about working towards her first major exams Sara guessed she must be fifteen or sixteen.

After the main course Aidan shared out a tub of Haagen-Dazs between the four of them, and all too soon the dinner was over, and the kids were excused to go watch TV.

It was now or never, thought Sara, though in truth it would have been now or later. What she had to say had to be said while she and Aidan were alone.

'Are you sure everything is okay?' Aidan asked aware that Sara was still tense.

'No, not exactly.'

'What is it?' he grew anxious.

'I don't want to worry you but…I can't remember anything since waking up this morning in bed.'

Aidan lifted Sara from the dining chair and wrapped her in his arms. 'Oh love. It doesn't surprise me that you don't remember anything after that blow you took to the face and the head.'

'Aidan. I don't mean *anything afterwards*, what I mean is *anything at all*.'

Aidan held her at arms-length as if that would help him hear her better. With his questioning expression he didn't need to say anything.

'I don't remember *us…this*,' she waved a hand. 'I don't even remember the children.'

'Right we're going back to the RVI.'

'But…'

'*Now!*' he whisked her towards the hallway, grabbing for coats. He popped into the lounge. 'You're Mum and I are just popping out for a bit, so how about you get that washing up done before we get back.'

'Oh sure,' said Lenny in a tone that made washing up twice in a day sound unlikely, while Lucy made no response at all, too caught up with face-timing a friend on her iPhone.

It took Aiden less than ten minutes to get them parked in the RVI multi-storey, but over an hour to be seen.

He was quite frustrated in his concern for Sara, even though she kept a firm hold of his hand the whole time. Luckily it was the same doctor on duty as when Aidan had brought her in the previous night.

Aidan made to come in with her but to his surprise Sara placed a hand on his chest and asked him to wait for her in the waiting room.

He was not happy about that, but she promised she would explain what was discussed when she came back out.

The doctor had her accident report up on screen including the x-ray and head scans that were taken. 'I take it you have been feeling the effects of the concussion…the dizziness and tiredness.'

'Tiredness no…It's more like anxiety.'

'Well it has been a shock to your system a trauma of this scale, although relatively minor compared to say a traffic accident. Head trauma can affect people in different ways…'

'Would you just let me explain?'

'Sorry, do go on.'

'Thank you,' Sara took a deep breath and sighed, deciding to take this in steps. 'I have no memory of my past here since I woke up this morning.'

'None?' It was clear from the doctor's tone that he thought she was exaggerating.

'Yes, none. I don't mean I'm a little fuzzy about what happened to me, I mean I don't even recognise my family.'

'Oh…You would seem to be experiencing some form of amnesia, though it is uncommon with such an injury as yours. However, I would expect it is only temporary and relates to your brain trauma,' he said pointing to the scan where the area of concussion lay.

'I looked up amnesia today, on the Internet.'

'Okay.'

'Although it said it might be temporary, it only seemed to talk about loss of memory of events not a whole life.'

'Well maybe you were not reading it clearly. Retrograde amnesia can certainly wipe from memory everything that existed before a certain point, except of course how to do things, like talking, eating, playing a musical instrument.'

'But I know where I am, and I recognise my house. I just don't recognise my family.'

'So what you are saying is that you are blocking out your family.'

'What do you mean?'

'Sometimes when there is a traumatic experience associated with something the mind simply blocks it out.'

'But my *whole* family? That doesn't make sense. They are lovely people…Well, what little I've learned about them today.'

'Maybe you have had an anxiety attack and wanted to be away from them.'

'No…'

'Are you on any medication Mrs Turner?'

'No…'

The doctor referred to her medical records. 'Yes you appear to be taking the Ziprasidone Geodon.'

'What? That's…Those can't be my records…I've never…'

'Yes yes, you have been taking these for some years…have you had your meds today?'

'No, because I don't take them.'

'Okay Mrs Turner, calm down, just listen to me, it's going to be okay. The blow to the head has complicated matters but you have a delusional from of Schizophrenia which is kept under control with your tablets. I can get you some to take now, save you waiting till you get back home.'

'No wait. I don't feel Schizophrenic.'

'And what *would* that feel like Mrs Turner?' he gave her his best quizzical look. 'The longer you leave it the more confused you will feel.'

'No. Listen to me. I have a husband called Paul and a daughter called Lucy. We have both been suffering domestic abuse from Paul who is alcoholic. He hit me, gave me this black-eye.'

'The report says you were struck by a garden rake. Are you saying that your husband hit you?'

'Yes, in the real world.'

'I will have to inform the authorities.'

'No listen. Aiden did not do this, Paul did. Paul is not part of *your* world.'

'*Okay*, Paul is part of your *delusion*.'

'No it is not a delusion, it is real!' Sara felt her anger getting the better of her. This doctor just wasn't listening.

'Calm down Mrs Turner....Delusions will feel real, like vivid dreams.'

'I've had vivid dreams before doctor. This is different. I can remember details going back decades.'

'You believe you remember them. The brain is very good at playing tricks.'

Sara began to sob, not knowing what else to say to convince the doctor.

'Let me get you the medication. Just take it and see how you feel in the morning.' Not waiting for agreement he wrote out a prescription and stepped outside the room to pass it to a nurse, asking her to run along to the dispensary desk, that this was quite urgent.

When he came back into the room Sara started once again to impress upon him that she was experiencing something different. 'I can hear my daughter's scream as I collapsed in her room...*No don't leave me Mum!*'

'Voices in the head, yes,' the doctor nodded. 'Typical symptoms, but nothing we can't help you control. What I want you to do is focus on the now, and on *you*. You need to keep yourself calm and don't worry about anyone else until you get yourself back to rights…Okay?'

'Okay.' Sara gave in, trying to focus on her breathing even though she could still hear her Lucy crying. She just wanted to wake up and reach out to her. She was still real to her.

Then, as much as she tried to focus on the *now* she began to think ahead. What if she started to accept all of this and forget about her Lucy once she started taking these drugs? This led her back to wondering whether Paul was trying to drug her and this medical support was the delusion.

She felt so drained that by the time the Geodon arrived with a cup of water she took it without question, and was shown back to the waiting room.

Aidan's worried face broke into a half-smile as he saw her coming back out and he got up to take her by the arm, thanking the nurse who'd shown her through. Aidan was shocked, Sara looked worse than when she went in as if she was carrying a massive weight in addition to her injuries.

'We'll get you home darling.'

'Thanks.'

'What did the doctor say about your memory loss?'

'Can we just wait till we are in the car?'

'Sure. Sorry, yes.'

A little later, they both sat in the car. Aidan put the keys in the ignition but then left them dangling there. 'So what does he think?'

'Do I take medication Aidan?'

'Your meds, *oh your meds!*' He put his face in his hands with shame. 'You must have missed your meds last night. I'm so *stupid!* Did you take any today?'

'Aidan. I don't believe I take any meds. This feels all wrong.'

'I'm sorry darling. Don't you remember, back when this all started we were told if you came off the meds you could start to think you don't need them, and possibly even while you were taking them. You must take them, *you must.* The distraction of the accident has messed things up. You'll soon be back to normal.' He leaned across, taking her in his arms, tears in his eyes. 'I love you *so* much Sara.'

'I have a husband called Paul, and a daughter called Lucy.'

'Yes Lucy, but not Paul, I'm Aidan,' he choked back a sob, sick with worry that he could be losing her.

'The Lucy I have with Paul looks and sounds different to the Lucy I have here with you Aidan.'

'You're just confused.'

'I checked out false memories on the internet today Aidan. It doesn't mention anything as extensive as my memory of Paul and Lucy. There is no Lenny there. I had wanted a Lenny, but never had a son. Paul is an abusive alcoholic and he has punched me to the ground in Lucy's bedroom. This is where this black-eye is from.'

'No, no, that's just a delusion darling you are here safe with me and the kids.' He clutched her hands. '*Please* believe me.'

'If I wanted to delude myself, don't you think I would have made it a dream-world not a nightmare?'

'I...I don't know.'

'From what I've seen of this reality today Aidan, this is almost my dream-world, but I know I don't belong here. I have to go back and sort things out...To save Lucy.'

'No, no darling.' Aidan held her tighter, tears streaming down his face. He had never seen her like this before. She seemed so convinced by what she was saying. 'I know...tomorrow, after a nights rest, we'll all go to Hadrian's Wall. You like it there. It will help bring back your memories, I'm sure of it...Okay?'

'Okay.' Sara said, not wanting to see Aidan Turner cry.

'Good, that's settled, and we'll go to that pub you like for lunch.'

'Right,' she didn't sound convinced, but was looking forward to seeing Hadrian's Wall. Paul, Lucy and Sara had never been.

That evening Sara noticed a book on the bedside table that she had read recently, except here the bookmark was near the beginning.

'Aidan?'

'Yes dear?'

'When did I buy this book?' she said showing him.

'Last weekend I believe. Why? Are you remembering it?'

'I remember it perfectly, because I finished reading it three weeks ago.'

'But…'

'Don't you see…This is proof that I'm not from here.'

'Have you taken your meds?'

'Yes I have, I was given some at the hospital, but they might as well have been paracetamol. They have changed nothing. Look, let me tell you how this book ends and then you have a look.' She went on to describe the ending handing it to Aidan to check.

He spent ten minutes skip reading the end of her book. 'You are right, but maybe you finished it before the accident and the bookmark has just gone back in near the front. I don't know.' He stroked her arm, but she took the book and placed it back on the bedside table, switching the lamp of and facing away from him frustrated.

Aidan began to run his hands over her back. He could feel the tension in her and rubbed more firmly, kissing the base of her neck, but she wasn't loosening up. He turned her over towards him and shifted his chest across hers before kissing her lips. Looking into her eyes he tried to read her.

'We don't have to do anything tonight if you don't want to.'

Sara had certainly fantasized about being with Aidan, but now that it felt so real it didn't feel right. 'Can we just spoon tonight? I'm still not…'

'Sure, of course.' He wrapped his arms around her to hold her back against his chest and pulled the underside of her legs onto the top of his, lying side by side.

Though Sara felt comforted by his closeness and support, it continued to feel wrong.

Sara had thought that she would wake from this dream to find Paul next to her that Saturday morning, but there was Aidan. She lay there thinking through the last day. It all seemed as clear in her memory as a typical day would have been, if not clearer.

Was it at all possible she could have imagined Paul? No, that just didn't make any sense. That would require her to have imagined a whole other life to fill a memory gap in her present reality where Aidan Turner was not a famous celebrity.

Aidan got up and went down stairs to put the kettle on. Listening to the sounds he made, Sara began wondering why she could not just accept this, *if* it was just going to continue. Maybe she could tell herself over time that the way things didn't add up was just because she had let her imagination confuse her, imagining problems.

Nevertheless, she could still hear her Lucy in the back of her mind screaming, but now it was simply 'Mum!'

Sara buried her face in her pillow, wanting to cry again, but this time no tears came, it just made her throat ache. Then she heard Aidan returning with the coffee, and turned over to face him. 'What, no toast?' she teased.

'Toast?' he looked at her unsure, 'so that we find crumbs in the bed?'

'I know. I'm grateful for the coffee. I'm just not used to it being brought up to me.'

'After all these years and you are still not used to it?'

'We often have coffee in bed then?'

'Yes. Doesn't it feel at all familiar?'

'No,' she took a sip of the coffee. 'Aidan…What was I like before the accident?'

'Essentially the same, but clearly less confused, especially once we understood you needed to be on Geodon.'

'You need the *other* Sara back.'

'Don't talk like that darling. You *are* my Sara, but give it time and you will be back to your old self.'

'What if I'm not?'

'Well we can adjust. I love you Sara. I'm here for you.'

'I know you are here for *your* Sara, but I do not believe that is *me*.'

'Believe it.'

'It is not that simple. I can still hear my Lucy crying out to me. It makes my heart ache. I feel torn apart.'

'But there is no need. Lucy is fine.'

'Our Lucy would appear to be, but my Lucy *isn't*. As I've said, they don't even look the same. My Lucy shares Paul's genes, this Lucy shares yours.'

'Okay there is some sort of logic to what you describe, but why would you imagine yourself married to an abusing husband by choice?'

'None of this *is* by choice. I'm just trying to work out how to deal with what I'm experiencing.'

'Maybe you need a stronger dose of your meds.'

'What?'

'Just for a while. You said they didn't seem to have any effect…But they did work before.'

'They worked for *your* Sara.'

'You *are* my Sara,' he insisted. 'People don't just switch places. It really is just your condition, worsened by the trauma with the rake. You need to give it time…Look it's a lovely morning, I think we should get up now and go to Steel Rigg before lunch, in case the weather changes. Fresh air will do you good.'

'Okay,' she conceded.

As Aidan drove the four of them up the A69 all Sara could recall was coming this way with Paul years ago when they went to Hexham. As Aidan turned off onto the military road going past Heddon-on-the-Wall the route became more scenic, though all new to Sara.

She appreciated that Aidan could walk to work from where they lived in Jesmond, but surely they could afford to live out west, in the countryside. She would love that.

'Have you ever thought of us moving out here?'

'We have discussed this but, until the kids are finished with schooling, and we've saved up enough we decided to stay put.'

'Something to look forward to then,' she suggested.

'Sure,' he beamed a hopeful smile.

Aidan turned up towards the wall near Vindolanda, and soon they were parked at the Steel Rigg car park and busy putting their walking boots on.

Sara's boots looked worn, yet she had no memory of wearing them before. She wanted this feeling to go away.

She needed resolution. She started to wonder again whether there was something she needed to do to sort it, like lay down in Lucy's bedroom doorway where she fell and close her eyes. Or maybe here she needed to lie down on the paving outside the shed. But would that have to be at the same time of day as the accident? When was that? What were the right conditions?

'Are you okay dear?'

'What?'

'You seemed to be staring at your boots.'

'Sorry,' she checked her laces. 'I'm ready.'

With her hip still clearly aching Aidan put Sara's right arm through his left and gave her support. Lucy and Lenny walked on ahead as Aidan remote locked the car.

'Thanks Aidan.'

'For what?'

'Being there for me,' she explained.

'In sickness and in health,' he reminded her of their vows.

Sara felt she should be telling Aidan she loved him for that, but she just didn't feel she had known him long enough for those feelings to have developed. If she was indeed suffering a mental illness did that mean it destroyed love between couples? What a sad thought. She decided to focus on something more amusing to share with Aidan.

'You know Aidan, where I'm from you are a famous celebrity.'

'*Where you are from?* That makes you sound like an alien.'

'I might as well be, right now. But you really are a famous actor. You have been in Being Human, and Poldark.'

'Hah! I wish…'

'You were even in the three Hobbit movies.'

'*Three* Hobbit movies? You do realise how daft that sounds, right?'

'Sure. There was only the one book but they made three films.'

'Not in this world they didn't, and as for my acting career, that never worked out.'

'Was that because of me?'

'No! Don't think that. If I hadn't started working at the uni we would never have met.'

'How did we meet?'

It saddened Aidan to think that memory was also lost to his wife. 'We met in the cafeteria. You were serving me roast pork but when I looked at what you handed me on the plate I said don't I get any mash. You took a massive scoop without comment and leaned forward to tap it out on top of what was there. Then to our amazement, as the serving spoon tapped the plate, it cracked from front to back, and emptied the gravy and half the dinner down my trousers.

'You were so apologetic about it you told me to come round to the side as you grabbed a damp cloth. Without thinking you started trying to wipe me down. Then you became embarrassed as you realised you should have simply handed me the cloth. As I looked into your eyes, I knew you were special. I explained that I had a change of clothes in the car in case I decided to go out after work, and made some corny remark about you coming for a drink with me after work so that we could laugh about the accident.'

'That sounds romantic.'

Aidan just smiled.

'Thank you for being patient with me Aidan.'

They carefully descended into Sycamore Gap and then up the other bank back onto the escarpment where Sara needed to get her breath back.

'Is this bringing back any memories?' Aidan asked.

'It is beautiful, but no. None.'

'Mum!' Lucy's voice came like a fearful warning.

Sara looked ahead to Lucy and Lenny to see a bright light, as bright as the sun coming from Newcastle.

Everyone shielded their eyes. They couldn't believe what they were seeing. It was a nightmare. Their hair stood on end with the terror of what this was, as a mushroom cloud thrust high into the sky, and then the hot blast of radiated air was upon them, blowing them from the escarpment into the tree. There was no time for reason only fear and anger at how stupid people could be. Sara lost hold of Aidan and her head struck a branch hard.

Sara was traumatised. She felt herself being lifted then struck a number of times, but as

Lucy's screams became louder and more frantic than the roaring in her ears, she became aware of a great anger welling up inside her, and a need to survive. She opened her eyes.

Looming over her with fist drawn back for another blow, the other hand on her collar was Paul, red-faced with fury.

With all the might she could muster Sara kicked her husband between the legs, and as he doubled over saw that Lucy was behind him thumping his back as hard as she could.

Sara followed through with the hardest punch she could to Paul's nose. Then as he crumpled to the side holding his bleeding face, Sara instinctively knew she had to act fast to end all this.

She searched his pockets for his keys, throwing them aside, then grabbed *him* by the collar and dragged him down the stairs, stopping only to open the front door before lifting him with muscle she didn't know she had and booting him out onto the front path.

'Consider this the separation before divorce. *We* are over Paul!'

She sighed long and hard, breathing out long held tensions, as if she had just experienced some life changing epiphany. If there was anything of any meaning Sara could take and share with Lucy from her time with Aidan, it was that life really was too short and unpredictable not to make the best of what you had, and there were far better people than Paul out there to make a future with.

Sara turned to see Lucy come down stairs crying, and took her daughter in her arms. 'It's going to be okay…I just need to phone the police.'

Beware of the Postie

Known affectionately by his mates as Big Ben on account of his height, rather than anything else, Sergeant Ben McGregor was surprised to find that he failed his Special Air Service reselection in the Brecon Beacons following Desert Storm III. He claimed that his failure was due to having grown far too used to running on sand in stifling heat, and being ill prepared for firm ground and a bit of damp. His sense of humour had always held him in good stead but he didn't think it would cope so well with being RTU'd back to the Paras.

When Big Ben's wife Meg heard his news she began selling the benefits of a new life in Newcastle upon Tyne, where he had grown up. He understood where she thought she was coming from. To her the outcome of the reselection was a blessing.

It would mean no more worrying about him crossing icy rivers and yomping across kilometres of tundra in the dark. No more need to evict spiders and scorpions from his jungle boots. No more ringing ears after the flash-bangs in the killing-house, and certainly no more evasion, capture and interrogation exercises. But deep down, Big Ben still wanted to know he could hack it, all of it.

Meg had tried to reason with him on a number of occasions previously, 'One day you won't quite manage it. *Our* luck will run out. You'll get injured or worse still fail to beat the clock tower, and what about *me* then? I want children. I want them with *you*, and I want you to be there to see them grow up.' He remembered how he just listened to her without saying a word. The Regiment was his family and his life.

Nevertheless, the time had come and with no better options in the offing they moved from Hereford to Newcastle, and once settled down they had their first child, Robbie. As much as he loved being with his family, he wasn't sure he was cut out to be a dad. He continued to miss The Regiment, the *action* and the crack with the lads even though in choosing his job in Newcastle he had thought it sensible to keep to something he was good at, walking long distances with a pack. So he had become a Postie.

One Friday evening Big Ben's sister Marion came to stay for the weekend, to hit the night clubs and of course to see her nephew Robbie before Meg took him down south Saturday morning to his only grandparents.

Then, as if it was thought that Big Ben needed even more company, out of the blue that Saturday afternoon Disney, one of Big Ben's troop mates, turned up. He had visited a couple of times before, but this time had appeared with a young woman. She had shoulder length black hair, and Big Ben was surprised to hear Disney introduce her as his fiancée.

'That's one for the books,' Big Ben said giving her the once over, 'what's her name then Disney, Snow White?'

They laughed.

'Actually, it's April Wilton,' she corrected.

'Pleased to meet you April, come on in…Oh and I suppose you better come in too Disney…Meg would have loved to have seen you both, but she'll be with her parents about now.' Big Ben said looking at his G-Shock.

'Taken the baby with her?' asked Disney.

'Yeah, it was to be peace and quiet for me this weekend.'

'Well not now we're here.'

'Why, what've you got planned?'

'Clubbing.'

'Clubbing? Aren't you supposed to wine'em and dine'em at this stage?'

April laughed. 'He's been telling me about your club scene in Newcastle.'

'Yeah I bet…As it turns out Marion is over too, with the same agenda. She's out shopping at the moment.'

'Oh, so what room can we have then?' Disney cheekily shook his Bergen in front of him.

'Well Marion's in the spare room, so I guess if you tuck your head between your knees Disney you can have Robbie's cot, and April can sleep with me.'

'Ho, ho, ho.'

'But, I guess if Marion pulls tonight she won't be coming back here, so you could find yourself with the single bed in the back room, which fits two at a squeeze, but then you know all about that Disney.'

April's smile faded as she turned to Disney and he in turn glared at Big Ben.

'Urr, yeah,' Big Ben brushed over his slip, 'the in-law's tried it once and didn't like it, so a single bed has one advantage over a double.'

Confident that Big Ben's very attractive sister would indeed pull, Disney gave April the Bergen and suggested 'Why don't you go up and take a look at the room.'

'There's always the lounge floor,' Big Ben's words followed her up, his alternative sounding like a non-option. 'I think I got away with that,' he said turning to Disney.

'Reckon so, but it's cost you a beer or three,' said Disney making a beeline for the kitchen and the fridge. 'Got any lager in, I'm parched?'

'Only a couple of packs.'

'They'll do.' Taking one from its plastic collar, and pulling on the ring, he emptied the whole can down his throat without swallowing. He crushed the can, lobbed it at the bin but missed, turned to the still open fridge, took another and opened it. 'Did you,' he paused to belch, 'want one?'

'No, you help yourself.'

'*Chee-arse*,' he belched the word out.

'Has Snow White seen you getting bladdered before?'

'Ha!' Disney shook his head, crushing the second can and getting that one straight into the bin, before taking a third from the fridge. 'April and her other HR colleagues are worse than me mate.'

Shortly after Disney and April had emptied the McGregor fridge of beer, Marion returned. Seeing Disney she dropped her bags and threw her arms around him. Only then did she acknowledge April, an action that resulted in both girls being unsure of one another for the rest of the evening.

It didn't help matters finding that her brother appeared to have double booked the single bed in her absence. Nevertheless, an hour or so later they were heading into town on the Metro, with plans to start at the Quayside before going up to the Bigg Market and heading on from there.

April began talking about the honeymoon that Disney had promised, in Cairns, with trips out to the barrier reef, and into the rainforests.

'Did Disney ever tell you the story of Black'n'Blue the Emu?' Big Ben asked.

'Ha. No,' April beamed an expectant smile.

'Big Ben is something of a storyteller,' Disney added.

Big Ben leaned closer and began, 'We were on exercise one time in the Australian bush, basically being taught bush craft by the Aussie arm of The Regiment. Anyway we had covered at least a hundred klicks before we….'

'Klicks?' April questioned.

'Kilometres,' Disney explained.

'Anyway,' continued Big Ben, 'we spotted a good area to make camp at the edge of some forest and set to, with our various tasks. Disney looked for water, Tic was following some goanna tracks, and I was helping the Captain, Shins, with clearing ground for sleeping and making a fire.'

'Yeah and Shins got bit by that snake he stepped back onto, didn't he,' laughed Disney.

Big Ben nodded, 'In fact it was while he was sorting himself out with the anti-venom that he told me he'd seen an emu in the bush, the thighs of which would provide us all with supper and probably breakfast too. The snake by then was already set to be starters.

'He told me he was going after this emu, and I was to finish making camp. But, he should have remained where he was for a bit, at least while the serum took effect.'

'Ha, yeah, you can say that again,' agreed Disney.

'So off he went, knife in hand. Shins wasn't gone long before the scuffling and cursing began, some distance away but clearly audible. The scuffling in the bush went on for some time before it eventually went quiet. Disney was back with water before Shins returned.'

'I'd heard the commotion, but thought nothing of it.' Disney put in.

'So anyway, Shins turns up and we both see him looking like he'd had the shit kicked out of him. He'd certainly lost the spring from his step, but he was dragging this massive bird by the throat.

'He tried to make light of it when he reached us by doing a Monty Python impression and commenting on the *beautiful plumage*. Its head was a brilliant blue, set off by its black body. I would have offered to help pluck and gut the beast, but thought Shins might have been looking forward to that moment, especially the disembowelling, since he'd come so close to it himself, as it turned out.'

Disney jumped in, taking over the storytelling, 'When we had the fire going and the first of the meat cooking, Tic turns up with some veg but no lizard. He asks what's up with Shins and we all hear his account of the fight with old Black'n'Blue the Emu. Then Tic piped up, *I've got some news for you. You're emu's actually a cassowary.*'

'A cassowary?' April didn't understand.

'Yeah,' Marion explained, knowing this story, 'Only the biggest, deadliest bird on earth. Closest thing we have left to a velociraptor, with gut-opening claws.'

Disney nodded, 'and because there's often a second one around, we didn't sleep easy that night.'

'However that meat *was* real tasty,' Disney remembered.

'Has Disney told you his happy New Year story yet?' Big Ben asked

'No.'

'Ha, well, a few years back Disney, Tic, Shins and I saw the New Year in on the Black Cuillins, on the Isle of Skye. There was the barest hint of morning through the low cloud when Shins wakes us up with a *happy New Year lads*.

'The next sound was a frantic shuffling, followed by *What Fucker?*

'*Easy Tic, we're on Time-Out*, Shin's reminds him knowing only too well what was up.

'*Fuck*, says Tic cursing himself. It wasn't easy for him to switch off. If only *ordinance* would let us sign out unloaded weapons, he wouldn't go through this sort of wake-up routine. It didn't seem to be a problem for the rest of us though. Our first thoughts were

140

usually *where am I positioned, and what's for breakfast?* Whilst Tic's was simply *Gun?*

'I remember peeping out through a crack in my snow-cam Gore-Tex bivvy-bag then peering over the ledge I'd slept on. Through gaps in the passing cloud I could just make out Loch Coruisk below. The Black Cuillins had seemed like a good idea back at Hereford. After all, this was the ridge that Sir Edmond Hillary and Sherpa Tensing had trained on prior to their assault on Everest.

'*Refreshing morning,* Shins continues, *Nice change from the Belize jungle don't you think lads?* which received a *piss off Boss* from Tic, who was never much of a morning person.

'Disney was first up, taking a leak over his ledge before putting breakfast on. The rest of us followed suit, looking forward to completing the ridge and then bagging the Red Cuillins before celebrating the New Year with a piss-up at the Sligachan Hotel back down the valley, where our transport was parked.

'Oh yeah, I took my thermal bag off my security line and was removing my boots to put them on when I felt cold pouring down my collar. Gasping and arching my back I turned to see Disney's leering face. *What the fuck you doing man?* I balled.

'*Thought you should have your bloody sand back,* he says.'

Disney nodded. It was true.

'*Sand?* I said, confused, getting up and shaking it down and through my trousers. At which point we both heard Tic laughing and sounding more like his wakeful self. Both of us twigged that Tic had switched the content of a food container for sand, to weigh Disney down more. *Twat!* I yelled, and returned to the task of getting dressed as Disney apologised to me.

'*Bollocks* I says.

'*It was an honest mistake!* Disney says.

'*No. I mean bollocks my other boot's gone over the edge.* I explained, to more laughter from Tic.

'Taking a rope, securing it on a large boulder and clipping my harness in, I grabbed a handful of friends…'

'Friends?' April questioned another term.

'Yeah, cam-geared climbing chocks.' Big Ben tried to explain with a mimed press and release motion of his right hand into his cupped left.

'Oh,' she still wasn't sure.

'Anyway, I abseiled down and found it caught between two rocks. I couldn't exactly have kept up with the others without it. But by the time I'd put it on and climbed back up, the other three had eaten and packed.'

'Ha.' Disney chuckled, remembering.

'*Come on, you're holding us up*, chided Shins. *Sorry Boss* I says. *It's warmer this morning and the ice is treacherous as fuck.* This warning was born out by our slow traverse across the remainder of the ridge. It was mid-morning before we took a break, and I finally got my chance to catch some breakfast. The cloud base had lifted somewhat and the end of the ridge was in sight.'

'This is sounding more like your own story than mine.' Disney jibed, wanting him to get to the best bit.

Big Ben continued, '*See those three sheep?* Disney pointed for the benefit of anyone who was remotely interested. A ewe and two lambs, way below, were grazing on an area of grass and heather criss-crossed by channels of water.

'*Watch this*, he says. He took a wedge shaped slab of rock, which looked too heavy to throw with any accuracy, and dropped it halfway into a crack in a massive block of rock. Then he lifted another rock, this one the size of a microwave, holding it above his head before slamming it down on top of the wedge.

'Shins had been looking at the map at the time and was too slow to realise what was about to happen. He attempted to call Disney off, but could hardly be heard over what sounded like half the mountainside coming loose.

'No doubt, in Disney's mind, the boulder was supposed to tumble down and chase the ewe and her lambs into the loch, or something equally entertaining, like some cartoon caper.

'However, in reality the awkward shape of the boulder made it jump from side to side, certainly succeeding in startling the sheep.'

'Ha. You should have seen them April.' Disney laughed, while Marion shook her head because she'd also heard this one before.

'As if attempting to predict the path from the sound and motion of the tumbling rock,' Big Ben continued, 'the ewe and lambs darted one way then the other. But then came that unexpected moment in the ensuing confusion.

'Gathering momentum on a steep section, the boulder dashed against an outcrop of rock and flew out into the air. For a couple of seconds there was only the sound of the smaller stones working their way downwards, which didn't worry the sheep so much.

'In that comparative silence you could almost feel them considering a return to chewing grass. In fact, there was consensus among the lads that the lamb in question had looked down immediately prior to the multi-ton boulder flattening it, with a crump that was just too soft to echo.'

April howled with laughter.

Big Ben led April and Disney from the Monument down to the Quayside, and on to The Crown Pasada, their first port of call.

While Disney went to the bar to get a round in, and Marion went to the ladies, Big Ben and April got settled in the snug by the door. Big Ben sat with his back to the window and wall looking towards the doorway, and April leaned across the table, with her low cut dress exposing her cleavage.

'I could give you one Big Ben.'

'What?' The surprise was obvious in his voice.

'A story…A funny story.'

'Oh. Right…' He sounded disappointed.

'There was this twelve-year old girl who worked part time at a stable mucking out the race horses. She was a buxom girl, but soft as shite. Anyway, she had a favourite, which wasn't the manager's favourite by a long shot, but she liked its temperament as some of the others could be a bit scary at times.'

'Right,' Big Ben thought he should let April know he was still listening, even though he was looking through the doorway. The story so far did not sound promising.

Then Marion returned helping Disney to carry the trays of beers, and April continued. 'So anyway, one day the horse is in a race and it breaks a leg. The manager immediately says he wants to cut his losses and send it to the knacker's yard, but the girl goes frantic and promises that her parents will pay for the vet bills and future maintenance.'

April paused to lift a glass, and all four glasses were clinked together with a chorus of *cheers*, before Disney and April necked their beers in one.

'You've been giving her lessons then Disney?' Marion asked, not looking as impressed as her brother.

'It's proved a good party trick on nights out,' April confirmed.

'Well I'm not rushing *my* beer.' Big Ben returned his glass to the table only half emptied.

'You're letting the side down mate. *Big Ben* being out paced by a *woman*.' Disney knew just how to wind him up.

Big Ben finished the glass, and downed the best part of the second, and resigned his body to a rough night.

'Now this girl,' April returned to her story, 'she got into show jumping with her horse when it was fit enough. She began with gymkhanas, with as much to learn as the horse and both gained in confidence. Though there were times that the leg seemed to be paining the beast, especially when it was cold and damp. Anyhow, along comes this major event, at an indoor arena, but on the night, the horse's stomach is

145

unsettled. By all accounts it should have been pulled out of the event but the girl had her heart set on getting a trophy, and they had been practicing so hard.'

Disney was smiling, but not at the story which he'd heard before, he was eyeing up some girls with very little on, who were coming through the door.

'The jump course was roughly a figure of eight, and as the horse came down from a jump in the middle of the arena, what appeared to be gallons of diarrhoea poured out of its back-end. The steward hadn't been paying attention for some reason, but when it was called to his attention he tried to call a stop but it was too late as the girl was on her way back round. She came to the next jump and the horse's legs went from under it as it reached this slick of shit. Everyone heard a snap like a gunshot, which was a taster of what was to come.' April paused only to neck half another pint.

'Get another round in will you love,' she fluttered her eyelashes at Disney.

'But I thought we'd hit the next pub, once you finished gassing,' he complained.'

'Okay, I'll be quick…So, the girl's parents came and took their weeping child further from the neighing beast, as the vet at hand rushed to inspect the situation. It turned out it actually had two broken legs so with a dramatic shake of his head he took the humane killer from his bag. The girl started screaming as he loaded it.

'He waved his hand and the lights went right down plunging the audience into darkness. The shot rang out followed by neighing and cursing. The lights came up too soon, to reveal the vet frantically trying to lean against the prone beast whilst hurriedly loading another charge, before waving for the lights to go back down again. He must have been really nervous. Bang. More neighing, more cursing. Lights up, lights down. Bang. Silence. Pause. Lights came back up, to see people leaving.'

April couldn't continue with her description for laughing. Disney and Big Ben laughed with her.

Marion however wasn't laughing, she was wondering how April could think this story, of a horse jumping to its protracted death, was so hilarious. April was definitely not a girlie type, not that Marion thought of herself as a typical girl either, but she had no idea what could make someone enjoy the pain and misery of another living thing like that.

Getting her breath back, April tried to finish her story knowing they needed to move on. 'Even now this girl flinches every time a light is turned off,' she broke into another howl of laughter.

'Where next?' asked Marion.

'Offshore's. Just round the corner.' Big Ben suggested.

'Sound's fine to me.'

The four of them left the snug with Disney pulling his still giggling fiancée behind him.

At Offshore's, April headed for the ladies to pull herself together, knowing that when she returned the men would be sitting in the little lounge to the right of the entrance, even though it was presently occupied.

'Where did you say you pulled Snow White?' Big Ben asked Disney.

'At a house party in London…She was being harassed by some twat on the landing as she queued for the loo. I'd just finished having a dump and then seeing this, well I took a disliking to the guy, and as it turned out he decided to leave after I showed him down stairs.'

'So you pushed him you mean?'

'Well, yeah.'

'I'll get this round. You clear some seats,' said Big Ben, edging closer to the bar, with Marion following to lend a hand.

Disney entered the lounge and found the two sofas were taken by a group of young lads who looked like students. So he squeezed in between two of them and belched loudly. 'So lads, what are you studying?'

'I'm doing Law and he's doing Engineering,' said the lad on Disney's left referring to the one on his right, but it was clear from his nervous tone he was unsure how to take Disney.

Disney tilted his hips and let loose a raucous fart. 'My mother was an engineer. She used to work on the trains. What about you?' He said to the lads facing him.

'Urr. I'm doing Medicine.'

'And I'm reading English Literature,' said the other.

'Well.' Disney announced to them all, whilst gazing at Mr English Lit. 'Any of you fancy coming back to my place now, for a good time on me. Mind you I'm not making any promises about the condition of my own arsehole.' He gave the lad to his right a firm squeeze of the thigh.

'Thanks, but we're just on our way out,' said the Engineer standing up like a shot, immediately followed by the other three.

'But lads, you've hardly started your beers!' He pointed to the pints on the table, but they seemed to have gone deaf in their rush for the door.

Big Ben and Marion arrived with the beers, with April hot on their tail.

'Where'd you get those y'bastard?' said April at the sight of Disney putting an empty glass down amongst three near full ones.

'Some nice lads let me keep'em'

'Have you farted?'

'Yes, dear.'

'Better get used to it.' Big Ben warned. 'He was a nightmare to share a tent with. Sometimes I swear you could taste it. Whatever you do, don't go feeding him onions.'

'I'm past that lesson. I'm on to not letting him eat cheese omelettes after beer.'

'Why what does that do to him?' Big Ben was curious.

'Near instant trots,' she explained.

'Funny, I don't recall that one.'

'Well you wouldn't,' Disney tried to explain, 'she cooks like a...'

'Like a *what,* dear?'

'I don't know. We need a whole new word for you.'

'Cook your own bloody meals then. I'm only marrying you for your body.'

Disney didn't respond. He gulped down another pint, slowly, for effect, and then started his own story. 'A few weeks ago I was making my way over a zebra crossing, on a bit of a corner and the green man was flashing. I'd only got two strides or so in, when the cars in front started to move off, and so I stopped.

'It was at that moment that I noticed out the corner of my eye this double-decker bus coming at me from the right, doing thirty plus, with some zombie in the driving seat.

'My mind made everything go slow-mo, just as it does in a firefight. Anyway, I figured I had to move and it was less distance to go backwards. I knew I needed my feet off the ground before impact or I'd be dragged under the vehicle for sure, so I jumped up and back, planning that if I didn't get clear I would push-off on the corner of the bus and roll free.

'I was surprised how much force the impact delivered though, straight into my chest. I was bounced off before I had chance to push. I came down into a rolling reverse break-fall, bloody grateful for my training, but hoping I wasn't rolling into the path of the bus.

'Then I was on my feet, only to find there was this woman next to me, screaming. I calmed her down and then noticed the bus had pulled to the side just down the road. So, I jogged down to it, to have words with the fuckwit driver, and you know what he says to me? He says *In all the times that's happened, I ain't never seen no one do what you just did*…In all the times!' Disney exclaimed, shaking his head.

Next they headed just along the street and up a narrow stairway footpath. They went up the steep bank and at the top they ambled over to The Bridge for their next round. April got the next round in with Marion providing support again as further opportunity for eyeing up the talent.

April shortly began another story about an old man who had been found by a neighbour, having been trapped in his garden shed for three days, with only grass seeds and meth's to keep him going. 'Apparently the blue dye they put into meth's makes you go blind. Makes you wonder why they do it. He's got a dog and stick now, and a garden like a jungle,' she laughed.

From the Bridge, they staggered up through the Bigg Market, dropping in at the George before heading up to a nightclub. They made sure to arrive just before closing time so they wouldn't have as much of a queue, or so they thought.

The thumping volume inside the club was not far off heavy shelling concussion and they fell silent, Big Ben and Disney used hand signals to converse. There were plenty of nicely clad women to eye up, Big Ben noted, and while April and Marion took to the dance floor for a bit, he and Disney propped up the bar.

A couple more pints later, and after a visit to the gents, Big Ben noticed a woman giving him the come-on as he returned to the bar. She was attempting to lure him onto the dance-floor, and her success was all down to the fact that she was the proud owner of the largest pair of breasts he'd ever seen. It seemed inappropriate behaviour *not* to take them for a spin.

After a fair few energetic tracks there was a slow one, and Big Ben found himself bawling the question into her ear, as to whether she fancied going somewhere else. She nodded and went to the ladies, leaving Big Ben to return to the bar to tell Disney that he'd pulled. But Disney wasn't there. He looked round, but couldn't find him or April, or his sister for that matter, so he returned for his busty playmate, only to spot her going off with someone else instead.

'Unbelievable…The morals of an alley cat.'

Acknowledging that the nights drinking was rapidly catching up with him, he decided against making a scene, and having mislaid his friends and his sister, he thought it best to make a move for home.

Keeping an eye out for them, he made his way out of the club and towards the Monument Metro to catch the last train back to North Shields. Coming down the station stairs, he heard a train pulling in and leaped the last fifteen steps. He span on his heels upon landing, and hearing the beeps of doors shutting he managed to dive through before they closed.

He picked a seat at random, sat down and closed his eyes. His head was spinning and his ears were ringing from the club experience. He wanted a drink, but made do with a power-nap, relying on his senses to tell him when he was due to get off.

However, he was shortly roused by a large group of loud-mouthed lads who had occupied the lower end of the carriage. They were shouting obscenities at one another, laughing, and generally being a bit boisterous. There was a sense of unpredictability about the group, but not like they were some sort of gang. This wasn't New York.

Big Ben had not heard of much trouble with gangs on the Metro, so these were probably lads out on a stag night. This was possibly borne out to a degree by the variety of accents, Cockney, Mancunian, and Glaswegian as well as Geordie.

As he watched and listened, the inevitable happened, being the only outsider left in that carriage, attention turned to him. Whether he was seen as a threat to their fun, to be encouraged to get off at the next opportunity, or that he *was* their next opportunity, this was not clear.

'Hey, big man.'

'What?' he chose not to ignore whatever was coming.

'How much y'gotonya?'

'I don't know.'

'What do y'say we count it out?'

'Why would I want to do that?'

'Maybe out of the kindness of y'heart.'

The others laughed at their peer's cheek, gathering around with natural intimidation.

'Well what makes you think I'm a kind man?'

'None of us have tickets y'see. And if you don't pay our fines, we will have to, and we're not up for that.'

More laughter.

'I think you have me mistaken, for someone who gives a fuck.'

The lad felt challenged now by Big Ben's attitude and peer group pressure. So he made the wrong decision on all their behalves.

The lad grabbed Big Ben's collar in an attempt to shake some fear into him, but Big Ben's body didn't budge, as the lad's balled fist just bounced off the collarbone a few times. Big Ben's reaction, though slowed somewhat by drink, was far more effective as he crushed the lad's testicles in his hand. As the lad cried out in shock and doubled over Big Ben head-butted him in the face, dropping him to the floor.

Before Big Ben could get to his feet, another foolhardy hand came at him from the right. He simply took the wrist as he stood up, twisted it and pulled, then side-kicked into the second lad's pelvis, successfully dislocating the youth's hip joint *and* shoulder.

Then an arm went round his neck and he sent another lad crashing into his buddies, upside-down. Big Ben looked over his shoulder to see another attack coming from behind and delivered a reverse kick that cracked ribs and hurled that lad backwards at great speed. The lad's head broke the nose of the lad right behind him, who then fattened the lip of the lad behind him as they went down like dominoes.

As Big Ben lowered his foot he could see that there was still more aggression to face down, so decided they all deserved a piece of the action. Spinning, he delivered a roundhouse kick to another target, sending this lad through the air to smack his head against a window putting a crack in the glass. At this, a number of youths clambered over seating to regroup on one side of him, not so confident of themselves now.

Suddenly, they charged as a group. Big Ben lifted up the body of the lad on the floor like a horizontal shield, grasping him by the neck and right thigh, meeting them half way. They went down like skittles and Big Ben just trampled over them, turning as he got to the pillar near a set of doors, throwing the lad he was still holding onto the heap behind for good measure.

Those lads who were able, and there were still half a dozen or so, got back to their feet.

'It Gauls me to say this, but I think we've crossed paths with Obelix.' One lad attempted to re-inject some of their previous humour, but no one was laughing now.

'Where's Les?' asked a lad at the back.

'Here,' came a voice from even further back.

'Okay Les, we've played about enough now. Take him out.'

Accepting the peer challenge the lad came to the front.

'You've done it now mister,' announced one of them. 'Les knows Ninjitsu.'

On cue the lad took up his martial arts posture, hands held as flat fists with fingernails pointing backwards set for tearing flesh.

'Howay man. What sort of name's Les for a Ninja?' Big Ben asked aiming to wind the lad up, as an angry fighter becomes a careless fighter.

Quick as a flash the lad was on the offensive. But Big Ben simply blocked the blows aside, turning the lad slightly, before delivering a palm-heel strike to his ear, deafening and dropping him unconscious all in one action.

Then a lad was coming at him with a knife, raising the stakes. Big Ben could have drawn his own larger knife from his trouser leg, but decided that it was not going to prevent what was still to come. It would only make things worse for him in court, since he believed the law would be on the side of these anti-social youths rather than a war veteran like him.

He needed to keep the lad out of reach without getting cut, but that was not going to be easy in his condition because it needed speed, accuracy and a bladder that wasn't fit to burst.

He delivered a forward kick to the lad's face, collapsing his jaw and dropping him, but as he bent to take the knife another hand beat him too it and then all the lads were onto him, kicking and punching.

With a roar like a bear, Big Ben gave his demonstration of a whirlwind, returning the rain of blows, cracking more ribs with elbow strikes then hurling bodies aside with heavy punches of his own. Finally, peace was returned to the carriage having successfully dropped all of them. It was at that point that he noticed the knife protruding from his right thigh.

'Shit!'

He drew it out, wrapped it in a lads cap and pocketed it in his jacket. Quickly he pulled down his trousers to inspect the damage. He was relieved to see that the running blood was not pumping, so the major artery had been missed. He just hoped the knife wasn't too dirty.

He knew he had to get off the train at whatever the next stop was and leave this lot behind, but before he even had time to pull his trousers up, he started to see stars, and passed out.

When he came round, he found he was lying on top of a lad in a compromising position. Blinking he got to his feet in a pool of his own blood and urine. His underpants were wet, but his trousers had escaped the worst of it. Taking off his jacket he made a makeshift dressing for his wound out of his shirt then pulled up his trousers pulled on his jacket and limped to the door.

One lad slumped in a seat was beginning to stir as the train pulled into the next station. Big Ben delivered a parting blow and put the lad back under. Exiting the carriage he stood for a moment alone, watching the train pull away, then noticed how close to North Shields he was.

'Fuck!...Bank Foot?!' he cursed his stupidity.

Not only had he somehow got on the wrong train, he had almost reached the airport, which was completely the wrong direction. He thought about getting a taxi but decided that, all things considered, he would be better off getting home on foot to sort himself out.

Getting two bottles of Lucozade from a vending machine to cope with his dehydration, he looked at his watch, and started out. It was one twenty-eight, and he wished he'd remembered to bring his mobile with him.

Ten minutes later he had reached a phone box, but dialling home there was no one in, or at least not answering. It most likely meant that Marion had pulled and since she had the spare key to get in, Disney and April would be waiting outside for him or gone elsewhere. He hadn't thought to tell them about the key hidden in the back garden.

He knew that if he just kept moving the pain in his leg would become easier. So, Big Ben maintained a cruise speed, heading back via Cow Gate. It was so tempting to go into the Royal Victorian Infirmary and get his leg attended to properly, but then there would be the form filling, explaining the injury. He didn't need that, but he also didn't need to be laid off work with an infected leg wound. The bleeding would help keep it fresh till he could treat it himself.

He trekked past the Hancock museum, along through Heaton and Walker. It was four thirty-two when he got to his front door, stopped and looked down at his feet. Deciding better of it, he went round the back. He had just unlocked the kitchen door when he detected a faint glow coming from the shed and thought it best to check it out before he went inside, or else he just might not bother coming back out.

Creeping over to the shed he noticed a patch of vomit on Meg's rose bed and threw the door open, confident now about the source of the glow.

'Surprise!' he shouted, loud enough to wake the neighbours.

'Fuck!'

'Didn't catch you *off guard* there, did I Disney?'

April was out of it, huddled up against Disney's shoulder, as they sat on a large toolbox wrapped in an old rug, against the chill air, with a paraffin heater onto its final dregs of fuel.

'April's dancing didn't agree with her.'

'That's the problem with dancing. You never get that with beer…Marion isn't with you then.'

'No, I believe she pulled in the club and must have gone back to his.'

'Shame she didn't hand you the house keys,' Big Ben sounded neither happy nor surprised as he turned his back on them and started back to the house. 'Turn that heater off and come inside.'

'Where have *you* been?' Disney noticed the limp. 'What happened to your leg?'

'Nothing much...Just got into a scrap.' He thought it best that no one knew about the Metro incident until he had chance to check the news. Knowing his luck he might be up for manslaughter.

'We lost you in the club and thought you had headed home...So tell us about the scrap.'

'Maybe later.'

By the time Big Ben came out of the shower and returned to the kitchen in his bathrobe, April had revived a little, with Disney encouraging her to drink more water.

'What you need is a good greasy fry-up.'

'There's an idea,' agreed Disney, heading for the fridge. But April just turned pale.

Big Ben had more important things to attend to. Preparing his sewing kit and dressings, he sat at the table, bared his thigh, and set to work. April caught sight of the thigh and was drawn to look closer, then was immediately up and dashing passed Disney for the sink, where she threw up long and hard.

'You'd have thought,' Big Ben said to Disney, 'being in HR, she'd be used to seeing people getting stitched up.'

Earlier, on the dance floor Marion had had a guy start dancing real close to her. At first she was tempted to turn her back on him but then she admitted to herself he was actually quite fit. After a good ten to fifteen minutes she turned to say something to April about him but she had disappeared, then she couldn't see her brother either. Turning back to the guy she saw him smiling at her *lost* look and signalling to her *did she want a drink?*

It was a short time after that drink that Marion felt like she might have been overdoing it, possibly to impress the guy. She was burning up.

She signalled that she was going out for some air and he followed. Outside in the cool air he introduced himself as Martin. He suggested they could try finding a quieter club where they could talk and drink, but Marion realised she wanted something other than drink and talk, and suggested they could go back to his.

He was okay with this and as Marion made to go grab a taxi he grabbed her hand, pulling her back in close. He explained that he lived in walking distance and then he kissed her.

The walk did little to freshen her up, which was unusual, and she didn't seem able to concentrate on what Martin was telling her, she was just fantasizing about getting in the sack with him.

To say Martin hadn't been completely up front with Marion would have been an understatement. The deception wasn't that his place was any further than he had claimed; it was that he had spiked her drink.

Martin considered himself an excellent judge of the effects of this particular designer date-rape drug. He could tell from a woman's responses to what he told them on the way back to his, the point at which they would no longer remember what he did with them.

Martin was not smart enough however to avoid a whole series of mistakes. His first was in ever following this approach; his second was in bringing women back to his own place, but then that was where he had everything prepared; the third was in doing things that any self-respecting woman would say no to; then there was the mistake of choosing Marion as a victim, and going further than ever in fulfilling one of his darkest fantasies, forcing her to become what he referred to her as his unlawfully welded waif.

Pulling Marion was to turn out to be like playing Russian roulette with a revolver and only one round *missing*. It wasn't that she was physically stronger than him it was the strength of her unclaimed connections.

Marion was roused from her drug induced stupor by splashes of weld that scarred her naked waist and hips to the rap lyrics of Blowtorch.

Her previous wails of amusement at the club had turned to wails of distress, and not just because of the excuse for music. Angrily she tried to pull at the metalwork but found her wrists and ankles already held fast.

'Don't bother struggling, yet,' Martin advised. 'Save your strength.'

'Who the *fuck* are you?!' Marion yelled looking away from his mask and torch flame to save her eyes.

He said nothing more, concentrating on finishing the task at hand.

'What are you doing to me?' She screamed as another splash of weld burned into her. 'You are hurting me!'

She knew then that this was the intention. The pain helped her focus and she tried to look around to get her bearings. She saw her clothes and bag tossed over the end of the sofa and then noticed the initials J.H. on the tool bag that the welding torch had come from.

This might mean that Martin was not this psycho's real name, unless a friend had loaned the tool bag to him, but it seemed to be becoming less likely that this person had a friend.

The contraption she was welded into appeared at first to be a number of large rings within rings, with an inner frame that held her in a star form with a collar, cuffs and ankle braces and then three hooped braces over her pelvis, torso and breasts. There was padding inside the constraints, and pins that held them closed. This was clearly a manufactured item, not something that Martin, or whoever he was, had managed to produce as a hobbyist.

The welding of the pins was obviously part of some trapping and vulnerability fantasy of his, serving to provide him with a level of arousal missing from approaches to sex more acceptable to others.

Standing back and removing the welder's helmet, Martin surveyed his handy-work for a moment, as if to be sure he had forgotten nothing. Then with a tug on a chain he hauled Marion, within her frame, up to connect with the support gantry above, where he finally connected the pivot pins in place and set her spinning. The rings rotated within one another. Vertical and horizontal movement was possible to place her in any position Martin desired. It soon became clear to Marion that he was also able to lock her in any chosen orientation.

From the horizontal and face down position she was now fixed in, Marion noticed a view of Eldon Square's roof through a gap in the vertical blinds, and was thankful she was still in Newcastle and knew roughly where she was. She just needed to get out of this contraption.

Martin wasted no time, with the act of welding Marion in and hearing her distress having provided a strong erection he threw his clothes off and mounted her, taking his pleasure from between her buttocks. Marion's tears flowed onto the rubber sheeting below, and she tried to remember all those things she had heard her brother say in his accounts of hostage situation survival.

The primary aim was to stay alive by conceding to some or all of the captor's requests. The secondary aim was to enter into conversation when appropriate to ascertain the captor's philosophies and needs. Third on the list of aims was to tell the captor what they wanted to hear. Doing all this gradually from a resistant or at least hesitant start, in order to gain greater trust. Fourth on the list was observing routine and potential opportunities for escape, evaluating risk of failure and consequences. Fifth, was attempting to stay fit, which might mean the use of subtle muscular movements to avoid stiffening up.

In the days that followed, as part of the last set of aims, Marion dearly wanted to stop swallowing the sedative Martin was now using on her. If it had been a tablet she might have feigned swallowing it, to later spit it over the back of the sofa by the wall, but it was liquid. She couldn't even spit that into the bucket on the mat where her urine was collecting, because Martin was simply mixing it with her drinks.

Martin was so pleased with himself and his captive he had rung in sick for the week, and spent his time taking all the psychological and physical pleasures of torment and sexual gratification he could dream up. In his own little world he had convinced himself that Marion was enjoying the experience as much as he was.

Realising the delusion her captor was under helped Marion with the conversations that she desperately forced herself to engage in, in the hope of reducing her torment. However, this did not work well.

Sadly, by the fourth day, exhausted and with no identified opportunity or plan for escape, Marion was taken by depression and was not as responsive to Martin's chatter.

She acknowledged that she was reaching her personal turning point in this situation. She had heard that long term hostages could be brainwashed into accepting their captor's beliefs and even develop a sense of love for them and their attentions once their own dignity and former spirit had gone, as part of a de-humanisation process.

She tried to keep her spirits up by imagining a rescue by her brother and his mates from The Regiment. Nevertheless, if they had had any idea where she was they would have been here by now.

She thought of how worried people would be and this just made her angry. Marion found herself developing ideas of what she would like to do to Martin in revenge for her treatment if she was ever rescued, but the rescue scenario remained a fantasy. The only realistic future she saw involved her dying in this flat which now smelled of her stale urine. For some reason Martin seemed to be waiting until the mop bucket was filled before emptying it.

Then one evening, when Marion had lost track of what day of the week it was, Martin had an accident with his contraption.

Thinking it was securely locked off in the horizontal, upward facing position, he made to climb aboard. Mounting Marion's upper torso, placing his erection between her breasts, he began a vigorous forwards and backwards thrusting motion, with hands on the ring frame above Marion's head.

The first that Martin knew that all was not as he intended was when the frame sent out a warning creak and quiver. It was as if the metalwork had been sharing Marion's abuse and had also had more than it could bear.

Martin froze, then began to relax as he decided he was safe but ought to check things out. At that point the contraption suddenly released, pitching him forwards. He put a hand out to break his fall to the floor and screamed as the metalwork over Marion's breasts tore at his penis. His right calf came down hard on the bucket of urine as he flipped over, spilling it under him. He rocked backwards, hands clutching groin, quickly lifting his head to look at the damage.

On its way back round the frame smashed into his mouth. The front teeth were instantly uprooted by the force which sent the tubing on to crack teeth at the sides. His lips instantly became swollen, and his gums bled profusely.

He rolled aside screaming like a madman. Up on his feet, he grabbed the wooden chair from his desk by the window and proceeded to discipline the contraption for its failure. Some of his blows missed their mark, bruising Marion's thigh and ribs. The unintended pain actually helped Marion, in rousing her from her exhaustion.

The attack ceased and Martin's screaming turned to sobs. His now sorry looking penis was leaning over to the opposite side from normal. This was due to the swelling still growing at its base, where he had sprained it against the metalwork. If this wasn't injury enough, he had also received a graze along the length, which was now bleeding freely.

The contraption had come to rest with Marion upside-down, a position she had already been subjected to a number of times, for her oral defilement. Seeing Martin's crumpled sobbing form, she knew she had to gather her wits. Whatever had happened to Martin, she had to turn his predicament to her advantage.

'What's happened Martin?'

No response.

'Martin?!'

'Abbruugh mmmnneeegguuhh!' he sprayed blood from his wrecked mouth as he attempted a vexed reply.

'Oh my God Martin you need help!' She'd known this for days, but now there was an additional sense of urgency.

Her confirmation that his condition was shocking only set him panicking.

'You must keep calm Martin. Free me from this and I can help you…I told you…I'm a trainee nurse… Remember?' she was pretty sure she had already fed him that one a few days back in an attempt to get him to open up about what was going on in that head of his.

'Arr carbbughh!'

'Don't try talking. I'm your only chance Martin. You could bleed to death if you don't get attention soon.' She hoped this was not really the truth, for her sake more than his.

He didn't reply, just scrambled up off the floor and hobbled in a half crouch to the bathroom. Marion noticed the two curved bruises on his right calf.

'I know how to stop the bleeding! But you'll have to free me to do it Martin!'

The sounds from the bathroom were those of loose teeth dropping into the sink, the spitting of blood, and then crying as Martin surveyed the damage in the mirror.

Marion's upturned position and the chemicals still in her system were not working in her favour, as waves of sleepiness washed over her. She fought with her rigid bonds, not in the vain hope of loosening them, but with the actual intent of causing pain to keep her adrenaline level up.

An age seemed to pass by. All had gone quiet in the bathroom, and Marion worried that Martin had fallen unconscious and was now bleeding out.

Screaming for help was not going to bring aid, she had tried that the first couple of days, all to no avail. It wasn't that the walls were thick. The sad truth was that people just did not want to get involved.

Martin emerged from the bathroom, but instead of coming to her he turned and shuffled to his bedroom.

'No, Martin. Don't go to bed! You might fall asleep and never wake up!'

He faltered in the doorway, turning to look at Marion, no longer interested in what she had represented to him. She saw that he had plugged the holes in his gums with toilet paper, which was already sodden with blood, but more shocking than that was how black his penis had gone. 'You might get gangrene if you don't get that treated.'

'Harr cugghaa?'

'Talking won't help, that's for sure,' she tried to play up her value to him. 'Look, if you are concerned about people finding out about what went on here, don't be. I can help you. You do need help Martin. I know a doctor, a personal friend, who will not tell the authorities and I can get him here to help you very quickly.'

But Martin turned his back on her, and closed the door behind him.

'Shit…Martin! Listen to me Martin!'

Marion soon slipped into a dream world, where she had a big motorbike and was flying down a country lane, wind in her hair, and life was worth living again, even though she had never ridden a bike before. However, when she took the next corner, the high hedges revealed an oncoming lorry and it all turned to horror. The truck took up the whole lane. She swerved and lost control, the bike going from under her. The lorry kept on coming and the bike was shuddering to meet it. She was going to die and she screamed as sparks flew all around her.

Marion continued to scream for some moments as Martin continued with the angle grinder, removing the accessible tack welds, in order that he might release the pins with his hammer. He accepted now that he had never thought this fantasy all the way through. It had always seemed that trapping a woman permanently for his sexual gratification was all that it was about, bar the feeding and toilet duty of course.

Driven frantic by pain, slipping in her urine and his blood, Martin put every effort into the grinding. The contraption was turned around to get better access to the welds, with no apparent plan of action, and Marion felt like a Catherine wheel, spinning one way then another ad nausea. Then came the hammering, then more grinding, then more hammering, then his energy began to wane.

This was the longest Marion had gone without her dose of sedative, and what with the wasp-like stings of the molten filings, she had not felt this alert in days. 'If you free my neck and wrists maybe I can help you with the rest.' She suggested. 'Don't give up Martin. You're so close to getting help,' she focused on the *you* references her profession had taught her to use.

This seemed to give him more energy, unfortunately, it didn't provide him with greater attention and the grinder caught a length of Marion's hair, tearing it out, as it wound around the shaft, jamming it and burning out the already hot motor.

'Uugghh ii airl!!' He balled over Marion's wails of pain.

Picking the hammer back up but freezing there for a moment it looked as if he were about to shut her up permanently. Then he focused on the pin to the side of her neck and pounded it until the welding fractured and the pin was knocked loose.

This step forward appeared to give them both hope and shortly a wrist pin was also loose. Then after another break for Martin, he freed the other arm. As agreed, Marion now took a turn hammering the pin at the side of her torso cage.

She wasn't able to do a very good job of it though, on three counts. She could only feel what she was aiming for; she kept hitting herself by mistake; and her arms were too stiff and weak to make an effective attack. She lost grip on the hammer and it landed squarely on Martin's nose with a crump.

Just as it seemed that the bleeding from the gums was slowing down, his nose smashed, opening the flood-gates anew. Hands cradled his now completely destroyed face.

'My God Martin, I'm sorry.' In honesty, Marion's sorrow only stretched as far as fear of reprisal. 'I'm sorry Martin. I'm weaker than I thought.'

He retired to the bathroom.

Not knowing what else to try, Marion felt for the pin to her side, found the lever end and began pushing and pulling on it. Then it gave a little, then a little more before finally coming loose.

'Yes! I have another one out!' she called to Martin, without giving it much thought. They were both so focused on the present task that, for a while, history seemed forgotten as they appeared to be working to the same end.

Marion tried to swing open the torso cage but realised there was another pin to deal with. 'NO!!'

She looked up to see Martin, his cheeks now puffing up to close those eyes which looked more evil than ever. The blood soaked ball of toilet paper, held to his nose with adhesive tape, had a look of Halloween meets comic-relief. To add to the sense of bad intent he stood there with the hammer in one hand and a cold-chisel in the other.

However, the chisel truly was the breaking point for the metalwork, and the moment came that Marion thought never would. She stumbled free of the miserable contraption.

This might have been the time to grab her clothes and bag from where they had lain the whole time on the sofa, and to run like hell. However, her ankles were weak and she reminded herself she had made a promise, and was a woman of her word. Unfortunately for Martin, Marion's promise had been with herself.

She played nurse, checking Martin's condition before getting herself dressed. The blood flow was slackening off. His pulse was coming down, and though he looked like he had lost a lot of blood he did not look worryingly pale. The main factor was that the tables had turned and in Martin's mind he had given himself up to her attention.

Soon, she had him resting in his bed, with orders not to go to sleep till after the doctor had seen him. Then as the kettle boiled, she put the radio on to muffle her activity.

She thought about pouring scolding water all over his helpless body. But, she had far worse in store with days of vengeance to sate. She made a mug of boiling hot black coffee for him and placed it at his bedside.

She finally went for a shower then got dressed. Next she went to the front door to check the number of the flat and for the first time took a good look out of the window, to confirm she was where she thought, then she rang Disney's number. He was surprised that Marion had rung him rather than her brother.

'Are you still with Ben?' she asked.

'Yes,' he muffled the conversation. 'We've been looking for you everywhere. Where are you?'

'Are you at Ben's?'

'Yes.'

'Are the police with him?'

'Not today no.'

'Okay, would you pass me across to him? Cheers.'

'Will do.' Disney wanted to know what was going on, but knew he would find out soon enough.

'Ben, it's Marion…'

'Where the…!'

'I need you to listen carefully. I need you to do something for me.'

'Go on.'

'I've been tortured by some psycho. I'm free now, but I want revenge bad, without the police getting involved.'

'What? No. Just come away. Leave it.'

'No. Listen. I've got it all planned. I've told the guy I'm a nurse.'

'Yeah, well, I suppose that was safer than admitting your real job.'

'Hey, don't knock social work.'

'The caring profession,' he said sarcastically.

'The system can't help people like this, Ben. Our job is to amend a failure in justice.'

'D'you mean it's a social worker's job, or yours and mine?'

'You're not talking me round. Days of thought have gone into this.'

'So what's the plan?'

She told him the flat number and the sort of things she wanted done. She went to Martin's room to reassure him that the doctor was coming, and to ask if there was anything she could get him. His eyes were closed, by choice or swelling. Either way he did not look at her, just gave a slight shake of his head.

Three quarters of an hour later the buzzer sounded from the foyer and Marion let Big Ben come on up. At the knock on the door she found him alone, but at least he was there. He took a look at the state of her then hugged her close.

'Smells like a fucking piss hole in here.'

'Tell me about it.' She led him to Martin's room reminding Big Ben he was the doctor.

Resisting the urge to beat the living daylights out of the guy, Big Ben made do with pulling the sheets back to expose the naked body below.

'Fucking hells teeth! What have you gone and done girl?!' his medical demeanour slipping.

'I haven't done a thing. Well except for the nose. And that was an accident.'

'Accident?! He'll be lucky if he can ever smell again.' He wasn't really paying attention to the face. He was more concerned almost to sympathy pain with the state of Martin's bloated black penis. 'You are going to need a lot of attention before we can put things right here matey.'

Martin's acknowledgement was just a gurgle.

The sheet was returned, his face inspected, pulse taken and then Big Ben returned to the lounge. He recommended to his sister that she only feed her victim soup.

Helpless in bed but slightly more conscious now Martin began to feel in two minds about the situation. On the one hand he certainly appeared to be being looked after now, though he hadn't received the level of medical attention from the doctor he had been led to believe he was in need of. Martin put this down to Marion's lack of experience as a trainee nurse.

Over the next few hours Martin slept as his body attempted to repair itself, and what with the constant noise of the television, he never heard Disney and Tic enter with *the equipment* the following evening.

Tic had hopped on his bike as soon as he got the CO's agreement to some time off, and had flown up the M6. The first thing Martin knew that some new plan was unfolding was when he was being put into some sort of space suit, in fact a hazmat suit to be precise.

Once he was sealed into the suit, he was walked into his lounge. He could hardly see out of his still puffed eyes but he could hear well enough the voices behind him. There were more people in his flat than just Marion and the doctor.

'It's going to be fine Martin. Just relax.' Marion reassured him. 'They know exactly what they are doing. We'll soon have that pain in your groin numbed.'

To his shock he felt water entering his oversized suit, through the air-line valve at the small of his back, filling his boots and racing up his thighs. But the cold water did not stop at his groin, it just kept rising, and he began to panic, shifting on his feet, becoming unsteady because of the weight of the water.

'Stay calm, and still.' Marion advised. 'If you fall over, things could get very difficult for you in there.' She heard herself laugh, and knew then that she was going to enjoy this.

Martin began to whimper as the water overflowed at chest level to fill his gloves and arms, weighing them down, then suddenly rose again up to his neck, where the flow was stopped just short of his chin.

'Okay lads. Who wants to brainstorm executions?' Tic's question was rhetorical as he returned from the tap in the kitchen, and the foursome sat down to begin the string of suggestions.

As part of SAS training in capture-evasion and counter-interrogation, the lads had been well exercised in psychological as well as physical warfare.

The suggestions started with all the simple obvious things, like shooting, hanging, stabbing, beating, hit and run. Then the suggestions progressed to drowning with weights in a quarry, and even being tied by the ankles to the spray arm of a sewage treatment pool and being dragged through the shit till Martin was overcome with the smell and exhaustion.

The panic grew in Martin with every suggestion, not understanding that this was purely aimed at destroying his spirit. His fate was already prepared and waiting for him near a recently demolished industrial site.

'I neee dur torut,' Martin complained.

'Plenty of room in that suit,' Marion answered.

Losing control Martin began to add sewage to his suit contents.

'How about we puncture him with hundreds of infected needles and leave him pinned out for the crows,' Marion went on to suggest, and for the first time she worried that maybe her sense of humour was becoming as warped as April's.

'Or wrap him in baking foil and put him in a bath of petrol then set fire to him,' Disney offered.

Marion's laugh didn't sound quite sane. In truth, the whole event was only serving to extend her period of trauma.

'How about we drain the water out of the suit and fill it with battery acid. It wouldn't leak out,' Big Ben proposed. 'And....It would only mean pouring Martin's corroded remains down the toilet then.'

'Mmm, I like that one,' said Marion.

All eyes turned to Martin. He made to step backwards, his bruised leg gave way and he buckled forwards to the ground, the water rushing into his hood. He tried to get up as the water and faeces gushed into his mouth, which he could no longer close. He turned to see his *guests* just sitting there, as if glued to a television programme.

There was a pocket of air at the back of his hood but he couldn't quite turn to reach it. He quit trying to stand up. Instead he tried to turn on his back. The weight of the urine and faeces tainted water was incredible. Through fluid dulled ears, he could hear Marion roaring with vengeful laughter at his helpless situation.

He was just losing consciousness when he felt the water draining out of the suit, and across his rubber mat and carpet. He coughed and choked as the hood was pulled right back, the makeshift bandaging from his nose now hanging loose down one cheek before falling completely free.

Initially relieved to be alive, the calm evaporated with a scream as Martin remembered the voiced intent behind draining his suit.

A swift kick to the head and Big Ben returned silence to the room. Then checking the flat for evidence and removing all the kit to the rental van parked below, Martin was carried down rolled up in his rubber sheeting.

Martin regained consciousness to the sensation of a tube being thrust up his bottom. He was disoriented but forced his eyes open to darkness. He seemed to be in some sort of trench.

There was a humming motor close by, and he noticed there was a chain around his waist. Then he felt something penetrate further inside him, and the tube was pulled free. He froze, in excruciating pain wondering what had been done to him now.

Tic, who had supported some of Martin's weight from the front, warned him that he should only move very slowly, as Big Ben and Tic scrambled out of the trench. It had been excavated by Disney the day before and hidden under a couple of four by eight-foot plywood boards. Hidden at the bottom of this trench was a half-buried heavy wooden gatepost with a length of barbed wire secured firmly to it. The other end of the barbed wire now rested up inside Martin's colon.

Between his legs he could just make out the barbs in the partial moonlight. He guessed the scenario was to be abandoned here till he was found, dead or alive. His miserable fate was in the balance.

'Well Martin, this is where I say good bye,' Marion's voice brought a sense of hope that the punishment was nearly over. 'I just want you to understand, I am not proud of this, but you turned me into the person I am now.'

'Just get on with it,' groaned Big Ben, uncomfortable with his sister talking this way.

She pulled a lever and the humming changed tone, accompanied by a slopping sound at one end of the trench, as she flooded it with liquid cement.

Martin had to make a choice, lacerate his bowls trying to escape and then have to contend with possible further torments, or just give up and let the concrete do its job.

Marion was enthralled by Martin's predicament. Whatever he chose to do, she felt she had now evened the score, but there was sadness too. She knew deep down that much of this had not simply been an act. This man's actions had awakened feelings of enjoyment in another's suffering. Her social work would never be the same again.

Minutes later the concrete oozed up the side of Martin's face as he held his position with regret, taking one last look at the stars before the desperate gurgling began.

Marion shut the cement mixer off, watching Martin's last breath bubble up from beneath.

'Satisfied?' Big Ben did not sound happy.

'Very satisfied,' she smiled.

'Right lads, raise the chain.'

'What are you doing?' Marion looked confused.

'We've done everything you requested. Now it's our turn.' Big Ben lent a hand to Tic and Disney, who were having more trouble than expected getting Martin back out. It was to be a close run thing.

'Leave him!' Marion seemed appalled with the lads. 'I thought the chain was just to weigh him down and you were going to throw it in after him.'

'We only agreed to scare the fucker, not murder him.'

'But what good will it do, letting him go? It has to better that he's left buried.'

'Yeah well, not according to the law of the land sis,' Big Ben countered.

Martin's body came up jack-knifed, with a haemorrhaging rectum. As he was laid out on the soil under Disney's torchlight, Big Ben cleaned Martin off with a water-filled extinguisher, then Tic as team medic attempted to get the heart pumping again.

'Okay, he's up.' Tic announced. They were lucky.

After Big Ben and Tic had loaded the gagging Martin back onto the rubber sheeting, placing the package in the back of the van, Marion climbed into the back with her brother.

Tic then hurriedly closed the rear doors behind them, and gave a double slap on the back door. Disney pulled away leaving Tic behind to fill in the trench with the hotwired JCB, return the stolen cement mixer, then pick up his bike from where it had been hidden nearby and head back to Hereford.

In the back of the speeding van, Big Ben and Marion put on black polo-necks and balaclavas by torchlight in preparation for the next step, whilst trying not to fall upon the groaning body. The RVI, in Newcastle, was to be the Drop Zone being only minutes away. As Disney pulled up outside Accident and Emergency for the drop, he hammered on the dividing wall to signal that they were at the DZ.

'If you have any parting remark,' Big Ben prompted Marion, 'now's your chance.'

Marion leaned in close to her tormentor and delivered her warning. 'We will do this and worse if we ever find you're back on the pull Martin.'

Big Ben added, '*When* the police talk to you Martin, you've been caught up in a gangland dispute, and you are too scared to talk further. Understand?'

Martin gave a weak grunt and then Big Ben turned him side on to the rear doors before throwing them open and delivering a heavy boot in the ribs which sent Martin tumbling to the paving, where his rubber wrapping saved him from a cracked skull. The doors slammed shut and the van, with its false number plates, sped away.

As they all headed out along the A69 Marion knew her brother was only tidying up her loose ends, but the way he was directing it all with calm and clarity was unnerving. She had given all too little consideration to having to talk to the police herself. Big Ben told Marion that when she reported her kidnap and torture story she would have to distort Martin's description, to avoid complications.

Leaving the A69 near Haydon Bridge, Disney took the Alston road and eventually there was another knock from up front as he got out and changed the number plates back.

'Okay, this is where we part company sis. Look after yourself, this time.'

Looking into the darkness and realising this was not North Shields, Marion became confused. 'Where is this?'

'Find out for yourself. It's more realistic for someone to play *dropped* if they have been. Walk down this hill towards those lights and phone the police. Tell them what we rehearsed about the abduction and that it was a dark blue van but you didn't think to look at the number plate. Got all that?'

'I think so.' She gave him a hug good bye. 'Anyone would think you did this sort of stuff for a living.'

Big Ben smiled.

Arriving back home with defeated expressions Big Ben and Disney were greeted by Meg and April with the good news that in their absence Marion had turned up at Alston.

The lads had not exactly been honest with the girls about what they had been up to the last couple of days. Meg and April had waited for news by the phone in the belief that Big Ben and Disney were continuing to scour the city for clues to Marion's disappearance, which certainly was the case before Disney took the call from Marion, a call he deleted from his phone log.

After being taken for a check-up at Hexham hospital, and then for a statement and description of her captor at the police station Marion was brought back to Big Ben's.

She only stayed another day just to rest up before returning home, spending most of it in the back room, vacated for her since Disney and April went straight back home following Marion's safe reappearance.

Big Ben considered that it wasn't often that an ex-SAS trooper got to rescue a family member in such a way, and this *really* should have been an end to such escapades.

Marion was not the only person to be affected by these events. They had also stirred a need in Big Ben. He missed the briefings, missions, and debriefings, with the excitement of living on the edge. He thought for a while about quitting with the post office and joining the police, but decided he probably wouldn't get along with them.

He had no particular interest in working for MI5 either, not that he'd been approached like some of his ex-colleagues had. He saw that line of career better suited to those who didn't have a family.

He looked forward so much to seeing his mates from The Regiment and hearing their stories and pranks that he came up with the idea of creating his own team of pranksters.

This idea developed to require a team of four people to individually plan, execute, and report their pranks back to the team. However, there were to be a number of key rules, and some operational differences to the way he had worked in the SAS of course.

Not only was Big Ben still bound by the official secrets act, he knew that in certain places you needed to watch what you said about your time in the forces. The general belief however was that if you heard someone claiming to have been in the SAS, most likely they hadn't been and were just lying in order to impress someone. The way Big Ben saw it the occasional mention of time spent in the SAS would actually be a good cover then, as just a bored postie.

The way the team was to work was that each member would have a month to plan, execute and then report their prank. They would meet up every two weeks at a prearranged pub with two of them reporting. If other people helped carry out the pranks they had to do so unwittingly, and other team members could not provide active support to one another, or be the target of a prank.

However, team members were expected to learn from one another's experiences, through the reviewing and judging of the pranks. Each prank had to be deemed funny by at least two of them, and could not be something simple and cliché. It had to have required real thought and planning, and in some cases guts to pull off.

If a prank failed it had to be reported as an embarrassing story, and if it had not been possible to do the prank in the time given then some other amusing account had to be provided. In some cases this would rely upon recounting past experiences, which would become limited over time, and so increase the pressure to carry out successful pranks.

In all cases of pranks or other amusing stories, evidence had to be provided to prove the account was fact rather than fiction.

If the humour or the evidence were called into serious question by two or more judges then that member was to be dismissed from the group. This was what Big Ben referred to as being Returned To Uneventfulness, and they were not to be communicated with again.

To set this up Big Ben had visited dozens of pubs in the Newcastle area over a couple of years chatting to people and sussing out likely candidates. Finally he got the team together and called it Admissions.

Each member he gave a nickname. One was an MD who became known as Medic, another was an Italian restaurant owner, who Big Ben called Leroy on account of his youngest son being born black. The fourth member was Erik a red-headed Norwegian. Erik's English was not perfect and at times there had been misunderstandings, but Erik was passionate about what Big Ben had named the *Admissions* group.

Erik was a little too passionate as it turned out and in his final prank he poisoned a local water supply, which Big Ben found amusing only because it was not *his* local water supply.

Leroy didn't find it funny because it affected his takings at the restaurant for a couple of days, and Medic didn't appreciate the humour because of the number of cases of extreme dehydration he had been called out to, on account of all the diarrhoea.

Big Ben told Erik that while it was unfortunate that he had chosen the one area that would impact both Medic and Leroy, rules were rules and he had to be RTU'd.

With Erik gone, Admissions needed to recruit a new member. It seemed the best way forward was for Medic and Leroy to help in the search.

After some weeks considering possible candidates and rejecting them for one reason or another the new member was finally decided on and brought into the fold of Admissions. Adam was a handyman who had done numerous jobs for Leroy, and Big Ben nicknamed him Odd Job.

Odd Job seemed to settle into the team okay at first but as time went on Big Ben noticed he wasn't always finding the pranks very funny, as if they were troubling his conscience. This made holding to the rules more challenging for everyone and Big Ben began to consider this as a threat to his group, and decided he had to do something about it.

One Sunday afternoon, Big Ben prepared and checked his kit, out of sight of Meg. The order of packing for the black thirty-litre backpack was essential to the smooth operation of his plan. Not that the plan was complicated, at least not in terms of Big Ben's military experiences.

His intention was to break into Odd Job's home under the cover of darkness, and check the place out, pinching a few items along the way, to make it appear a straight burglary, whilst finding out more about him to inform a follow-up plan.

Nevertheless, there was a secondary benefit to Big Ben's initial plan. What he was intending to do would hardly count as a prank, and would not be valid for Admissions since it involved another team member. He wanted this to be seriously intimidating, the sort of experience that might cause a person to re-evaluate their life, up-sticks and move away.

It could hardly have been easier for Big Ben to track Odd Job's address. He had asked Leroy for Odd Job's contact details, and then checked the PO Box number on the computer system in the sorting office.

Meg had noticed an excited manner about him though, like he was going on a shout, and not just another of his usual group activities, details of which he never shared with her. She didn't like it. 'So what did you say you are up to this evening?'

'Just taking the car to pick some stuff up and then going to a mate's,' he said as if he had actually told her once already.

'Well I don't want anything *else* happening to my car Ben. You still haven't fixed that wing mirror.'

'No worries pet.'

Big Ben drove slowly past Odd Job's house, but not suspiciously slowly. His speed was just slow enough to get some sense of the surroundings, though it was too dark to pick out much detail in passing. The lights were off, but there was a van round to one side, its light colour just visible through the trees at the front.

Some way further down the unlit country road, he came across a wooded area that had no wall or fence separating it from the road. Slowing almost to a halt, he picked his spot and pulled up.

He took his first item from the pack. Night vision goggles. Taking them from their case and donning them, he returned the case to his pack then went into the woods to investigate.

Listening out for vehicles on the road, or people in the vicinity, he checked the ground and the spacing between the trunks some way into the wood. When he returned to the road he ran along the edge of the wood in both directions checking for any sign of official or unofficial footpath. Satisfied, he got back into the car, and with its lights off, reversed a little, then turned to the right and entered the wood, sensitive to the car's movements on the rough ground.

Reaching the spot he had chosen, down a bit of a bank, he switched the engine off. He could hear a stream or river close by as he got out of the car, locking it. He removed the second item from his pack, a camouflage net, which he covered the car with, and pegged securely to the ground. Then he quickly cut a broad branch from a large bush with the knife he always had strapped to his right leg, and returned to the road at the point he had entered.

He used the branch like a broom, erasing and covering the tyre tracks as he returned once more to the car, where he placed the branch in the netting.

Using his knife again, he cut more branches to weave into the netting. Only branches facing away from the road were cut, so that no raw wood could be seen by road users. The spot he had chosen for the car was tucked round the side of a rhododendron bush, so he only really wanted sufficient branches to further mask the right and rear of the vehicle.

He wasn't planning to take long on this break-in job, but this camouflage was about risk reduction. Besides which, he was enjoying himself again.

Satisfied that no one would find the car, Big Ben turned for the road. However, before he got there he heard a sound and froze. It sounded like a dog, by the sound of the shuffling, so he dropped immediately to a crouch.

Wherever there was a dog there was bound to be an owner out walking it. But there was no sign of torch light, or typical owner-pet chat. It turned out to be a badger. He kept still, taking the opportunity just to watch it for a few moments with his green tinted tunnel vision. Then he focused back on the job at hand and moved on.

Returning to the road, Big Ben switched off the goggles and put them back in his pack. Putting the pack on, he jogged along to Odd Job's house. His footfalls were soft on the tarmac, not just because he was running lightly, but because he wore hessian boot-socks he had made, the thickness of which softened and disguised the tread of his soles.

Half a mile down the road he spotted another animal. Smaller and moving slowly, it was a hedgehog, which gave him an idea. Taking a tucker-bag from a side pocket of his pack, he put the pack at the side of the road and went after the animal. Hedgehogs were relatively easy to catch, and provided they weren't noisy in transit, they had proved good for testing security systems and even creating diversions on occasions.

By tying a bit of nylon fishing line to a rear leg in order to keep possession of the animal, lighting or alarms could be set off a number of times in quick succession to create a 'cry wolf' scenario. Alternatively, if the situation arose, they were also a source of protein.

With the hedgehog bagged and quiet, Big Ben continued on his way and within a couple of minutes was outside Odd Job's house. To complete his black attire he took his balaclava and tight gloves from his pack along with his lock picks. Pulling his goggles back on for the last time he switched them on and moved in.

Big Ben began his infiltration by scanning the property for signs of security and signs of life. There was one PIR security light for the driveway, another for the side of the house leading to the back door, but as far as he could see no other infra-red trips or CCTV.

He considered climbing the garage or shed roof to avoid the security lighting and to attempt access through an upstairs window, which were often the least well secured. Neither structure was connected directly to the house, which would mean jumping the gap, gripping the window ledge with one hand while trying to make access with the other. He regretted having let his training lapse with the climbing wall at Eldon sports centre, but decided he might be better off bluffing it out with the security lights.

He was glad he had thought to pick up his little helper. He *or she* could prove useful yet.

Big Ben continued to investigate before deciding on a plan of action. Returning to the road he checked the other side of the house, which had a field adjacent to it. This point of entry was more exposed. Nevertheless, it did give him a small gap of opportunity between the back of the garage and the back of the house to get around to the kitchen door.

Squeezing between the bushes and stepping over a barbed wire fence, he crossed the back of the garage to the passage that ended at the door to the house. He placed both bags at the corner of the garage, and with lock picks in one hand he took a suckered microphone from a trouser pocket and then moved very slowly across the end of the passage. Extremely slow movement could fool PIR sensors if time was not pressing, and with this being such a small distance it was worth a try.

Big Ben obviously was not slow enough for Odd Job's system and the bright light came on almost immediately. The green tunnel vision was flooded instantly. Big Ben shifted the goggles to his forehead and quickly set to work making his entry.

He placed the microphone on the kitchen window to the left of the door, put the ear-piece in and switched it on. This kit was sensitive enough to use to crack tumbler safes, and was also highly effective for listening out for, and to, occupants of buildings.

As he listened he turned part of his attention to the door lock. If he kept still for long enough with his back to the PIR, the light would go off again and in the shadow of his body he would then be able to work without triggering the sensor. However, Odd Job's choice of lock told Big Ben that this would be no easy job. He made an attempt but soon decided against wasting further time, and turned to his contingency plan.

Standing straight again he removed another suckered device from his trousers. This one was a diamond tipped circle cutter, used for fitting ventilators to windows. Before he placed it, he checked the hinged window panel for internal sensors and locks. Then deftly scored a circle and used a little rubber coated mallet to tap the glass out. The sound of the glass being scored should have been enough to remind him, but Big Ben was focused too much. When the mallet hit glass it turned into an explosion of pain in his left ear.

'Shit!' He cursed under his breath as he ripped the ear-piece out. Pulling the microphone free of the window, he returned the device to his trousers with his free hand.

The disc of glass was suspended inside the kitchen window on the end of the cutter strut. He reached inside with his free hand and removed the disc of glass, placing it to one side of the sill. Then he returned the kit to his trouser pocket and reached through the hole. Feeling round the window edge for wires, then around the window catches, he identified through the thin material of his gloves that both catches contained lock mechanisms. He found the catches locked, but within a couple of minutes he had them picked and the window open.

He put his tucker bag, with its active but sympathetically quiet little friend, through first onto a section of handily placed and thankfully clear worktop then climbed in himself.

The house sounded eerily silent. He decided that Odd Job was either not in or was sound asleep. What he hadn't appreciated, because Odd Job had chosen not to mention it to the group, was that he actually lived in a barge he had renovated, on the river at the bottom of his property. These living arrangements were to support him while he renovated the rather unsafe house he had inherited from his recently departed father.

Big Ben pulled the window shut, but did not lock it, then swung his goggles back in place and surveyed the kitchen. 'You sneaky fucker, Odd Job,' he muttered under his breath as he spotted and then proceeded to study a blackboard covered in action plans.

Odd Job had been planning to prank all of the Admissions members in one go, as his own exit strategy. Big Ben's opinion of Odd Job rose as he read all the detailed jottings, but finally shook his head at Odd Job's overconfidence, especially in leaving his blackboard so open to view.

Odd Job could have turned it round to face the wall when he had finished working on it but he hadn't. Well he had lost out. He would not catch Big Ben with that prank now, and he decided that as soon as he was finished here he would call Medic and Leroy and warn them about what was intended for them.

This was all he needed to know to be rid of Odd Job by the rule-book, so he could have could have just turned and left, but since Big Ben was now inside he felt a need to investigate further. He headed out of the kitchen for the stairs, with his pack on his back and his tucker bag in his left hand. He was barely out of the door, vaguely aware that the messiness of the kitchen was nothing compared to the hallway, when he trod on something that moved underfoot. He froze, thinking *trip mechanism*, and looked down to see it was just a bicycle saddle. He moved on, paying somewhat more attention to the mess on the floor as he headed for the stairs. The staircase looked old and creaky.

Odd Job's home improvements had clearly been limited to the kitchen so far. Big Ben ascended cautiously, listening to the wood, as well as for any signs of Odd Job. His assumptions about the condition of the stairs proved correct, forcing him to keep to the edges of each step to reduce the creaking.

He had almost reached the landing when he grabbed the banister post at the top of the stairs. It wobbled causing him to lose his balance. Stepping backwards to regain his balance, the force of his step cracked the step he trod on, and his balance was compromised completely.

Twisting sharply he reacted immediately and violently to the vision of another balaclava-donned burglar with night vision goggles at his side. This burglar made an identical response falling through disintegrating banisters away from the landing mirror towards the floor below.

Amidst the splintering and crashing timbers Big Ben fell heavily. The tube of the bike frame, in need of its saddle, received Big Ben's skull instead, penetrating the left side of his head. The tilting bike forced his body over to the other side of the passage, where it went into spasm for one long moment then fell limp.

When conscious movement broke the long silence it was only from the tucker bag. A snuffling nose poked through the noosed top, and with scratching and clawing of paws the opening was forced wider. Soon the hedgehog was free, sniffing its strange surroundings including the head of its abductor. Intrigued by the fluid pooling on the floor, it began to lap happily.

Big Ben woke with a shiver. The shiver felt like it was confined to his right side though. He felt for his gun. No gun. He heard birds and caught the musty smell of woodland. In the early morning light he could see he was under some dirty plastic sheeting, covered with fern leaves.

He moved his head a little more on the makeshift pillow which was the tucker-bag stuffed with more ferns, and acknowledged the pain in his head. Lifting a hand to investigate, he could feel the circular protective dressing around the injury below his balaclava on the left side. He felt the opposite side of his head. No exit wound, but his lips were swollen badly into the bargain, no doubt from falling after taking the hit.

He had absolutely no memory of acquiring these injuries, or how he had got to the woods, nor what he was supposed to be doing, or where the lads were.

He sat up slowly, groaning and blinking, wondering if this was escape and evasion on reselection and somehow he'd acquired a bad head injury. He spotted his main pack within reach and drew it close. He pulled all the contents out: Night vision goggles; a first aid pack; survival pack; vehicle keys; lock-picks; glass-cutter and mallet; and four flasks, two of which were already empty. He had hoped that there might have been some rations and extra clothing because he was conscious that he was losing heat.

He was dehydrated, and had no idea how long he had been unconscious but he desperately needed a drink. He opened a flask and began to gulp. But stopped, almost choking, trying to control his shock, and return what contents he could back into the flask.

'Bollocks!' he spluttered.

It was urine. That could only mean one thing. They were on a hard-routine insertion mission. No sign of their presence could be left. They would be carrying no forms of identification, in case they were captured. Even this makeshift cover was questionable. He should be on the move, but he didn't know where he should be heading. Maybe the others had gone for support. But why would they leave the vehicle keys with him? And anyway, they could have carried him out themselves, *unless* they were also badly injured, taken captive, or dead. He was confused. Something had happened which had lost him most of his kit and all his team.

'Fuck. What a mess.'

He opened the second full flask. This proved to be urine too. He calculated he must have been here for twenty-four hours or so. What little of the terrain he could make out appeared to be Northern European, but he would need to find some local signage to get a clue.

No note had been left by the lads to prompt him what to do next, but by the rule book he must stay at the camp, till they came back for him. However, he had less than twenty-four hours before the empty flasks would be full too, and he would have trouble not breaking the zero-trace directive. In fact he realised he needed to take a leak right there and then.

Meg rang the mobile. Big Ben had not come home and she needed the car to get Robbie to the University nursery and go on to work. The mobile was ringing but it was just going to answerphone.

'Ben! Where the *hell* are you?!'

She tried phoning round her husband's friends, but those who were answering had not heard from him either. Looking at her watch she saw she was late, or would be by the time she had walked with the pushchair to the station to catch the Metro.

'Ben McGregor, you are in *so* much trouble!' she promised.

Big Ben could not light a fire for fear of being spotted but he had to keep warm, and with no additional clothing the options were to keep eating and get some sun. He could not leave the wood during daylight, but there were sections of the wood, not too far from his makeshift camp, where the sunlight streamed through the canopy and crept across the leaf litter.

As for food, he found a few handfuls of berries and ate enough youngish Beech leaves to see him through to the evening. If the lads had not returned by then he would just have to make a move without them. The question was, if he did move on, in which direction would he go?

Moving towards signs of habitation would increase the risk of capture. Away from habitation was little better than staying put. At least towards habitation he might better understand his situation, and possibly find further survival opportunities.

Water was the immediate concern. There had been very little water content in the vegetation he had consumed, and he had not located a potable source of water within the wood. Since he could not make a fire he could not use heat to release water as steam, and since there was no suitable vegetation to draw water from, this left the hole digging option.

His right arm and leg seemed to be exhausted and twitchy, which he considered a disturbing sign, considering the cracked skull he had sustained. He therefore used his left arm to dig a hole in a suitable spot, using his knife and fingers. Unfortunately he found nothing but roots, stones, and weariness. He left the hole just as it was, unfilled, in case it collected moisture later on.

On his way back to the camp, he made some string from nettle stalks and set a few noose traps for rabbits. He would have to make sure to remove these before leaving, as they were signs of occupation too.

At his camp he laid back down under the plastic and ferns, looking up through the canopy, watching the leaves move one way then another in the breeze, then suddenly his body went into spasm. He vomited over his shoulder and fell limp.

Meg had tried the mobile again at lunchtime and the sorting office. Her husband had not shown up for work, so her concern grew. She knew he could take care of himself, she just wished he would let her know where he was.

By five o'clock Meg had collected Robbie and was heading down Northumberland Street to the police station to report her husband missing, but came to a halt. She started to consider whether her husband might have simply left home.

She found herself wondering whether she had been too hard on him recently. He was not the sensitive type. He tended to bottle things up. She decided to leave it another twenty-four hours, before she went to the police.

Big Ben woke with a shiver and he had a strange sense of déjà vu, as he tried to figure out where he was and felt for his gun. No gun. He caught the musty smell of woodland and in the late evening light he could see he was under some dirty plastic sheeting, covered with fern leaves.

He moved his head a little and his right cheek touched something wet, which smelled like a mix of compost and vomit. Then he acknowledged the pain in the left side of his head. Lifting a hand to investigate, he could feel a doughnut shaped dressing below his balaclava and his lips were a bit swollen.

He lay there wondering how he had acquired the injuries, how he had got there, and what the mission was. There was no sign of the lads.

He sat up slowly, groaning and blinking. He spotted his pack behind him and drew it close. He pulled all the contents out: Night vision goggles; a first aid pack; survival pack; vehicle keys; lock-picks; glass-cutter and mallet; and four flasks, one of which was already empty. He had hoped that there might have been some rations and extra clothing because he was conscious that he was losing heat.

He had no idea how long he had been unconscious but he desperately needed water. He opened a flask and began to gulp. But stopped, almost immediately, choking, trying to control his shock, and return what contents he could back into the flask.

'Bollocks!' he spluttered.

It was urine, and that could only mean one thing. They were on a hard-routine insertion mission. Checking the other flasks he confirmed his suspicion. He had no water.

He did have a need to urinate though, and half-filled his only empty flask, which decided him, he would have to move on in the hope of relocating the others. However, before he broke camp he had to defecate. The turds and accompanying leaves were placed in a bag from his first aid kit and put into a side pocket of his pack, where he discovered another bag full. The tucker-bag was emptied and placed into his pack along with the folded up plastic fertiliser sacks, which had been cut to form ground and upper sheets. There was little he could do about the ground impression to mask that someone had pitched there for some time, even when he had brushed leaves over it. At least he wasn't leaving any definite clues behind, or so he thought.

He put on the night vision goggles and followed his intuition, with no idea about the rabbit that was slowly strangling to death only ten meters away. But nature took its revenge that night. Before he reached the edge of the woods, Big Ben's left leg went straight down the deep hole he had dug earlier, badly wrenching his left knee.

'What sort of *fucking* animal digs a vertical hole, for *fuck's sake*!' he yelled forgetting he was supposed to be operating in silent mode.

Hobbling out of the wood it was lighter out there, but only for another twenty minutes or so. He decided to switch off the goggles to save the batteries and stowed them away, then he made his way across the field ahead.

At the far side he came across a well-worn path. He looked one way, then the other, and turned in the direction that the horizon was lightest.

Soon he arrived at a stile from which he caught the silhouette of a footpath sign at the far side of the next field. His heartbeat increased with the prospect of answering the key question of whereabouts.

The signpost sadly did not appear to be in a language Big Ben recognised, so he concluded he was in a foreign place he had not been before. These people even seemed to use different number symbols. His heart sank. But different to *what* he wondered, since he realised he couldn't even recall what his own letters and numbers looked like. He *so* wanted to be back at base now, or even home.

Big Ben woke with sore testicles. He no longer remembered the incident with the electric fence. He felt for his gun. No gun, but he did have a sense of déjà vu. In the early morning light he could see he was under some stone archway, huddled in a ball, with plastic sheeting wrapped round him and his pack in front. His head ached. Lifting his right hand he investigated the left side of his head.

He had no idea that by rights he ought to be dead by now. He also had no idea how he had acquired the head injury, or how he had got under the arch. He got up to stretch his aching, injured legs, and to take a leak. Urinating against the stonework Big Ben recognised the structure as similar to a typical Northumberland lime kiln.

Retrieving his pack he began pulling out the contents: A case for night vision goggles, but looking through his pack he found no goggles; a first aid pack; survival pack; lock-picks; glass-cutter and mallet; and four full flasks. He didn't feel thirsty. He had no recollection of the stream he had found and drunk from, having to use one of his survival kit's purification tablets.

He was feeling exhausted, but sadly he found no food rations and his stomach was making audible complaints but he was confident he could turn something up. Without searching the pack further he set off to look for tucker.

Before long he was on a lane heading east, feeling happier. His exhaustion was such that he had reached that phase when it is possible to become delirious, with death close at hand. No longer thinking things through as effectively, it took something as blatant as a road sign to raise his concerns once more. He stopped at a junction, staring at the signage, but he couldn't even recognise what style of writing it was.

He took a flask from the pack and took a swig, immediately spitting it into the hedgerow.

'This is fucking piss!'

Then his previous conclusions occurred to him again and he scrambled to get off the lane.

Big Ben had experienced being trapped in an avalanche on exercise in Norway, and had a chute fail to open for him in Bosnia. He had been under *friendly fire* from American artillery, and even been in a helicopter crash in Iraq, but as he watched the traffic below the footbridge on the dual carriageway he experienced real fear.

He recognised Fords, Nissans, Rovers, and Peugeots, by shape, but their number plates were all alien. He sensed he should know this place, which suggested to him more than just memory loss, it almost certainly meant *brain damage*.

'I can't fucking read, I can't *fucking* read!' He lifted a broken hand to the side of his rolled up balaclava, his inner voice telling him to remain calm.

He took a flask from his pack and began to drink. His thirst was so great that he did not stop till it was emptied. He had no memory of the spring, or his decision to lose the urine. Nor did he remember the incident with the barbed wire and the fall from the wall that tore open his trouser leg and deeply cut his left leg, which he had since bandaged. This had been the incident where he broke two fingers on his left hand and landed so heavily on his shoulder that he had passed out.

He was now so weak and confused he could no longer consider whether or not he was on a mission. He had trouble remembering his name and rank, and had moments where he felt like he was floating. The only thing driving him now sheltered deep in his subconscious, whispering which way to go next.

He put the pack on his back, and lifted his right hand to adjust his night vision goggles, only to discover they were no longer on his head. Too tired to look around for them he set off again, across the footbridge, limping now with both legs.

In town police were attempting to intercept and stop a car, when one of the units was involved in an incident. Suddenly a tall man in black had stumbled into the road. The police driver took avoidance measures, swerving into the clear opposite lane. Unfortunately, the shocked limping man managed to execute a very athletic forward dive, in an attempt to get out of the way, but coupled with the vehicle's swerve his body landed on the bonnet. He crashed hard against the windscreen, shattering it before spinning over the roof and coming down somewhere behind.

The WPC in the passenger seat was getting out of the door before the car was even stationary, running back to attend to the injured person, leaving her colleague to call in the incident. But there was no sign of the man. It was as if he had vanished into thin air. There was only his pack, lying between two parked cars. The WPC picked it up as she began checking the front gardens and under cars.

'This isn't possible,' she said when she had walked back to the patrol car and sat inside. 'He's not out there.'

'What do you mean, he's not out there?' her colleague frowned.

'The man's vanished. I could only find his pack.' She opened up a pocket in an attempt to identify its owner and wished she had not been so curious, as the smell of the burst food bags hit her full in the face. '*Shit!*'

The three lads were disgruntled to say the least, heading for the pub with the intention of getting legless. Their four days of landscaping labour had resulted in the client's refusal to pay up, on the grounds of dangerously uneven paving and gaps in the lawn.

Their suggestion that it would settle with weathering only served to switch the client into 'legal proceedings' mode, with the demand that they return and make amends, or suffer the consequences.

They had not walked far when they noticed a body collapsed in the front garden of a derelict house, with one foot resting awkwardly on the top of the low wall. Normal behaviour here would have been to ignore the man, after all this was Benwell and it was often best not to get involved. Nevertheless, their attention was caught first by the unusual sight of the big boot covered in some sort of hessian sock. Then they noticed something more important.

'Hey Al, this is that fucker from the stag night metro a few years back.'

'Is it? I can hardly tell with the state of him. I'm not sure I can remember back that far,' Al peered closer in the near darkness before turning to their other colleague. 'What do *you* think, Den?'

'Does look a bit like him, I suppose,' said Den.

'Why aye man. I can understand Al not getting as long a look at him as we did, but that face is unmistakable.' Col nodded then suggested, 'Why don't we load him in the back of the truck and….'

'No, let him find his own way to the fucking hospital,' Den didn't want to hear it. 'I'd rather get beer down my neck than help that git.'

'No man. I mean, we could take him out to some waste ground, maybe Newburn Haugh, and give him a good kicking. What do you think?'

'I think you need that beer before you lose it totally,' Den shook his head. 'We'd be better taking him off our patch. Somewhere like Heaton Dene, by the allotments.'

Al touched Big Ben's face, with no idea how to check for a pulse. 'Well he *is* still warm.'

Den looked around. 'I'll nip and get the truck then. You two stay here with him.'

'He looks close to croaking, Col,' Al commented as Den legged it back along the road.

'Y'divn't want to wait till he gets better surely?'

'No. I just thought we might be better off mugging him and getting on to the pub, that's all.'

Concerned that Al needed a bit more motivation for this, he decided to wind him up a bit. 'Y'know, we didn't tell you this before, but this bastard said you collapsed on that metro like a swooning gay boy.'

'WHAT!'

'Yeah, remember how he was taunting us all. He said that he'd have to remember to wash his hands afterwards in case he caught AIDS off *you*.'

'THE FUCKER!' Al stuck the boot into Big Ben's chest, just as Den arrived with the box van.

Big Ben groaned and stirred, but little more.

Den jumped out, went to the back and rolled the shutter up. There was space in amongst the gardening equipment for the body. 'Right lads, sling him in the back.'

Al grabbed shoulders while Col grabbed legs and they lifted Big Ben over the garden wall and round to the back of the truck. After a couple of swings they committed on the third, and heaved the body up onto the bed of the van. Al clambered in, and with a shove against Big

Ben's boots by Col, Al dragged the deadweight inside.

'You two might be best in the back, while I drive,' said Den. 'But don't go starting anything till we get there. I'm not in on this just for your benefit…Right?'

'Right,' they echoed.

Col climbed in and took his position, as Den rolled the shutter down, flipped the lock and went round to the cab.

Den drove them along Elswick Road, heading for Gallowgate, but when he reached the Rye Hill roundabout there was a bumping in the back. All the tools were secured so he knew it would not be those. Then Den laughed, concluding that one of the lads must have fallen with his cornering.

However, as he came to the lights on Westgate Road he was aware that not only was the noise continuing it now involved some loud cursing.

'Hey Guys! I said wait till we get there!'

The crashing around continued, the vehicle being rocked with the violence.

'Al, Col!' he yelled like a frustrated drunk in a bar queue demanding another short.

But he was ignored as the blows kept coming.

'Wait on y'bastards! Or I'll stop right now!'

Den thought it possible that they could not hear him in the cab, which decided him. He pulled to the side of the road believing it quiet enough, and hopped out.

Sliding the shutter back up, in the light of the street lamp, he made out the looming figure just prior to receiving a boot in his throat, knocking him backwards off his feet to the tarmac, with a crack of his head, where darkness took him.

Col's backside was wedged into the lawnmowers cuttings-bin, while he wore a steel bucket on his head, dented from repeated impacts of a size 12 boot. While Al was suspended by his ankles with orange electrical flex from a support beam running across the ceiling. He dangled there unconscious, dripping blood onto a pair of lost teeth, complete with nerves, which only minutes before had resided in his upper jaw.

In the darkness neither of the men had seen the attack coming. Despite their frequent experiences of late night fighting in pubs and clubs, they were not trained in close quarter fighting, in pitch black, while moving like this. They never stood a chance, despite Big Ben's injuries.

Big Ben looked from his captors in the truck to the prostrate body outside. He was confused and so terribly tired now. He just wanted to curl up and go to sleep. To let it all go. But the firm voice in his head from his past wouldn't let him.

He quickly went through the lads pockets, removing phones and wallets, then he lifted Den up off the road and piled him into the back of his truck, where he slapped his face a few times to rouse him.

'I have your ID's here.' Big Ben flapped the wallets in front of Den.

'What's…?' Den tried to get a grip on what had happened.

'If I hear you have even mentioned me to anyone I *will* find you and I *will* kill you,' Big Ben gave him his favourite line from Taken. 'Understand?'

Den nodded and was immediately knocked unconscious again by a blow to the side of the head.

Big Ben pulled the roller shutter down and locked it off, and then with keys in hand drove them away. He couldn't risk having them get to the hospital while he was still there. He had a feeling he knew where the hospital in this town was; somewhere near the football ground his subconscious was telling him.

So, in a secluded backstreet near the football ground Big Ben reversed the van up to a high wall till the rear bumper was pressing hard up against it. If the lads did find a way of breaking through the shutter they would be faced with bricks.

Leaving the van and locking it, he threw the keys over the wall, along with the wallets, minus the money and the driving licences. As he moved away he could hear some mumbled questions from the confused occupants inside.

He stopped, but only to discard the driving licenses down a deep drain. He could do without those being found on him.

Twenty minutes later, with his hessian boot socks off to look less suspicious he staggered into the RVI A&E, where he found himself standing behind a drunk in the admissions queue. The drunk was getting aggressive with the receptionist.

'Why don't you take a seat and calm down sir,' Big Ben suggested.

'Wait a minute pal, *I* was here first.'

Big Ben simply trod on the drunk's left calf behind the knee folding him down to the floor, with an 'Upsee-daisy' as if he cared, causing the man to smack his jaw into the reception desk, putting him out cold.

He dragged the drunk aside just as two security men who the nurse had called earlier turned up to deal with him. Big Ben turned back to reception.

'What seems to be *your* problem sir?'

'Head injury,' he said, pointing at his bandaging.

'How did it happen?'

'I don't remember.'

'Okay. What's your name?'

'I'm not sure.'

'Do you have any ID?'

'None.'

Trying

It was early summer and still exams time, but Geoffrey sat on the carpet with his back against the sofa in front of the widescreen smart TV playing with the latest release of Crime-Spree.

In this game, players could do more than make their characters take a variety of drugs, commit rape and kill people. With this latest version there was the added functionality of being able to torture useful information out of background characters and other players.

He and his friends found this acceptable because they believed that these games helped vent people's darker needs. Besides, hadn't research sponsored by the games companies shown that such games only negatively affected those people with a propensity for anti-social behaviours?

Nevertheless Geoffrey *was* becoming aware that he had been getting a kick out of developing his new interrogation techniques. Right now however, he was just trying to evade police interceptors who were close to catching up with him. He was so engrossed with trying to stay in the lead that he barely heard the sound of the key in the front door as his sister Jessica returned home.

With no word of greeting as she closed the door behind her Jessica dropped keys into a bowl by the door, which had normally caused a metallic-ceramic clatter but was now dulled to a flat jangle as the keys landed on a growing collection of unopened letters.

'I can't believe they've put the fuel up again,' Jessica moaned in her brother's direction to no response. 'I said I can't believe they've put the fuel up again!'

'Mmm.'

'It's ridiculous. Up another fifty pence a litre. It's like they haven't thought it through, yeah?'

'Uh huh.'

'They'll just make clothes and all the other essentials cost even more.'

'Mmm,' Geoffrey continued with his disinterested responses.

Jessica placed her carrier bags on the chair next to the sofa then began to pace back and forth between Geoffrey and the TV screen looking for something on the sideboard and shelving, shifting ornaments and photo-frames, causing Geoffrey to growl with irritation, craning his neck one way then the other to see around her.

'I'm just glad Dad pays me back,' she added, sounding like she was responding to a missing bit of conversation.

'If the fuel prices really concerned you, you could try walking,' Geoffrey suggested in the hope of hitting a nerve as payback for her interference in his game play.

'Says you...I had shopping to do. I'm not going to walk one and a half bloody miles home with bags of clothes.' The truth, which Jessica so far had managed to keep to herself, was that she was buying what appeared to be top brand clothes on the black market and with the false receipts getting extra pocket money out of her father. This extra money was used to support her designer drugs habit. She was also given extra drugs by her supplier, whenever she had use of her father's car, for distributing drugs to the local pushers.

'Ah Jess man, will you keep out of the way!'

'I've lost the receipt for the top I got at Warehouse last week.'

'And this game will be lost if you don't stop blocking my view.'

'So? I'm dealing with the real world here. Now that I've worn the top I want to take it back and exchange it for another one I've just seen.'

'Whatever…but isn't the receipt more likely to be lost in your sty of a room than here in the lounge?'

Jessica stopped, turning with hands on hips obscuring a vital third of the screen, and there came the sound of a crash and explosion in addition to the police sirens behind her.

'You bitch! Why did you have to stand in the way?'

'Mmm. Just let me think a minute.'

'It isn't me inhibiting your brain cell.'

'You should be revising.'

'I'm taking a break.'

'Well it sounds like you've had some major breakage. Crashed and burned in fact, so back to your books.'

'Sod off. You sound like Ms Hedges.'

'You know what Dad says.'

'Yeah well he's not back yet.'

Jessica moved away from the screen and slumped into the empty chair to the left of the sofa. 'I expect you'll fail your A-levels anyway, and then you can join me on benefit.'

'Thanks.'

'That'll piss dad off, showing him that, even with the two extra years of school he's supported you through, you're just as thick as me.'

'You're far from thick Jess. You just don't like the idea of work.'

'That's *so* not true. I'm more than willing to work, more than you'll ever be. They just haven't given me anything that really suits my skills yet.'

'I guess there's not much call for complainers.'

'Oh do shut up…Though, that does remind me. Last time the job centre set up an interview for me, I fell and hurt my knee, ruined a good pair of tights, and worst of all cracked the screen on my iPhone.

'The wankers phoned me to tell me that I was late, *as* I was coming up their stairs. And I reckon they must have put in an extra step at the top since I was there last. I'm thinking of trying one of those *no-win no-fee* companies.'

'I think you'll find those are only for work related injuries.'

'It *was* a work related injury! I was going for a *bloody* interview.'

There came the sound of another set of keys in the lock, and the door swung open with a bump as their father, Len, staggered in with two suitcases clattering over the doorframe.

'Hello?' Len gasped his greeting over the sound of the taxi still outside.

'Hi Dad,' Geoffrey and Jessica said in unison but didn't get up. They were used to their father's trips.

215

Jessica went on to ask, 'How was ur…Calcutta?'

'It was Uttar Pradesh.'

'Oh dear, that bad?'

Len frowned but then turned to the sound of someone else following him in. 'I'd like you both to meet someone.'

A young woman entered, carrying a large rucksack, and as the taxi was heard pulling away she closed the door and turned to face Len's son and daughter.

'This is Spring,' Len announced.

'Hi.' Geoffrey responded with mild surprise.

'Okay.' Jessica responded with concern.

'Hello,' Spring greeted, unsure what more to say, looking to Len.

'This is Jessica, and Geoffrey.'

There followed an awkward silence so Spring put her rucksack beside Len's cases, and Geoffrey got to his feet. Tossing his game controller on the sofa, he shook Spring's hand, rattling her collection of bracelets and bangles. 'Nice to meet you.'

Recovering herself, Jessica followed suit, but at a loss quite what to say said 'Urr…Nice top.'

'Thanks. It's handmade.'

'*Really?*' Jessica's tone betrayed the meaninglessness of *handmade*. Then she turned to hug her father. 'I've missed you Dad.'

Len flicked open one of Jessica's shopping bags to glance at the contents. 'I think you mean you've missed you're Daddy bank, by the looks of these.'

'Oh that's so not fair. I've been limiting myself to essentials, a new dress and a pair of shoes, for going out with the girls…And maybe a few other odds and ends…this time.'

'Could I use the loo Len?' Spring asked, placing a hand on his arm.

'Sure. It's up the stairs and then right in front of you.'

'Thanks.'

Spring had a confident motion to her as she walked away. The squeaky third step was heard as she went upstairs.

In a slightly hushed tone Jessica asked her father, 'What were you thinking Dad? Hikers go to hostels. Maybe *this* trip has addled your brain.'

Len sighed 'Spring will be staying with us…for a while.'

'What?' Jessica didn't want to hear this.

'She seems nice to me,' said Geoffrey

'She would.'

'She is,' Len defended.

'But…but dad she's…she's…ginger.' Jessica protested.

'We met about a week ago,' he ignored her remark, 'and she just seemed to click with me.'

'Clicked to your *wallet* more like,' Jessica snapped, feeling threatened by the unexpected guest.

'Are you suggesting I cannot interest a younger woman with my looks?'

'Sure you can Dad.' Geoffrey looked to provide support, in his sister's silence, but then admitted, 'it's just a surprise that you brought her straight home that's all.'

'There's just something…strange about her.' Jessica pointed out.

'Yeah, you're right. She's good company… You've spent too much time with those bitchy friends of yours to connect with someone pleasant.'

'Dad!'

'Well *I* think it's good that you're finally taking some time for yourself.' Geoffrey said with a caring smile.

But Len looked surprised. 'You think I haven't been?'

'No Dad, I don't. For too long it's been work, work, work, ever since Mum died. These trips haven't been holidays, but I think maybe this trip might have done you some good.'

'Well I *have* been making sure we could afford to stay here…The sooner you're both working, of course, the sooner things will ease up.'

'Oh Dad it's not *that* bad…So did you bring anything back for me?' asked Jessica

'I have…but it's going to be delivered later.'

'Delivered later? Ooo, what is it?'

'Wait and see.'

'Oh come on, tell me.'

'A rug.'

'A *rug*?'

'For your room.'

'Why the hell does my room need a rug?'

'I thought you should have something that has been hand crafted. It's really good quality.'

'*Hand* crafted? I see…Did *she* choose it?'

'Well…Spring wanted to look round the craft market, but *I* chose the rug,' he explained, then turned to his son, 'and for you Geoffrey, I bought a hand carved statuette of Shiva. It's *really* detailed. A lot of time must have gone into it.'

'Fantastic,' he sounded unsure.

'I just wanted to remind you both that there's a wider world out there.'

'Thanks,' said Geoffrey.

'I'll give it to you later when I unpack.'

'No rush.'

Spring returned to the lounge.

'Anyone for a cuppa?' asked Len.

'Yes please,' Spring replied.

'Yeah, go on,' said Geoffrey, 'I haven't had one for a while.'

'Not for me,' Jessica shook her head. 'I'm going to take my stuff and try it on again.' Grabbing her shopping she turned and went upstairs.

'Why don't you make the teas Geoffrey,' suggested Len, 'while Spring and I put our feet up.

'What?...Oh okay.'

Len took Spring by the hand to the sofa, but as he sat down he reached behind and pulled out a note book. Not recognising it he started to flick through it, sighing and shaking his head, his mood changing.

From the kitchenette came the sound of running water and cupboard doors opening and closing. 'Does Geoffrey often make tea?' asked Spring.

'Urr,' Len looked up from the notebook, 'Not often no. Why?'

'He seems to be looking for the tea, and has forgotten the tap is running.' The kettle could be heard being filled and then the tap was turned off.

'Well it's not like we're still in India now, we don't have to worry much about water *here* do we. In fact, look out there it's raining again. We got back just in time.'

'Mmm…But we *should* think about water usage *everywhere* Len.' Spring argued.

'But what with all the rain we get…*surely*?'

'You need to think of water like it is energy.'

'Oh that's crazy talk,' Len said a little gruffly. 'Why?'

'People in developed countries forget that the water we get through our taps has been processed, and *that* requires energy, and most of our energy generation is still pumping out CO^2.'

'Right,' Len grudgingly nodded finding Spring's constructive criticisms rather trying at times, and took that moment to vent on Geoffrey, waving the notebook. 'What *are* these scribbling's Geoffrey!'

'What?' Geoffrey returned to the lounge.

Instead of repeating himself Len said, 'I thought you had been doing your homework!'

Geoffrey made no attempt to defend himself, so Len continued.

'Now I find while I've been away you've been wasting your time on some sci-fi nonsense in this note book…in addition to your gaming!' he said pointing at the controller on the sofa next to him.

'*Hey* I only played for an hour…or two… today… and anyway, those are just notes… for a novel I'm going to write.'

'You can write novels when you've got a job. Till then you've got to focus on you're A-levels.'

'What will the novel be about?' asked Spring.

'Aliens,' Len's tone was condescending.

'Actually…' Geoffrey tried to explain, 'it is more about us, and what extra-terrestrials might make of us as a race.'

Len began to read some of the notes out with a mocking narration. 'Early Glian explorers of Earth learned the most effective method of entering the heads of humans, without causing major damage, was through the optic nerves. Not only were they able to share the human experiences once resident, they could also suggest thoughts and behaviours, as drivers of their hosts,' he scoffed, 'very original.'

'I happen to think it's a good idea to use adaptations of the familiar, Dad, or else there could be difficulty for some in imagining the story, which could lead to a loss of credibility.'

'*Credibility*?' Len continued with his mocking narration, 'In such relationships, especially over protracted periods, there were some noted side effects of *hosting*. In the main the human would be unaware of their Glian driver, but their presence created unfortunate dysfunctions, including a disruptive influence upon nearby electronic equipment, plus food intolerances, recurring headaches, stomach aches and… *flatulence*… Geoffrey… This is rubbish!'

'As I said Dad, it's just the notes.'

'You've got to think of your *career* Geoffrey.'

'I am. I want to be a *writer*.'

'You won't make a living at this. Who do you think would want to read this stuff?'

'I think *I* might,' said Spring.

'*You* keep out of this. Geoffrey is lazy. He needs to focus on things that matter.'

Spring persisted, 'It seems to me that maybe his writing *does* matter, at least for now. And I would expect that something like writing might be a good vehicle to developing interests in other things.'

'*Yeah*,' Geoffrey agreed with her defence.

'Where's that tea!' Len barked.

'I *was* making it and *you* called me back.' Geoffrey returned to the kitchenette. With the kettle now having boiled, he popped a bag in each of the three mugs and poured the water in.

'You need to understand Spring,' Len tried to explain himself, 'my two need discipline or they take you for a ride.'

'I think they need inspiration.'

'Mmm, well they certainly need something.'

Geoffrey brought the teas through on a tray. 'Dad, yours is the one on the left, and yours is in the middle Spring. I'm guessing you don't take sugar.'

'No…But a tip for the future, you could have saved two tea bags if you'd put one in a pot.'

'Yeah, well, we don't have a pot now. Dad…broke it.' Geoffrey said as he sat in the chair to the right of the sofa, putting the empty tray down beside it.

'Well I could get you a new one. In fact, I could even show you how to make tea with leaves from the UK.'

'I didn't think you could grow tea here.' Geoffrey sounded interested.

'Tea is a form of rose leaf actually. But there are a whole load of leaves and petals you can make some really quite delicious tea from here, and if you find a plant that you like it would save you buying tea bags, and more importantly reduce the number of imports you purchase.'

'Oh that'll save the economy,' Len said sarcastically.

'It takes lots of little changes to make a big difference Len. Sharing ideas helps improve the way we see, think, and do things...To become resilient.'

'So you've been saying, but sometimes your ideas seem too inconsequential to be worth bothering with…It's just tea.'

'Like, *it's just water*…'

'Well…'

'It's the freedom to explore ideas, instead of following blindly. All the easy to do little things adding up to something bigger… and better.' Spring slipped an arm around Len as if that would help him appreciate her point better, just as Jessica returned wearing her new dress. Len and Spring watched her as if half expecting a twirl.

'So *this* is the new dress?' Len asked.

Jessica just dropped into the chair to the left of the sofa with a disgruntled growl.

'What's up… now?'

Jessica pointedly turned her attention to Spring. 'I don't know how they do things where *you* come from Spring, but in our house we *flush* the toilet.'

'Jessica!' Len barked.

'Sorry. Habit,' Spring apologised.

'Looks like a *sorry habit*.' Jessica retorted.

'It's for water conservation.'

'Well you're back from India now.'

'But it's just as important to conserve water wherever you are in the world.'

'You missed the lecture.' Len pointed out.

Spring continued, 'Consider the energy you can save over time if you follow the saying 'If it's yellow, let it mellow. If it's brown flush it down.'

'Oh…My…God…Who is this person Dad?'

'My family are travellers.'

'Gypsies?!'

'Travellers… I'm originally from Southern Ireland, but I've spent the last ten or so years travelling the world, living in eco communities.'

'*Eco communities*? You mean like eco warrior feminist brainwashing caravan cults?'

'No.' Spring was used to defending her way of life. 'Before I went to India for a year I was living in Findhorn.'

'Hmm…Sounds like somewhere in Norway that you go to get randy.'

'Randy?... It's in Scotland, near Inverness, and a wonderful place to experience an alternative life to city hustle.'

'Hmm… I think I'll pass. Sounds like it would be full of *crazies*.'

'I think you'd find you have more *crazies* living under the strain of city life. These communities are about healthier and more sustainable approaches to living.'

'Haven't you just been brainwashed to believe that though?'

'You mean by them using suggestive advertising, and everyone close to you talking about the next new thing?' Spring said with irony.

'Yeah,' said Jessica, the point missed.

'People judge for themselves, from life's experiences, which things makes sense and which don't. Anyway, there is very little advertising in these places as few people have televisions. They use radio to keep up with the news.'

'No TV?' Geoffrey gasped, 'Sorry Spring you're not really selling it to us.'

'A few people do have problems adjusting to the simpler life at first, but there are plenty of things to keep you busy.

'Like what?'

'Community tasks, like the cooking and washing, running workshops, constructing new buildings, those sorts of things.'

'And,' suggested Len, 'if you don't pass your exams, I'm sending you there Geoffrey!

'Dad!'

'Len! That's the wrong attitude…' Spring turned back to Geoffrey. 'It might help with your writing Geoffrey.'

'Help with my *writing*…How?'

'Well it seems to me that the best way to get inspiration is to go places that are new, to see different things, different people. Maybe you could come to some arrangement with your Dad, to have a trip after your exams, before you get a job. A lot of youngsters do that. It can be easier for some to travel then, rather than in mid-career.'

'Would you let me travel if I pass all of my exams Dad?' Geoffrey asked hopefully.

'If they are good grades I'll consider it, but not for you to be away for a whole year, just a few weeks.'

'Oh that's great!' Jessica complained, 'you never let me go touring after school.'

'You left school when you were sixteen. I'd have worried about you. I still would.'

'Oh, thanks.'

'It's a bad world out there.'

'*She* went on her own I bet. Didn't you Spring?'

'I did, yes. But there were some scary moments.'

'Like what? Finding a town with no caravan park?' she snickered.

'No. Like one time finding I was being followed by three Eastern European men, who clearly had gang rape in mind…It's always best to travel with others.'

'So what did you do?' she wanted to know more.

'Some quick thinking on my part. I wasn't sure how good their English was, but I took on an expression of being ill, and started to slow down. In fact I focused so much on the act I must have looked too sick to be frightened. One of them grabbed me, and I said *I have AIDS*. They looked disgusted called me a whore and left.'

'Oh…'

'You shouldn't joke about things like that,' Len looked concerned.

'It wasn't a joke.'

'But you don't…You don't have AIDS do you Spring?'

'No…I've been careful…and lucky…I saw a lot of people, including children, dying of AIDS when I was in Africa. As if their life was not difficult enough. There is truly nothing fair about life. We make of it what we can, but preferably not at someone else's expense.'

'Have you ever thought of being a teacher?' Geoffrey asked.

'Not as a full-time career, no,' Spring shook her head.

'I reckon you'd make a better teacher than Ms Hedges at my school. She just seems to think teaching is about making the kids practice the answering of previous exam papers, and shouting at anyone who gets bored and talks.'

'Dear me. Teaching ought to be about inspiration and opening the mind to enquiry. What does this Ms Hedges teach?'

'Math.'

'Oh, not my subject. I used to think algebra was created to make adding up more challenging.'

'Ha ha.'

Len got up from the sofa and went to the bowl with the keys in, and began looking through the pile of letters there, stopping at one in particular and opening it.

'Bollocks!... Bastard.'

'What is it?' Spring asked.

'Urr…Oh, nothing…Someone's cocked up while I was away… Excuse me while I get it sorted.' He dug his mobile out of his pocket and went upstairs for some privacy.

'Someone's in trouble,' Jessica smirked. 'So Spring, how did you meet Dad?'

'In a market, he saw me buying some fruit and warned me I should wash them in clean water before I eat them unless I enjoy the shits. He assumed I might not already know. It made me laugh. But he must have thought I was laughing at him, because he just walked away.

'But then we crossed paths again a few minutes later. He was looking at some T-shirts with local pattern prints made for western tourists. I told him they were made by child labour. He said he wasn't against kids earning money to feed themselves. I said I agreed in principle but I'd be happy to describe these children's working conditions over a cold drink.'

'Nice,' Jessica said with sarcasm.

'So *you* picked *him* up.' Geoffrey confirmed.

'Well yes I suppose I did.'

'But you can only be a few years older than me.' Jessica suggested.

'Really? That would make you in your early thirties.'

'Would it? I'm nineteen…But you don't look…that *old*.'

'Thanks, but I don't think that age between adults should matter…when it's right.

'When it's *right*?'

'Sure. When you just *know* that you've met someone for a *reason*.'

'Hmm…Like he's rich.'

'No actually…Like, I'm supposed to…be there for him.'

'What does that mean? He's got *us*.'

'To be honest I'm not totally sure yet, but maybe we'll see.'

'Are you one of those fortune telling gypsies?' Geoffrey asked.

'No, not me. But if I were, I'd predict there are some tough times ahead.'

'Oh you're an optimist then,' Jessica piled on more sarcasm as her father returned. 'So what's up then Dad?'

He breathed a long sigh of exasperation. 'The haulier I use…he went belly up while I was away. He said he's lost just too much business with the recent rocketing fuel prices, making people unprepared to pay his costs.'

'I was just saying about the fuel earlier wasn't I Geoffrey. It's like the government's decided to self-destruct. You can bet the Americans aren't paying these prices.'

'I think the government may be trying to encourage us to reduce our dependency on oil, but the economics are too complex to manage it well.' Spring suggested.

'Why bother?'

'Because fossil fuels are running out Jessica, which means either we can keep it cheap and use it till it's suddenly all gone, or restrict its use by increasing the cost over time.'

'Yeah, as long as the government still gets its tax on top,' Len muttered bitterly.

'At least this way we get to feel the pinch and respond to it, rather than get surprised by the crash,' Spring pointed out.

'I think,' decided Jessica, 'I'd rather have it easy and go out with a crash.'

'Would you? *Really*?'

'Meanwhile,' said Len, 'in the real world, I have two containers of merchandise stuck at the docks costing me for being there, and making no money because they didn't get to clients who are doubtless as cross as I am. They'll want a reduction on their late order, and I'll end up with little if any profit.'

'So sell to someone who will pay,' Jessica thought she was stating the obvious.

'These items were made to order. It will be difficult to find a buyer who won't also want them on the cheap.'

'So…' said Geoffrey thinking on from what Spring had said earlier, 'tough times ahead then?'

'Get on with your homework.'

By the autumn the family unit *included* Spring. Nevertheless, for Jessica there was still some way to go in coming to terms with this woman's presence.

Though Spring was trying hard to fit in and provide support, Jessica did not want to see her as a replacement mother, or having any influence over her father. When Spring had stayed behind during Len's next business trip abroad, Jessica tried to encourage Spring to leave, but surprisingly grew a little closer to her as a result of their discussions.

This particular evening, when Len had returned, they were eating dinner at the table in the kitchenette. Geoffrey was first to finish and put his knife and fork down on the plate. 'Mmm, that was good Spring, thanks.'

'Here. Have some more of mine,' she responded.

'No, no.'

'I gave myself too many peas,' she scraped some off her dish onto his.

'Ur Dad, tell her!' he pulled a face of disgust.

'What's the fuss?'

'Spring's just given me her peas.'

Jessica's scornful laughter at her brother's poor choice of words suddenly turned to choking.

'Oh for God's sake stop it, both of you!' Len didn't seem to acknowledge his daughters plight.

Spring quickly poured more water into Jessica's glass, but Jessica waved a hand at it, mouthing a 'No', but appearing more panicky. Spring slid her chair back, got up and carried out the Heimlich manoeuvre on Jessica, and a chunk of potato ended up on Len's plate.

Len looked at the addition to his plate shaking his head with a sigh of disappointment, 'I'd have preferred the peas.'

'Cool,' said Geoffrey. 'Where did you learn to turn people into Nerf guns?'

'I learned first aid when I was part of a commune in Germany.'

'Thanks,' Jessica gasped, reaching for the water she had previously waved away.

Len decided he'd had enough and took his plate to the sink, then looked for a beer in the fridge, but remained with his back to the sink drinking from the bottle.

Spring turned to Geoffrey. 'So how's it going with that novel?'

'Oh still just notes. Shame I couldn't have gone on that trip to Findhorn, or anywhere, but I guess a B and two Cs wasn't good enough.'

'Well at least you got that job at PC World. You can save up for your time off now.'

'I suppose so. I might even get a Christmas bonus. We're having record sales of home-office equipment at the moment.'

'I guess more people are looking to work from home, to save on travel expenses.'

'Maybe people are copying you Spring. Trading on e-bay,' Jessica commented.

'Maybe,' Spring agreed.

Len shivered. 'Have you turned the heating down again Spring?'

'Not me Luv...' she said with a smile, 'I turned it *off*.'

'Well then, I think it could be time to christen that wood burning stove you got us.'

'Oh it's not cold enough for that yet. Put a jumper on.'

'Are you telling me I can't dress how I please in my own home?'

'Dress how you want. The way we dress is a show of how much we care.'

Len banged the bottle down irritably on the worktop and went upstairs.

'Did you know,' said Geoffrey, 'between 1945 and 1992, we were sending a signal into space that said this planet contains dangerous life forms.'

'Were we?'

'Yeah.'

'Why would we bother doing that?' Jessica sounded exasperated with her brother's mine of useless information.

'It was the un-natural radiation of atomic blasts...It was realised this might seem bad, and that the accompanying TV and radio waves since 1912 might be a bit confusing to any intelligent extra-terrestrial viewers. With it being a mixture of fact and fiction. So SETI started sending out a repeated signal to declare we are intelligent.'

'So more fiction then,' Jessica said with a smirk.

Ignoring his sister, Geoffrey continued, 'That means that our evidence of atomic weaponry reached the first of our neighbouring star systems, known to have planets, Gliese 876, in November 1960.'

'Gosh,' said Spring.

'If any of those planets had intelligent life, and if they had space travel, and could only average even half the speed of light, they could have been with us since the 90's. If they had worm-hole technology they could have been with us earlier still.'

Len could be heard cursing upstairs, 'Damn it!'

'The *atomic age* sign just keeps spreading, and the further it goes the more likely it is to be received by intelligent life as it expands. With an end to the radiation, since the last weapons test, they may conclude we have either quit testing, or have destroyed ourselves.'

Len returned, now wearing a jumper.

'You missed the aliens arriving Len,' spring told him as she looked at what he was wearing, making a mental note that the elbows needed darning.

'Oh well…I hope you've charmed them into doing the dishes.'

'They probably wouldn't understand what dishes were, would they.'

'How's that?' Len found himself asking.

'Well the Glians are a *lightform*…right?' she winked at Geoffrey.

'That's right, and if you've seen any strange lights Dad, they're probably already in your head.'

'Seen any strange lights while you were upstairs luv?' Spring teased.

'Now you come to mention it, I did.'

'Oh?'

'Yeah, pulling this polo neck on I banged my head on the wardrobe door,' he felt for a lump but there was nothing there, so changed the subject. 'I noticed Alf across the way has put a 'for sale' sign in his car window…He'll be lucky.'

'How much is he asking?'

'A thousand…You're not thinking of buying it are you?'

'No. Just thinking *difficult times*,' Spring sighed.

Len took his beer through to the lounge and sat on the sofa. With no one volunteering to do the washing up, the others followed him through.

'Anyone for the news?' Len enquired, TV remote in hand, looking through the guide listing.

'To get our daily dose of depressing stories?' Jessica groaned. 'Oh that should help us get through another evening.'

Len cursed Jessica under his breath and took another swig from his bottle.

'What's up Len?' asked Spring.

'Nothing.'

'Which means *something*.'

'*Everything*, more like… It's the business… It's becoming very difficult to profit from it now… I think I'm going to need to change profession… Solar panels and rechargeable batteries are the businesses to be in these days I reckon, but I know nothing about those industries.'

'Or,' suggested Spring, 'you could help me with my e-bay work, while it lasts.

'Mmm, I suppose. And of course Dan down the road said he could do with a hand making his biodiesel.'

'I'm sure we'll survive.'

'We better do.' Jessica began to whine.

'And *you* are going to have to take whatever job you get offered next.' Len told her.

'What?!' she protested.

'Yes, even if it's washing up.'

'You could, of course, try clothing modifications,' suggested Spring, 'by using your interest in clothes, and your father's contacts in the industry to buy in seconds, and second-hand garments and modify them into something more appealing.'

'Well Dad's mates might make a good market for his biodiesel, but don't expect any of my mates to want anything *I've* made.'

'They don't have to. The garments will be just another thing we could sell through e-bay.'

'Right,' Jessica didn't sound convinced.

'Do you have anything that you could have a go with now, just to see how you get on?'

'I might…I suppose I could go take a look,' she said grudgingly but thinking it would be better than washing up. She headed upstairs in no rush, considering that her search would give her time to chill with something from her stash.

Len finished his beer and put the bottle by the sink. 'I'm going to take a walk to the supermarket to get some bread and milk. Is there anything else we need?'

Spring knew this probably meant *and pop into the pub on the way.* 'Oh I've put a list by the breadbin.'

'Oh, okay, I've got it.' He picked up his coat from the corridor then left.

While Geoffrey made further notes in his book, she watched a programme on the latest animals to become extinct due to human expansion and interference. It was criminal how people were mismanaging their countries with such global impact, all attempting to blame others.

With a creak of the third step Jessica came back down stairs, looking overly enthusiastic about her find. 'What do you think Spring?... A long sleeved T-shirt. Could we do something with that?'

'Sure…' Spring took it and spread it out on the carpet. 'We could do *something* with it yes. The question is *what*? What sort of garment do you want, or can you imagine selling?'

'Urr well I'm sure I could sell anything *really*,' she sounded as if she had taken an attitude transplant, 'though I'm more used to selecting stuff for people than making conversions.'

'I'm off to my room.' Geoffrey said in a rather bored tone.

'No interest in women's wear then?' Jessica teased.

'Huh. The only interest in women's wear I have is seeing it worn by a fit lass, then seeing it come off.' Geoffrey went upstairs, laughing at his own joke.

'Okay then…' said Spring, 'We could make it into a sleeveless dress.'

'Could we?...How?'

'Well…We could remove the sleeves and open their seams to give us the material for front and back panels, and then cut across here, below the breast line to insert the extension, below which the remainder of the T-shirt forms skirting.'

'Right…but won't it look odd…I mean with those seams across it?'

'We could make a feature out of them so that they stand out like ribs…In fact we could replicate the detail like a false seam around the middle of that panel to add further interest.'

'Yeah that could work,' she smiled.

Spring had been pretty sure for some time now that Jessica was taking drugs. Her mood swings seemed abnormal. She had tried to talk about it with Len, to get him to talk with his daughter, but he wouldn't have it that Jessica would take such risks.

For now Spring tried to work on the underlying reasons why Jessica would want to be experimenting with drugs.

'Did your Mum never do anything like this with you?' she said pointing at the garment they were about to attempt converting.

'What?'

'Sorry… Nobody says much about Erica… I wondered what she was like.'

'Oh Mum was great… Not like you… What I mean is she was different… She was wonderful. Not good at making stuff though, or cooking come to that.' Jessica paused in thought about the food, 'Dad never balked at what she made, but Geoffrey and I would get a frequent telling off for not finishing our meals and that included her puddings. Dad was so undiscerning. He loved her that much I suppose. I swear she could have served up wet kitty litter. He'd have happily eaten it if she explained she'd overcooked the rice pudding and raisins… She always seemed to be explaining her cooking to us as she served up, in case we didn't recognise it as food.'

'I'm sure she was good at lots of *other* things.'

'Oh sure… There was this one time, Mum had promised Geoffrey and I that she was going to get a clown in for my birthday party, like they do in America. The thing was, having promised, she couldn't then find anyone to do it. So what she did was to hire a clown costume and bought some face paints, to be the clown herself.'

'That was nice.'

'But things didn't go to plan. She made us all laugh with her fooling about after we'd eaten, but there was a complication… Geoffrey.'

'Geoffrey?'

'Yes. He liked painting and had wanted to use Mum's new face paints, but she told him no, and he had a tantrum. What she didn't know was before the party food was served, Geoffrey and another boy, Alan, had been doing some painting with Geoffrey's paints in his room, and Geoffrey had decided he was going to try some of Mum's paints anyway.'

'And used them all up?'

'Ha no. It would have been better if he had because when Mum called the two of them down for tea, he bundled all her paints together and quickly put them back on her dresser, only he'd mixed a couple of his own in with them, and Mum never noticed…Till much later…when the red around the mouth and circles on cheeks wouldn't wash out… For days… That's when she got her nickname at work… The Joker.'

'Oh dear.'

'When she'd be sorting out the schedules they'd say to her…*Ha. It's all part of the plan…Mmm*. And when she tried to laugh it off they'd go, '*Hoo ha hah hoo ha. Sinister, isn't it.*'… Which Heath Ledger as the Joker didn't even say in that classic Batman film… Apparently.'

'So what did she do?'

'Grinned and bared it I guess.'

'Sorry, what I meant was what *work* did she do?

'Oh…She was a midwife.'

'Huh. Not what a woman in pain wants to see I guess. Her baby being delivered by a clown.'

'Well I think Mum's face was pretty much hidden by the face mask, which she took to wearing *most* of the time, till the colour wore off.'

'Of course.'

'You know, I think with her working in a hospital we thought she'd never get sick, and that her colleagues would see to it that if anything ever did happen they'd save her… It was a shock when she got cancer, and how fast it spread.'

'I'm sorry Jessica.'

'It felt, at first, like our lives ended with hers... I guess being younger Geoffrey and I coped better, but Dad became very bitter. He wasn't like he is now, before Mum died.'

'I've sensed that.'

'Between you and me, if I had a boyfriend and he acted like that around me I'd tell him to get lost... I don't get why you are with him...*us*... really.'

'As I've said before...It's like I feel I'm *supposed* to be here...I care about you all.'

'I guess that's why I don't have a boyfriend then.'

'How do you mean?

'I think I only care about myself.'

'Well you can't expect anyone to love you if you don't love yourself first.'

'Who said anything about *love*? I just want some sex. Love leads to pain. Sex leads to more sex.'

'Does it?'

'Sure. I read this book once called The Secret. It basically said that those who have get more. The rich get richer, because their money attracts more investment. By the same token the more sex you have the more attractive you become.'

'I guess, but that would have to depend on how tired you start to look.'

'Ha! Shagged out... I wish.'

'So why aren't you meeting boys?'

'I don't know. They always seem to be elsewhere. When I'm out with the girls shopping, we eye lads up but never get talking.'

'Why?'

'Well there's typically between three and five of us and usually only a couple of lads so they are outnumbered. And anyway, why don't *they* come and talk to *us*. If we talk to them it looks like we're desperate.'

'And they wouldn't be?'

'Oh thanks!' she laughed.

'What I'm saying is that this attitude is part of the negative sexist culture of labelling people as sleaze balls and slags, which makes friendships more difficult to initiate.'

'I don't follow.'

'Boys and girls just want to talk and see what happens. If nobody makes a move, even if only to set up an opportunity, then nothing does happen.'

'Well sometimes things have happened for my friends when we go to the night clubs. Lads approach them on the dance floor.'

'And are these friends in relationships now?'

'Well no... meeting in the clubs is based on looks, because you can't hear anything inside, unless you scream.'

'Sure.'

'And when they do get chance to talk later, outside, or the next morning, these guys are usually wankers.'

'Naturally... Most people *are* wankers. So what are you looking for exactly?'

'Someone with a good job so that I don't have to work, and who likes me dressing up, so is happy to pay me to go shopping.'

'Ha.'

'*What*?'

'Sorry... Is that *really* what you want?'

'Yeah... Why not? Isn't that what we *all* want?... Rich good looking guy... Life of luxury.'

'Huh, oh sure... But it's a bit unrealistic though isn't it... So how were you planning on catching Mr Dreamboat?'

'Well… I don't have any plans… I thought only desperate girls planned. I thought I was supposed to wait.'

'Wait? Who gave you that advice?'

'Mum.'

'Oh…Sorry.'

'She used to say *everything comes to he who waits.*'

'*He,* yeah… But what about *time waits for no man*?'

'Well I don't know.'

'You need to consider your proverbs wisely, and who they were meant for.'

'Right.'

'Why wait, if you can be creative.'

'You mean like creating that opportunity?'

'Yeah. Some of the best opportunities for getting to know potential partners are through work…'

'But I don't have a job.'

'Or socialising with neighbours.'

'But I…'

'I've been talking to a few of the neighbours and I'm considering setting up a community where we might support one another better… You could help me with that.'

With the change in conversation leading further away from Erica, Spring realised she had lost her opportunity of asking Jessica how she coped with the loss, and whether she took anything to help with it. Then Len returned with the shopping, placing the bag by the breadbin before going to the corridor to take off his coat.

'Busy there Luv?' Spring asked.

'Usual… Though the shelves are looking emptier… I expect people are starting to hoard, and they can't restock quickly enough.'

'Especially with imported goods I bet.'

'I wouldn't have thought things could get like this so quickly.'

'They say that the average supermarket only holds sufficient food for the community it serves to cover three days.'

'Three days?!' he put the milk in the fridge, closed the door, then opened a cupboard and started to put can's in it from the bag.

Noticing this Spring reminded him, 'You know what I told you to do with tinned stuff Len.'

'Yes... Fill out the fridge before the cupboard, as long as it leaves circulation space. It saves energy by retaining the cold better when the fridge is opened,' it sounded like he was reciting a text book answer. 'It's just that old habits die hard.'

'Well I think some old habits are going to need *putting down*.'

'Anyway, I don't like the way it makes some of the sauces go funny.'

'Well then, keep those ones in the cupboard.'

'And some of us could open the fridge less often looking for something to nibble on, that isn't there,' he suggested to no one in particular.

'I don't know what you mean,' Jessica went on the defensive then laughed making it sound like she did.

'Yes. That's what the fruit bowl is for,' Spring prompted.

'But I don't like eating fruit all the…'

The lights went out without warning.

Geoffrey was heard coming down stairs slowly. He bumped into the door as he entered the lounge. 'What's happened?'

'Power cut I'd say,' Spring guessed.

'Not dad blowing a fuse then?'

'No,' Len sighed.

'I don't suppose you have any candles tucked away anywhere?' Spring prompted him.

'Other than our mobiles I've a torch somewhere,' Geoffrey offered, 'but I don't know what state its batteries are in.'

'You know what…I just saw packs of candles on offer, on a pallet at the front of the supermarket, and didn't think to get any… I'll get my coat.'

Winter was upon them, with its darker challenges. It had a way of making life feel that much bleaker, whether you suffered from Seasonal Affective Disorder or not.

Spring and Len were sat on the sofa writing, she on her tablet, while he used a paper note pad, when they heard keys at the front door. They both turned to see Geoffrey enter, then heard a police with car sirens blaring pass by as he closed the door after him.

'You're back early,' Spring commented.

'Did you lose *your* job?' Len asked anxiously, after hearing about so many job losses on the news.

'Worse,' Geoffrey grunted.

'Worse?'

'I spent the day sweeping up broken glass and putting damaged goods into skips, after the looting.'

'Looting? I wouldn't have thought people would bother with somewhere like PC world, now the power cuts are so frequent.'

'Well looting's what the police were calling it, but I don't think much stuff was missing, just wrecked. More stuff was taken from Halfords, a WPC told me. Bikes mainly.'

'Well you'd have to be a bit dim to pinch the car stereos these days.'

'Mmm.'

'So is that you out of work now then?'

'They haven't exactly said, yet... But I expect so.'

'Well, just keep your ears to the ground for any other jobs going.'

'Oh there're plenty of jobs *going*.'

'There are?'

'Yeah, the problem is, they're not *coming back*.'

'Oh *right*... Maybe you should join the police. Get talking to that WPC again.'

'I'd rather not. I'd have been home earlier but we were kept inside this afternoon because youths had started stoning the police. It was like a scene from Crime-Spree. You don't expect it to happen in the real world. Not *here* in Newcastle anyway.'

'What happened?'

'They'd kicked off when the police had arrested someone from the estate across the way. They were identified on the CCTV footage apparently. Then one of the military units opened fire and everyone scattered.'

'Martial law has been one hell of a Christmas present,' Len was saddened that this was what it was coming to.

'There're a lot of desperate, frightened, and angry people around who don't know what to do,' Spring remarked. 'They are little better than spoiled children.'

'Spoiled children?' Len looked in disbelief at Spring.

'Yeah. When people haven't had to scavenge or forage, or even hunt or farm for their living, they've never had to learn the natural life skills. Without the familiar easy life of modern civilisation, it's like being told *game over*.'

'Hell Spring, I don't think it's that bad.'

'Maybe not yet, but I think it's getting there.'

'What's gotten into you? You're normally the optimist.'

'I know, but I'm just being realistic about the changes ahead, so that we have a better chance of adapting.

'For example, I'm not sure how much longer the parcel services will keep going, to support our e-bay opportunities. They've already lost a number of packages... I think we're going to have to focus on more locally marketable things, which we can source and make, and deliver on bike or by foot. It is in our interest to develop our sense of community. I've already been talking with the neighbours.'

'Great... Don't expect much from them.'

'The thing is not to expect much from anyone, at first. We all have to manage our expectations... You have to *give* before you *receive*. To help them adapt.'

'I can't see Audrey and Philip adapting. I remember when TV turned to digital. They told me technology had gone too far. Their programmes were breaking up in giant pixels and stuttering. Worse than watching analogue interference they said and quit watching TV altogether… Bought the ten-season box-set of Friends, and just kept that on in the background, end to end, and on again… Said they barely noticed the difference.'

'Well doesn't that show that they *can* adapt?'

'Well…Okay…What about their child then?'

'I didn't know they had a child.'

'Exactly.'

'Sarah,' Geoffrey piped up.

Len nodded. 'She was a bit of a tomboy.'

'I liked her.' Geoffrey admitted.

'When she was fifteen…'

Geoffrey cut in again, 'she suddenly decided she wanted to go live with her Uncle.'

'No actually, it wasn't like that. It turns out that even at fourteen she had been trying to explain to her parents that she was a trans-boy and desperately needed the ops, but they said they didn't want her around if she did that.'

'That's dreadful,' Spring was saddened by the intolerance.

'How did you find that out Dad, if they didn't want anyone to know?' Geoffrey questioned, 'I didn't know.'

'The uncle, Steven, came round to see the two of them to talk sense into them. They told him to leave, and then wouldn't let him in the second time he tried to visit. I saw him standing on their driveway, pretty cross. I went out and asked if everything was okay, and I guess he saw me as a way of foiling their secrecy plan, and told me all about it.'

'And so did you spread the word?'

'No… Not till telling you… Otherwise I doubt they'd have ever spoken to *you* Spring.'

'Well maybe it's not too late to bring them back together.'

'Oh *don't* go meddling Spring.'

'But Len, it wouldn't be meddling. It would be seeding an idea, which ought to make them think again about the way they have behaved towards their child. I would simply be talking about my experiences abroad. Some of my stories would relate to how people learned that their life improved when they accepted people for who they are.'

'And what happens if you get it wrong? They could think you are preaching, and you could alienate yourself. People don't like being preached at… The word would spread, and there goes your community.'

'Do you really think I could be that tactless?'

'I…'

At that moment they heard the sound of more keys in the door as Jessica returned home, excited, her face glowing as she put the keys in the dish.

'Did you get through to South Shields okay?' asked Spring.

'Well they are still bulldozing the main streets clear, after last week's blazes, but I took some back road detours to make the delivery, and got back without trouble.'

'Good,' Len was pleased.

'But better than that, I think I've got some additional work, and well paid at that.'

'Oh?'

'Yeah, the guy I delivered to asked me to deliver something for *him*, which wasn't too out of my way on the way back, to an estate over by the Angel of the North.'

'What was it?'

'Don't know. It took up most of the boot. Looked heavy though…He and this other lad put the canvas bags in, and at the other end two blokes took them out, but look…' Jessica took a wad from her pocket, and with a twist of her thumb fanned out twenty-five ten pound notes. 'Two hundred and fifty pounds and he wants me to do more driving for him. He says he'll provide the fuel in addition to paying me.'

'I'd rather he paid for the fuel, and then that would help with Dan's biodiesel sales…Though we're having difficulty finding anyone with chip fat they're chucking these days.'

'Well I don't think Jessica should do this extra work, Len.'

'What?!' Jessica couldn't believe what Spring was hearing.

'Why not?' Len was surprised too. 'It seems like good money.'

'I doubt that…Why does he want a female driver?'

'I don't believe it… Is this you actually being sexist, Spring?'

'Not at all… Think about it. He must have loads of lads his end that can drive.'

'So? Maybe they are all busy filling his heavy canvas bags.'

'Yeah, heavy with what?' To Spring's mind it was a question Len needed answering for his daughter's sake.

There came the distant sound of heavy gunfire.

'I don't know.' He didn't seem to care. 'That's his business. It's hardly going to be big bags of drugs is it? Reduced drug supply is one reason for the rioting… I think the police and soldiers will have more on their minds these days than searching cars.'

'Oh Len,' Spring sounded very disappointed.

'What did Jessica take down there from us?'

'Mr Pearce wanted that old carriage clock I restored.'

'There you go then… Maybe he's a jeweller.'

Spring shook her head. 'In Africa, I saw…;

'Oh *in Africa*!… Here we go…' Len said frustrated by more of her pearls of wisdom from foreign contexts.

'Yes… *In Africa* I saw good people getting caught up in black market trading. First it was food, but it led to drugs and guns, by which time these folk couldn't get out, as the law saw them as transporters, guilty from the first job onwards.'

'Get real Spring! This isn't Africa. This is England!'

There came a distant boom, and dust fell from the ceiling, but the conversation continued regardless.

'My experience tells me we should steer clear of this.'

'Oh for fuck sake Spring! This sounds like some good money to me. Which we need right now! I could do the driving if Jessica got uncomfortable.'

'Though, Pearce *asked* for Jessica.'

'You know what, I'm pretty sick of all your know-it-all advice. It's as if you think you're never wrong.'

'Dad!' said Geoffrey shocked.

'I can't just let us get into a mess,' Spring tried to reason.

'*Let*?!... We *all* have to take more risks to survive now.'

'Sure, but not stupid risks.'

'Are you saying I'm stupid?'

'I…'

'Is that why you're always telling me how things ought to be done?'

'No Len…'

'I'm so sick of it… I think you've out-stayed your welcome. You should leave.'

'Dad?...' now Jessica was protesting.

'Why?' Tears welled in Spring's eyes.

'Have you not been listening to anything I've said?'

'Please Len. Think about what you are saying.'

'I have thought about it. I guess it's been building up in me for some time. I suppose I didn't start to notice your annoying habit till I brought you back here, and watched as you tried to take over as Mum.'

'No Len! I haven't! I've just been *trying* to…'

'Oh you have been *trying* alright. Just stop it! My mind is clear now. You really need to go.'

'Where to?'

'How about *Africa*!'

'Africa, why on Earth…'

'I don't know. Go back to Ireland then, or hitch back to India. Where do you want to go?'

'I don't *want* to go… I want to stay here with *all of you*.' Spring began to sob. 'The truth is… I grew tired of moving from place to place. I started to feel lost. I don't want to go back to

Ireland. When I met you I thought, felt, here's someone I think I might settle down some place with. Someone who might *need* me… And I still feel that I'm supposed to be here, to do something… I can't leave.'

'Sure you can… Just pop what you arrived with back in that rucksack of yours… Head down the garden path… And keep going.'

Jessica's eyes were filling with tears now. 'No Dad. This isn't right!'

'Why are *you* defending her? I thought you really wanted Pearce's job?'

'Not as much as I really want Spring to stay.'

'Me too,' agreed Geoffrey.

Len fell silent, not knowing what to say, but clearly still unhappy.

'What's really wrong Len?' Spring asked.

There was a long pause. It was as if Len was trying to force the words up from deep inside. 'It's just…' he sighed, 'When I used to look into the future I saw my plans like a well-lit road stretching out in front of me. For some time now those lights have been going out, and for the last few weeks, as business fails, there's almost nothing there. I guess I'm scared of the darkness that we're heading into.'

'But I…*We* are here for you,' Spring took his arm.

'I know… It's just… I miss Erica… *So* much… The world seemed a better place before she took ill… Before she died… It's like her cancer kept growing after she'd gone, sickening the world that remained… It's grown to fill me with despair.'

Spring put her arms around him, then with Jessica and Geoffrey it became a group hug.

Outside there was the sound of a heavy diesel engine and sirens of a passing fire engine.

There was Spring to provide hope and encouragement. The sound of a blackbird's song could just be heard out the back. The third step creaked as Len came down the stairs and through into the kitchenette carrying three hot-water bottles in fluffy jackets.

He placed them on the worktop to one side, then sidestepped to the sink where he had a load of dishes stacked ready. He squirted a little washing up liquid into the bowl, causing a bubbly flatulence.

'Not much of that left now,' he muttered to himself, checking under the sink, 'and only one left in the cupboard. Looks like I'll have to learn some soap-making skills soon.'

Next he emptied the contents of the hot-water bottles into the bowl. They were still quite warm, thanks to the fluffy jackets and double duvets on the beds for those frosty nights. He began to wash up the dishes by hand, with a chinking of glassware. 'Wonder if I'll have time to skin the two rabbits before... Oh here they are.'

Jessica entered through the kitchen door, followed by Geoffrey and then Spring. All three were laughing. They remove cycling helmets as Len looked over his shoulder from the sink.

'How'd it go?'

'Jessica beat us back,' Geoffrey announced.

'But she *so* cheated,' said Spring.

'That wasn't cheating,' argued Jessica, 'that was advanced driving technique.'

'You mean a gap in a hedge and a fallen wall.'

'Ha. That house is abandoned, so as good as a thoroughfare now.'

'Did you find any then?' Len asked hopefully.

'Loads,' said Spring.

They remove their back packs, and Spring opened hers up first putting a gardening fork on the worktop, then with another rummage in the pack she showed Len a handful of roots. 'We only dug up the ones without flowers, with the youngest of leaves. It will be much better when we gather them in autumn of course, but these will do for now. They should chop easy and roast up fine in the stove, and then we'll have Dandelion coffee to sell.'

'As well as drink.'

'Of course.'

'Not the same as real coffee beans though,' Jessica sounded a little glum.

'But close enough when roasted right,' said Geoffrey.

'I've had a thought while you were out Geoffrey.'

'Oh?'

'Yeah, about your writing.'

'*Really*?' he asked expecting a wise-crack from his father.

'I think you should have a go at writing for street performance.'

'*Street performance*?'

'Yeah. Either storytelling for a paying crowd. Develop it into theatre maybe, if you get some people to act out the parts.'

'Do you think?... Would they really pay?'

'It's up to you to find out. It could be like the festival they used to have in Edinburgh. You would gather a crowd give your rehearsed story, and then offer your cap round.'

'Wow. Yeah…But do you think I'd really gather a crowd?'

'Well with lack of reliable electricity for TV, cinema, or the Internet, I'm predicting a comeback for live performances.'

There came a sound from the letter box as something was put through the door.

Len turned, 'Is that post?'

Spring went to investigate, picking up an envelope and opening it. She drew out a booklet, and turned it from front to back, with a frown.

'What is it?' Geoffrey asked, 'A government survival guide?'

'It looks thin enough,' quipped Jessica.

'It's… a ration book,' said Spring.

'Oh,' Len didn't know how he felt about that.

'Like they had way back in wartime?' Geoffrey asked.

'It feels to me like it's been wartime for months,' Len reflected.

'Humankind at war with the legacy of its stupidity… What will those Glian's think of us,' Geoffrey pondered aloud.

'Will it ever go back to how it was?' Len stared out of the window.

'No…' said Spring, 'I don't think it will. And we shouldn't expect it to. Resilience is all about expectation management; Looking to move to something better than before; Learning new ways, and sharing them, providing and profiting from services to one another.'

'Is this another one of your lectures dear?... Should we all sit down?'

'Very funny… No… All I'm saying is it's about being inspired by our challenges, to *spring forward* rather than looking to *bounce back* to the way things were. We just have to keep trying.'

Shark Bait

Trish Fullerton looked at her grey complexion in the dresser mirror. She looked tired and hardly ready to be going outside never mind putting in a day's work at the cancer charity shop.

Nevertheless she just got on with it, adjusting her auburn wig before putting in her contact lenses. Her eyes looked bright and full of intent to continue, but she knew she would not be here much longer. She had taken care of everything now, and the way things were going it was almost time.

Like many people she did not look forward to going to work, but it did fill in the time, even if it failed to pay all the bills. She found stepping into the shop particularly depressing. It always looked untidy because it was limited to irregular sales of other people's unwanted belongings; though she knew underneath all the tat what they were selling was *hope*.

Nevertheless what disturbed Trish about the cancer charities now was that the cure for certain cancers were already out there but prohibitively expensive. This meant they were only available to the *haves* unless charities could be convinced to provide support to the *have-nots*.

The problem was that most of the profits and donations went to running the *service*, very little went to actual support, and only those applicants whose *proposals* were believed to offer future benefit to the charity stood a chance of getting the financial support they desperately needed.

The charities had come to operate more and more like banks with their focus turning to *investment*. The whole system reached a tipping-point when the NHS could no longer afford to deal with the number of people suffering from a growing variety of cancers.

If this increasing number of people were unsuccessful even with charity applications it meant they had to rely on bank loans, or worse still loan sharks.

The loan sharks often claimed they also had access to the required meds like a one-stop-shop, however, they were little better than drug-pushers. As users debts typically spiralled out of control it led to other forms of abuse. Trish had ended up involved with such people.

As she went down her front path she stopped at the sight of the red Ford, recognising Benny in the driving seat. She had managed to avoid him the previous night, coming home late having spent extra hours in the shop sorting stock. Now here he was, waiting for her. She wanted to walk to work, but as she closed her gate the passenger door swung open.

'Want a lift?' asked Benny leaning across the passenger seat.

'I'm fine thanks.'

'Get in,' the politeness was gone from his voice, now a demand.

'I have to get to work, and I can't afford to lose my job *if* your dad wants his money back.'

'I'm heading your way.'

'Why?'

'Just looking after our *client*.'

Placing a hand on the roof of the car and leaning in as Benny straightened up, she repeated '*why*?'

'You sound like a three year old with the why-whys. Just get in.'

Trish got in and closed the door. Benny pulled away even before she had managed to get her seatbelt fixed. Her movements were slow and laboured.

'You know you are two weeks behind with your payment.' It was a statement rather than a question.

'Yes I'm sorry about that, but I haven't been paid yet.'

'You said that a couple of weeks ago. We gave you a week's extension. You agreed to the extension, remember, with its raised interest level.'

'Only because I had no other option,' she protested. 'If I'd had the money you would have been paid.'

'So here we are. When *are* we going to get our money back?'

'We've been told that there has been a problem with accounts and the money should be through shortly.'

Benny shook his head with a sigh, 'How old are you Trish, forty-five?'

'Thirty-two,' she replied honestly.

'Really?' he sounded truly surprised. 'Wow… Well think how good you are going to look once you get the rest of those meds… I might even want a piece of you myself.' He placed his left hand on her right thigh, but she brushed it off.

'I'm going to need those meds next week Benny. Soon the widening gap in the treatment will mean I have to start over again, and I can't afford that.'

'Well you better be good to me then,' he said replacing his hand on her thigh.

Trish wondered if he had some perverse thing going on for him involving sick-chicks. She had read about that somewhere. 'What are you suggesting?'

'Moonlighting, in something more *profitable*,' he hinted.

'Like what?' her tone sounded like she was asking but not about to listen.

'Prostitution,' he suggested simply with a shrug.

'Bastard,' she spat her disgust.

'Hey! I'm trying to help you… What're a few blowjobs here and there, if it means keeping up with your payments and getting your meds? And who knows you might find some better earners once that body is healthy again.'

'You are a sick man, Benny.'

'Watch what you are saying Trish. You wouldn't like to see me ugly.'

'*Uglier.*'

'What?'

'Just helping you with your English,' she said looking at the hand still on her thigh and wishing she could burn holes in it with her eyes.

'What?'

'You know, like you're helping me with my meds.'

'Right,' Benny wasn't sure how to take her. Sometimes she sounded like she had more fight in her than she looked capable of. She had attitude, and he liked that. 'Here we are… Charity Street.' He pulled up by the row of shops, all owned by the same holding company, claiming their support of different causes.

'Thanks,' her gratitude sounded grudging as she got out of the car awkwardly.

'I'll be round tonight so I suggest you get *something* together for the old man or it could get tough.'

Trish said nothing just slammed the door on Benny's threat.

He watched her go to the door and knock in front of the closed sign then wait for the manageress to let her in before he went on his way to play bailiff with another *client*.

The smell of damp and old possessions hit Trish as it always did first thing in the morning. She was never sure whether it was because her nose had been rested overnight or whether the contents of the shop had gassed-off in some way, whatever the reason she knew she would not miss coming here.

Trish was halfway through her evening meal of baked beans and pork sausages with a pile of chips when there was a knock at the front door. She ate a couple more mouthfuls hoping it would go away, looking longingly at the Danish pastry she had picked up from the reduced shelves, but the knock came again, harder.

Trish got up and made her way to the front door. At first the person appeared to have gone, and she wondered if it was just kids having a laugh, but it was Benny standing to the side of the door. As soon as he stepped in front of her she tried to close the door again, but he had his foot in the way and shoved it open.

'Hey that's no way to greet a friend Trish.'

Giving up the struggle she turned her back on him and shuffled along the hallway to finish the meal in the kitchenette.

'So, have you come up with the cash?'

'Some of it,' she mumbled.

'Only some of it Trish?' he said with mock sympathy. 'When will you learn? It won't go away till you *clear* all of your debt. You seem intent on *increasing* it.'

'Increasing it?!'

'Sure. You were into us for fifty thou, but after tonight, if you don't pull a rabbit out of the bag the old man says it goes up to seventy five.'

'No!!' she wailed.

'Yes Trish. I've been warning you to sort it, but would you listen? No. I can see I'll be taking your Smart TV and microwave away with me, and we'll be lucky to get five percent of the going rate for them.'

'No you can't do that!'

'How are you going to stop me? You owe us.'

'This is fully furnished accommodation. Nothing here is mine. It is all rented. If you take anything I will lose my thousand pound deposit.'

'Well you know Trish, you should have thought of that before you went and got the big-C.'

'You *are* a miserable bastard.'

He shook his head. 'As the old man likes to say, it's nothing personal, it's just good business.'

'I want to see your father.'

'What for?' Benny frowned.

'To talk things through, and work out some win-win opportunity.'

'He's a busy man. That's why he has me helping cover *collections*.'

'I just need to agree a different way I can clear my debt.'

'Well I'm open to ideas Trish,' he said opening his arms wide as if to embrace her. 'Lay it on me first, and I might tell him.'

'*Might* is not enough. I need his buy-in.'

'What is it then?'

She paused, clearly reluctant to share but with little option she bit the bullet and launched in. 'It concerns how to rob the security van that comes to the shop at the end of the week,' she started to explain.

'The shop's *security* van?' he scoffed.

'Hear me out, please. The van collects from all three of the company shops on a Friday afternoon, and comes to ours last. And as…'

'They collect your bag of coppers and wonder why you even need a fucking security van! Don't be a silly bitch Trish. Each of the shops brings in maybe fifteen hundred, on a *good* week, that's urr what thirty five hundred in total. Nowhere near what you need in order to clear your debt. No it's a *shit* idea.' He said it all with a smile, clearly enjoying putting her down.

'Let me finish.'

Benny turned away and looked in the fridge. It was almost empty. 'Bollocks woman! You don't even have any beers!'

'People bring bags of stuff to the shops and walk away. Mostly its clothes and Blue-Rays, but occasionally it can be half a dozen bags of possessions from a dead relative.

'When people are emotional about a person's death they don't always think to check the value of things, they just bag it all up and clear the place out to put the property on the market. But at least some think to drop it off with a charity rather than taking it to the tip. What the charity shops do is sort it all through and clean it up. Some of the old stuff goes to auction and can raise a lot more money for the company.'

Benny yawned. 'Is there an end to this story? It's got dangerously close to triggering my boredom intolerance.'

'Yesterday, I stayed late because we had one of these house clearances to sort through, and I came across a wooden box with a puzzle lock.'

'Bored now,' he was more interested in winding her up. He wanted to see her squirm; caught so wickedly in his father's trap.

'And when I figured out how to open it, it actually contained a necklace and earring set that I thought would fetch quite a bit in auction. When I came home and checked on the Internet I figured the set could raise between one and two hundred thousand.'

'So…just take it.'

'I would lose my job.'

'Who'd know?'

'We work in pairs, and all items are inventoried with a scanner as we sort through them.'

'You should have nicked it before it got scanned.'

'And risk being seen on the CCTV… I had no idea what was in it till I figured the lock mechanism out. So anyway, what I was thinking was that if the van just happened to be raided for money and the auction items, it would look like a coincidence rather than an inside job. The inventory doesn't get prices put against things till they've been to valuation.'

'Mmm, I don't know,' Benny feigned his disinterest badly, sounding more interested now.

'Look I have a photograph of the jewellery,' Trish said pulling a picture out of a draw.

'So where's the box?'

'These aren't the actual ones Benny. It would look a bit suspicious, me photographing possible valuables in the shop, or downloading the scan data from the computer for that matter. No, this is the same thing but off the Internet.'

'Right…Well…Maybe you *should* come and see the old man,' he said, more convinced at the sight of the jewellery and reaching for his smart-phone.

Benny pulled-up around the back of his father's garage and impatiently led Trish up the fire escape to the office. There they first entered a short corridor which led to two doors and an internal staircase which went down to the garage workshop. Benny knocked on the first door, and they heard a '*Come*' croaked from inside, then he showed Trish in closing the door behind them. The air was thick with cigarette smoke, and together with the sound of the garage still working in the evening all added to the sense that here was a less than legal working environment.

The old man looked like he was in his seventies, and had very mean eyes. 'So, you have a proposition to resolve our *issue* over repayment.'

'I believe so,' the quiver in Trish's voice suggested nervousness.

'Please, take a seat,' the old man pointed to the chair in front of his desk.

Benny stood behind her as she sat down. She wondered if his intention was to intimidate. It certainly didn't feel like he was standing there in support. The old man offered her a cigarette. She shook her head.

'She's got cancer Dad.'

'So there's nothing stopping her then,' the old man responded cynically, before replacing the half empty box back on the table, as Trish coughed.

'I know how to bring an end to my debt with you, but it will mean moving fast,' she said with a smile, please by the cleverness of her choice of words.

'Go on then, explain this robbery Benny mentioned.'

'On Friday the van turns up to secure our takings and the week's collection of items for valuation and auction. This week there is a necklace and earring set which I estimate would fetch around one to two hundred thousand pounds. The wooden puzzle box and jewellery are recorded on the inventory but not their value. If you can get me something that will create smoke by remote control I can place that in with the items and you can set it off when it goes inside the van, forcing whoever is inside to bail out, then you rob it.'

'And where do I get this incendiary device?'

'I don't know. I thought you might know about things like that.'

'What are you saying?' he feigned offence. 'I offer a public service to those who cannot get loans any other way. I'm not into robbery.'

'Oh. Don't you have any guns either?'

His eyes didn't stray from hers. 'Listen lady, either you have a simple failsafe plan for getting those jewels or we don't have a deal.'

They paused watching one another expectantly.

'And I thought my son said your plan was to avoid making it look like an inside job, so that you would be in the clear.'

'Yes.'

'But if the device goes in with your money and items then they will work out it was an inside job.'

'Oh.' Trish sounded desperately disappointed. 'What if you have a device thrown into the van when the door is opened?'

'This isn't like the old movies Trish. Things get loaded into these vans through an airlock hatch with a scanner.'

She gave an exasperated sigh, 'Well do you have any suggestions?'

'Me?... I suggest you show me what you have on you today and I might just think about your robbery idea overnight.'

'But…'

'What's in the bag?'

Trish didn't move. A nod from the old man saw Benny pick up her hand bag and rummage inside.

'Hey!' Trish protested.

Benny hoped he would find nothing so that he would get his chance to frisk Trish, but he located something bundled up in a corded plastic bag from a shoe shop. He took a look inside. 'How much is this Trish?'

'Four hundred and fifty,' she replied, keeping her eyes on the old man.

For a split second, at the mention of the money, the old man's eyes flicked to the cabinet to his right. 'This *pin money* really isn't going to cut it Trish, you really are going to have to do better than that or things could get *difficult* for you.'

'That's all I have. I need my *meds*.'

'And I need my *money*. You knew when you took out your loan with us that we are not a charity.'

'But I thought if you got your hands on the jewellery everything would be sorted.'

The old man gave a triple tut as he shook his head at her naivety. 'We haven't got the jewels yet. But say we got two hundred thou from them, after the expenses incurred in doing the job and you getting say twenty-five percent of the profit, by my reckoning you'd still be in debt by maybe ten thou.'

'No! That can't be right!'

'Face it Trish, it looks like you are in with us for the long haul.'

'But I'm not sure how much time I've got left!'

'That's *your* problem.'

'Surely it is *ours*. You won't get your money when I'm gone.'

'I hear bodies can fetch quite a bit for harvesting these days.'

'What? You can't be serious,' Trish gasped.

'She has *cancer* dad.' Benny reminded him again.

'Oh yeah… Well…It seems to me that you need to be thinking about other side-lines if you don't want to be missing those meds.'

'But please…' She pleaded, reaching out for the old man's right hand and appearing to play with it for sympathy.

Frowning, the old man told her 'You could however consider selling shares in your *recovered* body.'

'What?'

'If we get you straightened out with the meds I reckon you could bring in enough to pay us off by selling harvesting shares in your body, then you could work to buy back your shares over say ten years and avoid forced harvesting, by providing sexual services.'

'No, please not that. Look I could do massage.' She became more attentive with his hand.

'Ha,' he barked his derision but acknowledged that her massage was quite pleasurable.

'You have knots in your hand and wrist. You seem quite tense.'

He opened his mouth to protest but only smoke came out. He didn't want to seem weak in front of Benny, but he hadn't had anyone touch him like this in years.

Keeping a hold on the old man's hand Trish stood up and shuffled round the desk only letting go of his hand at the last moment to place her hands on his shoulders. 'Oh yes you do need loosening up. I was a physiotherapist once,' she explained.

The smell of his sweat stained shirt combined with the smoke to make Trish want to gag but she remained focused and the old man began to relax. Nevertheless, he must have noticed his son was looking on, jealous of these attentions. 'Go down and check with Terry how the lads are coming along with tonight's jobs.'

'Okay,' he sounded reluctant to go, starting to wonder what his father was going to have Trish doing when he was out, but he knew better than to argue.

'Couldn't I provide massages for you and certain friends and colleagues maybe, to earn my meds?' she asked as Benny left.

'Well,' the old man contemplated the idea, as he enjoyed the probing of Trish's fingers, 'I would...' He never finished what he was about to say, as with one massive pull on his jaw and push to the crown of his head she snapped his neck.

Wasting no time Trish moved quickly to the cabinet to the right which the old man had glanced at when money was mentioned, the door was locked. Coming back to the desk she reached to the bottom of her bag and pulled up the false bottom to remove a memory stick and a blue-tooth microphone sucker with ear-pieces. She slipped the stick into the desktop computer's USB4 port automatically activating its programme. She let it run.

Next Trish pulled open the draws feeling underneath them for items stuck there whilst eyes scanned the draw contents for keys and other items of interest. She found what looked like the cabinet key first in the top draw but continued her search. On the underside of the bottom draw was taped a key she expected to be for the safe. Going over to the cabinet the old man had glanced towards she opened the doors. It was full of accounts files, but pulling these out onto the filthy carpeting Trish revealed that the cabinet had no back and the wall behind held the safe. The second key fitted the safe lock, but there was still the combination dial to crack.

She smiled as she put one of the ear pieces in and placed the blue-tooth microphone sucker on the safe door. She loved these analogue safes, but she could have done with a little less noise from the workshop. Leaning into the emptied cabinet and listening intently as she turned the dial, she kept a wary eye on the office door for Benny. She expected him to be gone for some time, but she knew that expectations could be dashed.

'Dee-Doo,' the sing-song signal came from the memory stick. Trish removed her ear piece and went to the computer. The first stage of its program had located and decrypted the safe code. Then it moved straight onto the second stage of the program to copy the hard drive content.

Trish memorised the seven numbers as she took the shopping bag with her four hundred and fifty pounds and went back over to the safe. Kneeling down again she dialled in the code and soon had the door open. With a cursory scan for trip alarms she quickly reached inside and began pulling everything out to go into the bag.

Trish only had half the stuff out when, with a knock on the door, Benny returned. His face was a picture of confusion. Trish was not where he expected her to be, and his father appeared to be unconscious at his desk. 'Hey!' he stormed over to Trish.

Rising from the floor to meet Benny's charge, Trish upturned the shopping bag, successfully distracting him with all the money falling out of it. He slowed, caught between a need to strike Trish but also grab the money. This was all the hesitation she needed.

The white plastic bag went over his head and she pulled the cord tight at his throat, twisting her hip into his backside, and lifted his feet off the ground in a half committed judo throw. The fact that there were four holes in the bag were not the main reason Benny was not about to suffocate, it was that he was in imminent danger of being strangled to death by the cord which bit expertly into his neck. His fingers scrapped uselessly at his neck, then as the panic increased he began to fling his arms and legs about, till he twisted off of Trish, but she was ready for this.

As his feet returned to the carpet followed by his hands Benny tried to push up, but Trish was pulling him backwards in a constant circle. The best he could do to reduce the choking was scramble backwards on hands and feet. However, he soon realised he would just die that way. He knew he had to grab her and stop her. He continued thrusting with his legs, trying to reach out for Trish's legs but she was too fast for him. There was no way this woman was even a little in need of any meds, and his last thought was how angry he was for being tricked.

As Benny went limp Trish stopped moving, but kept the cord tight for another sixty seconds, listening to the workshop sounds continue. Satisfied she removed the bag turning it inside out and drying the condensation of Benny's breath off it on his shirt before searching his pockets, taking his wallet and car keys.

She returned to the safe packed the bag with its contents, closed the door, shutting both its keys in it and twisting the dial. Then she replaced the accounts files and closed the cabinet doors. That done she returned to the desktop computer.

By this time her stick had finished the third and final stage of its program having wiped the computer's hard drive. She put the stick and listening devices in her jeans pocket, gathered up both bags to leave then had an after-thought.

Swivelling the old man's chair so that he faced to the right, she parted his legs. Then she took his son by the arms and dragged his dead body across the carpet, turning him over to kneel before his father, and finally placed his face into the old man's piss soaked crotch. She knew it was needlessly gratuitous, but it brought a smile to her face.

'What goes around comes around, grief merchants,' Trish said in parting as she picked her bags back up. Returning to her cover persona she shuffled down the fire escape to the Ford, to put Manchester behind her and head to her real home in Cambridge.

Leaving the car at Manchester Piccadilly train station, where she changed her appearance in the toilets with practiced ease she walked to the national express depot to catch a coach.

Trish Fullerton now looked at Zoe Innes in the mirror once again. While it was a relief to look at her real self in reflections around her house she knew this feeling never lasted long. It didn't help that she had pictures of her twin sister Chloe and her husband Mitchell up as reminders of life's injustices and Zoe's need to do something about it.

Mitchel had been in the Royal Marines until he had been killed in action in the Indian Ocean on anti-piracy patrol, and Chloe had died some two years after because the inappropriate medication for her grief had somehow led her to alcohol and drug abuse and associated gambling and debt. The loan sharks had finished her off before Zoe had even realised her sister was falling apart.

Zoe was tormented by guilt. She had always thought she and Chloe were telepathically close, and yet she clearly had not been there for Chloe in her time of greatest need. In actual fact she had been working in Saudi Arabia. Things had become easier there for women since the mid the 20's when women were allowed a little greater freedom, like finally being permitted to drive.

In some respects her decision to blame loan sharks, came as a coping strategy for her own grief. To her mind if these sharks had not been there to provide money and contacts with drug suppliers, Chloe would surely have turned to her before it was too late. It seemed possible that once Chloe had started on that slippery slope she felt she couldn't admit to Zoe what she had resorted to.

It wasn't that Zoe felt Chloe would have condoned what Zoe was doing now, or that she thought her actions were putting anything much to rights. It was just a burning anger that needed controlled venting and this was the only way that pleased her.

Nevertheless, it did more than please her if she had to be honest, the planning and execution *excited* her. These very controlled actions used a wide range of prior experiences she had gained over the years to become what she was today.

From performing arts to martial arts, from IT skills to detective skills, she wasn't sure whether she was a self-styled assassin, or had simply become a serial killer.

To friends and neighbours Zoe was still doing IT security contract work across in the Middle East, which worked as a cover for her being away for months on end and not easy to contact.

When she was back she was never one to lounge around. She was regularly going for runs, and training in her gym room with martial arts weapons and targets. When she did stop it was either to investigate files she had removed from criminals, or to develop ideas for her next vigilante mission. Otherwise it was of course eating, sleeping, and other mundane necessities.

After a couple of months her mind was made up. She would be heading for Newcastle upon Tyne as Shelley Denton. She had been letting her hair grow back its natural dark brown. It would be quite short, but with the LED nose stud, metallic blue lipstick, and more youthful looking clothes it would appear *on trend*. She would of course be taking a new make-up kit for the tired eyes look of a student, and had been practicing her new voice.

She used differing modus operandi for each killing, hoping to reduce the likelihood of the deaths being linked and therefore attributed to a serial killer. To further confuse any pattern she also targeted drugs suppliers, and had used all the obvious techniques of separating people from their lives.

She had often taken full advantage of the weapons which people brought with them and tried to use against her. She had stabbed and shot people before but had also moved into the realm of the *less usual*.

She had slit open target's throats with glass finger nails and choked one woman to death with a squash ball forced in with her racket handle.

On one occasion before she was ready to complete her mission, which typically involved removing gang money and destroying their business, a couple of men had busted their way into her rented accommodation. Their intention was to beat a warning into her. However, Zoe was not into taking a beating just to maintain her cover, nobody else was depending on her and she could do without unnecessary injuries if her personal mission became compromised.

Once it was clear that aggression was their only language she subdued the two heavies by a series of leg and arm deadening nerve-point attacks.

One of the men she left strangling on the cord of her iron which she had been using when they had entered, leaving the plate of the iron burning into his back as he was unable to move his arms and legs to get free. The other died like a macabre piece of art as she smashed bottles of her alcoholic cover's collection of spirits over his head till his skull plates revealed the brain within. Finally, with a bit of help from her nails she had opened his skull like a Terry's chocolate orange.

Zoe felt no remorse for these actions, then or since, only frustration on that particular occasion knowing that the incident with the two heavies meant leaving immediately with her *dash-bag* full of essentials, and aborting her mission. She often found herself considering returning to finish that job as the crooks were still out there making a misery of people's lives, but she knew she shouldn't.

The mission in Newcastle didn't just require a new *dash-bag* and getaway strategy it also required contingency plans for attack and defence.

As much as she thought the details through she knew only too well she had to stay open and alert to new information in real-time and that meant remaining fluid in how she operated. In this instance one of her back-ups involved having to hide eighteen inch plastic zip-lock ties on her person. For this she resorted to customizing her bra, and hiding the plastic strips in with the support wires in the lining, with each ratchet head protruding for ease of removal. Nevertheless, she accepted that if she allowed herself to get drugged or otherwise taken by surprise she could find herself stripped of her clothes and devices.

There was something about such thoughts that disturbed Zoe these days. The more she thought about what disturbed her the more she started to wonder whether she might actually *enjoy* the prospect of getting caught.

Such thoughts were making her heart race and it thrilled her to fantasise about various scenarios. Deep down she wanted to either see how she met such a challenge, or maybe it was about wanting an end to this macabre existence. What worried her most was that such thoughts might subconsciously lead her into messing up and getting caught.

Zoe, now Shelley Denton, looked the part as an exhausted mature student, who was putting too much effort into living night-life to the full and not putting much time into sleep or study. Most students couldn't afford to have their own flat, whereas Zoe could not afford to share one. As part of this cover she did not clean the flat and only washed up if she needed anything clean to cook or eat with.

Most of what she ate came from tins anyway and was simply heated up in the microwave in the same glass bowl. The condition of her kitchen made her want to gag, but it was potentially more of a health risk not to play the part in case she had uninvited visitors. The landlady had dropped by once and complained that if she didn't *sort her shit out* she would lose her deposit.

Loss of deposit was the least of her concerns with all the organised crime money she had amassed so far. However she understood that this sort of lifestyle would in time take its toll on her health and fitness and put limits on how long she could carry on with her personal vendetta.

She promised herself that next time she would go under cover as a rich person down south somewhere, maybe Brighton, and focus on taking out a drug supplier. The one concern she had over the occasional drugs mission was that unlike the loan sharks, there was a risk of coming across under-cover police, and she didn't want them getting caught in her traps.

Thanks to the false passport and other paperwork she had bought she had enrolled at university to do Travel and Tourism, but had not turned up to any of the morning lectures. Like many students, her day didn't appear to start till after lunch. In truth she stayed in with the curtains drawn and television on, doing exercises and some Internet searching.

Though she did occasionally pop to the shops she mostly had purchases delivered, this acted as cover if she had to explain how she had been getting her drugs supplied if someone had been watching.

Nevertheless, Shelley Denton was out at the clubs of an evening trying to suss out the scene to check how it related to what she had pieced together on the Internet in terms of access to drugs and more importantly loans.

She held to the scripted sob story with people she met that she had used the best part of her student loan on a deal that had turned sour and wasted her money. She couldn't get more money from the bank, or come clean to her parents or the police for obvious reasons. She was going to get chucked off her university course next term if she was unable to pay her fees.

Eventually word got back to her of a man who might be able to help, called Kirk, who she would meet in Fenham at a park on the edge of the town moor, where he fed the birds for an hour around mid-morning if it wasn't chucking it down.

Kirk turned out to be a very scruffy looking man with a walking stick, smoking roll-ups as he flicked out his mix of seeds to a gathering flock of filthy looking feral pigeons. Considering that these birds were reputed to carry around sixty diseases it seemed madness to encourage them.

Kirk looked and behaved like someone in need of care not someone about to offer a sizable loan. Either he was just as he appeared or it was also a convincing cover.

The latter was confirmed as the introductory discussion developed into what felt more like an interview. Shelley answered a number of probing questions about her childhood as well as her present circumstances.

Zoe was ready for this and had fully rehearsed the persona of Shelley and believed in it, for her own safety. She could not afford to sound like an amateur. To do this well though also required some obvious lies because people were never totally honest with one another. These were ridiculous claims about stuff she had got away with in the past, as if she was trying to impress Kirk how capable she was of paying back a loan.

As Kirk emptied his bag of seed he asked Shelley how much she needed. She asked for twenty-five thousand, and he didn't even blink, just stood up and said 'Same time tomorrow.'

The next day she met him again. He didn't just hand over the money but engaged her in what felt like another interview, at the end of which this time he wanted to know her address. She gave it to him wondering if he intended to bring the money round later, but at the end of the meeting he told her to go to Erikson's chip shop that evening and explained to her what to ask for.

'Davie, the blind guy, sent me to collect his supper,' said Zoe to the woman at the counter, hoping it was the right person to ask, and handing over the tenner as arranged. The woman popped out the back and returned with a plastic bag with two paper wrapped bundles and a can of Coke.

At home she opened the bundles to find twenty-five thousand in a mixture of twenties and fifties, and upon checking further she determined that they were all counterfeit. This was often the case even with notes she took from loan sharks safes, as a number of them were involved in money laundering of counterfeit as well as ill-gotten legitimate notes.

This did not bother her because the money was not the goal, only a means to an end. She had two months to pay the money back with an extra ten thousand, but Kirk made no suggestions as to how she was supposed to make the extra money. It didn't matter because Shelley was just not going to be able to pay back that loan, and this is where things would start to get exciting.

Close to the agreed repayment deadline Shelley met with Kirk and his greasy flock of flying rats and confided in him that she was worried she was not going to get the money together in time. She had resorted to gambling what she had left after paying for her last batch of drugs and lost it all. She asked whether there was any chance she might get another loan but Kirk just chuckled at her stupidity.

She requested an extension, sounding more desperate, but all Kirk said was that she would need to talk to Jerry who ran a local club in the city. She was told where to go. It involved going down a back alley full of industrial wheelie bins and knocking on a fire escape door at exactly eleven-thirty the following evening. Kirk had knocked the special knock on the park bench and she had repeated it to show she had got it.

Half eleven the following evening, having found the place early and hung around the bins for quarter of an hour, Zoe knocked but nothing happened. Deciding that people's watches didn't all run to the same time she knocked again. When it still wasn't answered, she wondered whether Jerry had decided she was late and had gone, but as she was about to knock a third time the door opened.

'Jerry?'

The man, who looked like a bouncer shook his head, then led her along a corridor and up some stairs, down another corridor and showed her into a very fancy office. There was a large aquarium to one side which, in character, Shelley appeared naturally drawn too.

'Oh wow. Are they for real?'

'Are *you* for real Shelley?'

'What?' she didn't sound like she'd heard him.

'I am rather disappointed in you.'

'Yeah, I'm sorry about that,' she apologised, her eyes still glued to the tank like a ditz.

'Hey! I'm talking to you!'

Shelley pulled herself away. 'Yes sorry. Those fish are fab. They must have cost a fortune.'

'Never mind the fish, I want to know how we are going to resolve our financial arrangement, which I have heard is going to be a problem for you now.'

'Yes. I'm real mad at myself Mr ur Jerry. I thought I could make up the money with online poker, but it's gone.'

'That was pretty stupid Shelley.'

'I see that now.'

'You do realise that gambling's sole purpose is to *take* the money from the players, not to give it away. And that was *my* money you lost.'

'But I…'

'I thought you were supposed to be a university student.'

'I…'

'I've done some checking and it seems you have not got a good attendance record.'

'Well they ask you to get up at a ridiculous hours for lectures and it gives me sleep deprivation issues.'

'How old are you?'

'Twenty-seven.'

'Well I've got news for you *Shelley Denton*, your acting like a seventeen year old, but you look like you are thirty-seven, and we both know what that is down to.'

'Well I…'

'Have you looked at yourself in a mirror lately? You are a mess,' he almost sounded like he was concerned about her welfare, but she knew he was just leading to a proposition. 'You look shagged out, and on that note have you got anyone you are going steady with that we should know about?'

'What? No.'

'You *are* a lesbian aren't you?'

'What the fuck business is that of yours?!'

'Hey. I'm just trying to figure out a way of earning your keep. I have some special clients who could be willing to pay big bucks for some special entertainment, if you know what I mean.'

'What *do* you mean?'

'Well for example, there are some men who consider themselves God's gift to women to the extent that they are convinced they could turn a lesbian straight. All you've have to do is be watched getting it off with one of my other girls and then sleep with one of these men and sound like you've never had it so good.'

Shelley stood there mouth agape at the stupidity of the proposition, but Jerry just stared back. 'I can't do that. Surely they'd realise they were being duped?'

'Not if we tell them you keep asking after them. These people want the fantasy so much they don't care how real it is as long as they get to do what they do.'

'But, I just don't think I can do that. Please, there must be some other way of me earning enough money to clear my debt?'

'Like what?'

'Well I don't know, do I? Or I wouldn't have needed to borrow money in the first place.'

'Okay then, so what I suggest is that you go home now and have a long hard think about your options, then drop by my friend Kirk and let him know what you want to do.'

His letting her think she had a choice was intended to put her off her guard. Zoe debated doing Jerry there and then but sensed there was more to this than met the eye; something she might miss if she just relied on stripping his computer system.

Anyway, once the killing started she liked to get it all done in a short space of time then disappear, and she just knew there would be more than Jerry to deal with in Newcastle. So, with the meeting over, Shelley sighed as Jerry turned his attention back to his desktop, then she span on her heels and left.

When Zoe got back to Shelley's she found that it had been broken into. It would have been Jerry's heavies sent to check her out. They wouldn't have found the money or anything that put her persona into question. Nevertheless, whenever this happened she still felt violated.

What little food she had in the fridge and cupboards had been dumped on the floor. Boxes had been ripped open, bottles smashed, and tins had been emptied. Liquid contents had run under the kickboards. It would take some time to clean up. But that was not the worst thing. Someone had crapped on her bed and then piled all her clothes on top of it. These people were sick.

She knew it was all part of their process of breaking a person, but she smiled inside, these people had no idea who they were trying to break.

'Some vandals broke into my place while I was at Jerry's' Zoe told Kirk.

'Sorry to hear that, Shelley.'

'It's like the whole world hates me right now.'

'But I hear you have potential for something better, and could leave all this behind, if you make the right decision.'

'I don't know that I can do what Jerry wants though Kirk. I've never had to fake feelings like that before.'

'Jerry's girls would show you what is required.'

Zoe sighed and wrung her hands in her lap for good measure. 'I can't think of another way out of this.'

'Just go through with it.'

'I'm thinking of running away.'

'Bad move. Jerry has contacts. They will just find you and bring you back to see what he's like when he's angry.'

Zoe whined in frustration. 'What do I have to do to let Jerry know my choice?'

'There is *no* choice Shelley. Either you do for Jerry whatever he asks, or he will do to you whatever he wants.'

'This is so unfair!'

'Look kid, you've made some dumb mistakes, and now you are paying for them, but look on the bright side, if you play it right it might just turn out fine.'

There was a long pause. Zoe stared at the ground at her feet. The birds seemed to sense her mood and didn't dare go for the seeds lying near her trainers.

'Okay, tell Jerry I agree.'

'Tell him yourself. Go to the same place as before, but be there one-thirty.'

'Lunch-time?'

'*No not lunch-time*, at night.'

The secret tap was answered first time but by a different bouncer who took her to Jerry.

'Shelley,' Jerry greeted her in good humour. 'I'm glad you decided to work off your debt.'

She gave what looked like a forced smile. She was still trying to decide whether to finish this now or wait to see if this could lead her to bigger fish to fry.

'Leona will be along shortly to take you along to our studio where you can take your pick of our girls for your promo video.'

'I…'

'Relax. Have a drink and chill,' he said pouring some liqueur into glasses for both of them.

'It's just that I've not done anything like this before.'

'You'll get shown what to do before any filming begins,' Jerry said, handing her a glass.

'How much *money* do you stand to get from this?' she asked taking a sip of the spirit whilst watching his eyes intently.

'That depends upon the clients,' he answered, his eyes not moving from hers. 'But I doubt you will be able to pay off your debts with the first few.'

'Oh,' she sounded disappointed. 'Well is it going to be *safe*?'

Jerry's eyes didn't even flicker. 'Depends what you mean by safe.'

'Well I don't want to get hurt doing this.'

'Hurt?' he laughed. 'You know what they say, *no pain no gain*.'

'Yes but…' Zoe felt her legs going from under her and felt a rush of panic as she couldn't stop herself falling. As she watched the remains of her drink spill she cursed herself for letting it go this far.

When Zoe began to come round it was to the sound of shouting. She did not recognise the language but she understood the emotion, it was fear. In the dim light she could see bars surrounding her and picking herself up off the floor she looked across to a woman some ten metres away shouting her frustration as she shook the door of her own cage.

'Who are you?' asked Zoe, but she could not understand the woman's response. She clearly did not speak English or she would have done so, unless she was acting.

Then she remembered what Jerry had said about the studio. Could they be being filmed right now? Was she supposed to act terrified too? The fact that there had been no explanation of what was happening suggested they were expected to do whatever came naturally, because they were considered helpless.

Holding to her persona of Shelley Zoe investigated the cage. The bars were too thick to bend. The caging could have secured a couple of tigers. The door locks were operated by swipe-card, and without the appropriate gadgets there was no way of forcing a release ahead of time.

The cages were on what appeared to be a stage, with some box placed midway between them and the stage front. By the dim light of two fire escape signs to the rear of the audience area she could make out a dozen dining tables set for dinner. Was this actually going to be *filmed in front of a live audience*?

Suddenly the stage lighting came on, making the two of them squint while their eyes adjusted. A door to one side of the stage opened and a woman came in. She was dressed very smartly like some big company PA or even an executive.

'What's going on here?' Zoe asked, but her own words were drowned out by the other captive pleading loudly, who she noticed now had wet herself. She raised her own voice for attention. 'When do we get let out of here? I'm dying for the loo!'

'In good time,' the Geordie woman replied with an unnerving smile.

'Who are you?'

'Sandy.'

'I want to speak to Jerry.'

'Jerry's not here.'

'He said I had to do a promo video. Is this the woman I will be doing it with?'

'All in good time my dear.'

'Well we're going to need to get cleaned up.'

'*All in good time*,' she repeated with a firmer tone.

'The woman seems very distressed.'

'Yes she *is*, isn't she,' there was a cold amusement in her voice.

'Shouldn't we do something for her?'

Sandy just moved closer to the foreign woman's cage and watched her plead for mercy. 'It is wonderful how a bit of knowledge can change a person don't you think?'

'What do you mean?'

'She's seen the show before.'

'Show?'

'Don't worry you don't need to have seen it to perform well. Our audiences like their girls straight of the street.'

'I don't understand.'

The foreign woman's demeanour suddenly changed from fear to disgust and she spat in Sandy's face. If the intention of this had been to get Sandy to open the cage up and attempt to strike her, offering a chance of escape, it did not work.

Sandy simply wiped the spittle from her cheek with a smile. She was confidently in control of something that was unlikely to end well.

As if suddenly bored, or remembering she had something important to attend to elsewhere, Sandy turned and left, switching the stage lighting off as she went. Almost immediately that Sandy left, the foreign woman began attempting to explain what she had seen.

She kept pointing at the box on the stage and making a sound like someone who couldn't whistle, hugging herself tightly and shaking her head.

'I'm sorry. I don't know what you are trying to tell me…Just stay calm, I will try and figure out a way of getting out of this.'

Zoe knew she should not have let things go this far. She should have taken Jerry out there and then on the second visit. It wasn't like she needed his money even. Money was just a perk.

The information on his computer and his contacts to add to her kill list should have been enough. Now she was paying for her poor decision, but the disturbing thing was she was getting a thrill from her dilemma. She finally felt that she was being tested by the *unknown* rather than simply reacting to rehearsed scenarios.

She hadn't seen herself as a *normal* person for some years now, and it wasn't really the death of her brother-in-law and then sister that had made her *different*. That had certainly been a major trigger for how she now lived, but she had known there was something different about her long before then, different between her and her twin even, since an early age.

She had spoken of it with Chloe in their childhood but stopped when her sister had said she found Zoe's thoughts of killing disturbingly boyish. Zoe had begun to fantasise about things she would love do to the bad people on TV shows and films if she were the heroine.

As she grew up she had become quite intrigued by different methods of killing. She developed an understanding of the human body's weaknesses; how everyday things could become weapons. It really wasn't about being seen to be a heroine. It was about maintaining anonymity and the taking of life; particular lives. It gave her a rush like nothing else, yet one that barely increased her heart rate. Zoe Innes was a psychopath.

Zoe was drawn back to being Shelley as the lights came on in the dining area and people began to file in. It was being treated as some black-tie event, and as she searched the audience's expressions they saw nothing untoward in having two caged women on stage. She got the distinct feeling it was not the first time these people had seen such a show.

The foreign girl began hurling abuse at them. Some of her words were in English, the most common of which was 'Fuckers!' But the audience only smiled in return, if they appeared to notice at all in their search for their reserved seats.

'Hey!' Zoe added Shelley's voice to the mix, 'This is not an act! We are held against our will. I'm just a student, and I want to go home.'

She was ignored and didn't bother wasting further breath on them, as Zoe watched and waited for her chance.

Once everyone was in and seated light music was played over the sound system and as if on cue waiters and waitresses began serving food and wine. The contrast between what appeared to be a civilised dinner and the misery on stage reeked of moral decay. In acceptance of the sickness of her own soul Zoe knew she was going to enjoy what was to come, *if* she got her own way.

In desperation the foreign woman shouted at the waiters and waitresses, and at times focused on particular couples as they dined, but if anyone understood her language they gave no sign of it. Eventually as coffees were being served the stage lighting came up again and Sandy walked on stage to tumultuous applause.

'Good evening ladies and gentlemen. We have a two act show for you this Saturday night. As promised last night, you will see Rachael perform first, having had a whole night to contemplate how her friend performed so obligingly for us previously.'

Laughter and gasps of appreciation could be heard among the audience.

'That will be followed by a performance from Shelley, who will have only had Rachael's prior performance to inform her own.'

The audience applauded the offered programme, some of them shifting on their seats with eager anticipation.

Two girls came on stage dressed as if they were part of a cabaret act, possibly magician's assistants, and Shelley recognised them as two girls who had been waitressing earlier. She wondered whether this whole performance was an initiation, and would be expected to waitress and assist on stage in days to come. Both girls were dressed in sequined short skirted police-like uniforms and had batons at their sides.

Rachael began to sob at the sight of them, and the hum from the audience was one of approval, as the girls moved to Rachael's cage door. One of them used a card to swipe the lock open as Rachael, still sobbing, attempted to plead with them.

Removing their batons beforehand the girls moved inside. Rachael backed away but there was nowhere to go, she was cornered. Her arms came up in a desperate attempt to defend herself but the first baton jabbed her in the ribs and she buckled over convulsing with an electric flicker and discharge. The second baton went straight to her head and Rachael was put out cold.

She was dragged from her cage to centre stage, in front of the box she had been so worried about. None of this was making sense to Zoe. How could Rachael be expected to perform anything on the box if she had been stunned? Maybe *she* was expected to do something to Rachael while she was in that state. But instead of coming to her cage next the girls headed off stage for a moment and returned with a trolley carrying a barrel, and the audience began to murmur again.

Leaving the trolley to one side the girls removed knives from their belts and expertly cut away Rachael's clothes to reveal her nakedness. She clearly was not expected to be going home in what she had arrived in. Next they returned to the trolley and took the lid off the drum pulling out what looked like gold Lycra footless tights.

With practiced ease they soon had the wet garment slipped onto Rachael, to just under her breasts. Then they returned to the drum and drew out a long sleeved top and pulled that onto Rachael's still limp form down to her hips. As the girls pulled Rachael's long blonde hair out of her polo neck top, Sandy used a remote to lower a chain from a pulley system high above the box.

The girls soon had Rachael's wrists secured in metal handcuffs looped through the end of the chain. Then Sandy was raising Rachel up out of her puddle to a metre over the box, to drip onto its lid. She ran a hand down the wet material from armpit to buttock and turned to her audience, with a big smile.

'Are we *ready*?!'

'YES!!' came the resounding reply.

The two girls removed the lid of the box to place it beside the trolley, and at the click of another button on the remote a motor began to whir, and from the movement of Rachael's hair Zoe guessed the box contained a fan.

The audience cheered as Rachael began to come round and realised where she was. The cheering brought adrenalin, and with it began her struggling. Zoe expected the girls to add to her torment with the batons but instead they moved off the stage taking the trolley and lid with them, leaving Zoe and everyone else to watch.

Considering that Rachael was only being hung out to dry she was putting up a fearful struggle, which could only mean she knew there was worse to come.

The air of the fan must have been cold because her nipples could be seen hardening beneath the thin suit which was beginning to cling to her like a second skin. She swung backwards and forwards and in one mighty effort got her legs up above her head and wrapped around the chain, then with sheer muscle power that she didn't look capable of Rachael began pulling herself up the chain, upside-down and away from the fan. It was like some sort of circus act she had been trained to perform.

Half way up Rachael began to weaken. Nevertheless, she spurred herself on with a few more choice insults for the audience, but then she slipped, and came down with such force that she dislocated her shoulders and brutally damaged her wrists in their cuffs.

'Stop struggling Rachael!' Zoe advised, but couldn't be heard over Rachael's screams of agony. Waiting for the screaming to die down she said it again. 'Stop struggling Rachael!'

Rachael was reduced to incoherent mumbling, but not for long, she began moaning and then crying with renewed pain that enthralled the audience and brought about a mixture of lip-biting and smiling with delight. Rachael's cries became screams of agony with intermittent gasping as if she was having a panic attack.

Zoe couldn't work out what was going on till she noticed Rachael's ankles were swelling up as well as her wrists. The material of the suit was being dried out by the fan and as it dried it was shrinking. They had put her in what could only be described as a constriction suit. Zoe began to bang on her bars.

'Hey! She needs to be taken down *now*. This isn't right! Quickly the suit is getting too tight! It could kill her!' But with that it became clear that this *was* what the audience had paid for, to watch someone die before their very eyes, a slow and painful death, for them to get off on, in their black-tie suits and evening dresses.

What could Zoe do? She felt powerless to interfere. She could not reason with anyone, she could not get out of the cage, and they had left her with nothing that she could use to save the dying woman. Zoe would just have to use Rachael's death to her advantage.

Shelley began to sob and plead for Rachael to be freed, but inside Zoe was plotting and her dry eyes were the only clue as to what was really going on.

As Rachael's feet, hands and face ballooned, turning purple, and her final wailing ended with a seizure. The audience applauded, and on cue the uniformed girls returned this time with an empty trolley. One of them discharged her baton on Rachael's left foot but there was only the natural cramping response of recently dead muscle in the leg.

Sandy shut down the fan and lowered Rachael so the girls could remove the cuffs and load the body on the trolley. As they left Sandy turned her attention back to the audience.

'I hope you enjoyed that as much as I did. I particularly liked her desperate attempt to escape the drier by climbing the chain. I hope our next girl has been taking notes and comes up with something even more entertaining to prolong the constriction.'

The audience cheered for Shelley as if to encourage her to go one better, not knowing that they might soon to be in for a nasty surprise. Opening Shelley's cage would be their Pandora's Box. In the cage appeared to be a frightened student, but what would come out was Zoe Innes.

The uniformed girls returned with another trolley containing a barrel with a second constriction suit. Leaving it by the fan they walked over to Shelley's cage door and swiped it open, their batons at the ready.

'Please don't. No, don't do this.' Shelley begged as they entered looking to corner her, but instead of her backing off as others had done she was upon them, but not in a desperate frenzied motion, but a lethally fluid attack. They hesitated as they looked into her dry eyes and saw a terrible darkness.

Zoe struck the first baton aside and moved inside of the second for a close quarters kill. Her left elbow ploughed into the throat of the girl to the left, collapsing the cartilage there and leaving her to fall forwards choking. Using the impact to pull back slightly and thrust then with her right hand, continuing its motion from the baton block she delivered a closed fingers strike under the other girl's jaw stunning her and allowing her to be turned in a spin as the same fingers went on to grip the girl's left ear.

The pull on the left ear coupled with a palm-heel strike behind the right ear was delivered with such speed and force that it snapped the neck. But the motion did not stop there as the lifeless body fell it was twisted further to present the waist belt, and its knife.

It was all happening so fast Sandy was having difficulty believing what she was seeing never mind remembering the drill for such an unlikely event. She turned away to shout for security but only got the first syllable out as the thrown knife bit deep into the back of the neck and dropped her over the stage and into the now screaming audience.

Zoe was working to the principle of destroying the command structure from the top of the pyramid down, if indeed Sandy had been the top, and not simply the entertainment host. Wasting no time and leaving no live enemy behind she snapped the gurgling girl's neck with a stamp kick, unfastened her belt, put it on and left with the second baton in hand.

As she moved to the edge of the stage to where Sandy had fallen, she saw the panicked audience were now heading towards the double doors at the back of the room.

A hefty security guard entered in response to the disturbance through one of the double doors. He was stunned by the crowd rushing towards him. It was sensory overload. He had never been trained for this, so he never spotted the flying knife before it planted itself in his forehead. He went down like a sack of potatoes against the door closing it and effectively blocking the double doors. The crowd could not move him out of their way, not just because of his weight but because of other people pushing against them from behind, which added to the panic.

Zoe removed the knife from Sandy and wiped the blood on the back of her suit jacket before frisking her. She did not find a gun but did find a key-card. Quickly she got back on the stage with the intention of locking the stage doors.

However, as she got to the first door two security men came at her, with batons of their own, only to discover that she was faster. Striking their batons aside and stunning them with her own they had barely hit the ground before their throats were slit.

Twice in quick succession the reacquired blade entered below a left ear, severing the jugular before drawing the blade backwards and round to sever the right jugular and exit leaving each wind pipe to gasp and choke on the fountains of blood.

Zoe used the two dying bodies to block the door. Before she frisked them she wiped what she could of their blood from her hands to improve her grip on weapons.

The blood now soaking into her clothes would be dealt with later. Finding a hand gun, key-card and radio on each of them she ran for the door on the other side, opened it with Sandy's card and stepped into a corridor. As she pulled the door shut behind her she used her heel to smash the swipe unit loose. It didn't spark like they always did in the movies but it was certainly no longer operational.

Running down the corridor, gun in each hand, safeties off and rounds chambered she arrived at the double doors just as two more security men were attempting to help open the doors against the mass of panicked bodies on the other side. However, it was a losing battle as Zoe delivered two head shots, pulled the doors closed and smashed the swipe unit there too.

This time she took their cards and just their weapon cartridges but smashed the radios before moving on. What she was looking for was the security control centre. She needed everyone dead and any record of her presence here removed.

The challenge was to achieve all of this blind, as she had no idea where she was, never mind the layout of the building or how many people she was up against. The only point in her favour was that the people here so far seemed poorly trained. A weapon was fired however, and the round did pass all too close to her head. She rolled aside, turning to face the direction of fire, raising her own weapons.

Four security personnel had run inside from patrolling the grounds in response to a code red on their radios. Although one of them got a shot off at the person crouched by two dead colleagues, two closer colleagues were felled by double taps before the remaining two could take cover in the curve of a circular stairwell.

Zoe was expected to dodge to one side to find better cover, but at the sound of her footfalls not going in the expected direction one of the guards took a quick look. The last thing the guard saw before his brain matter covered the female colleague behind him was Zoe sprinting towards them.

The woman who remained was the one who had fired the first shot that missed, and now she was wondering what she had got herself into here.

From the cover of the stairwell she fired blindly round the corner in the direction she expected the woman to be coming. The shots were deafening in the stairwell until she began clicking on an empty chamber. She listened but there was no sound of the woman only the ringing in her ears. She hoped she had killed her, but no such luck she looked up and was shot dead from the stairs above.

Zoe searched the bodies and stocked up on ammunition and security cards before smashing radios and continuing up the stairs. Halfway up Zoe saw through the windows a number of mean looking German Sheppard guard dogs outside, caught in security lighting listening to the commotion inside and clearly frantic for a piece of the action.

Then Zoe's attention was drawn away by the sound of the radios she had taken.

'The intruder is coming upstairs now.'

'Intruder? *You* bloody brought me here,' she pointed out under her breath. Clearly she was on CCTV and had to find the security control centre quickly to blind it and hamper communications. She also needed to know how many more security personnel there were, and the layout of this place.

'She appears to have at least one of our radios,' the voice continued. 'Do not state position when reporting in…Oh and she is now armed. If you are presently unarmed report here immediately before attempting to engage.'

'So I should track staff to the control centre. Thanks for the advice.' Zoe heard movement on the floor above and raced up the remainder of the steps. The landing led to corridors to the left and right. The running sounded to be receding to the left so she followed at a sprint. The corridor seemed to be full of bedrooms, going by the numbers on the doors. In a perfectly planned operation she would have been looking to clear every room before moving on, but that would not work in this scenario. She would have to watch her back as she attempted to make it to the control centre.

Running as quietly as she could in her trainers she turned a corner and saw a figure turning another corner. Then as she closed in Zoe heard the person stop running.

'Reg, it's me Mary.'

Reg had already been waiting for Mary having seen her coming on his screens, and knew Zoe was close behind. He whipped open the door and grabbed Mary to pull her inside and close the door. However their momentums were turned against them as Zoe bundled them both inside.

Mary screamed as she got Reg's boot in her face as they both sprawled onto the floor. Reg turned on his back raising hands in surrender. He had already seen how dangerous Zoe was.

'Don't shoot. Don't shoot!'

Zoe kicked the door closed behind her and scanned the room whilst pointing both weapons at her targets.

'Please, I have children.' Mary pleaded.

'Maybe you should have thought of *them* before you got into this line of work,' Zoe retorted. 'When are the police due to turn up?'

'Police?'

'You *have* called the police?' she asked in the hope of tricking the guard into volunteering information about their actual procedures, since they had appeared unprofessional enough to make such a slip a possibility.

'Are you kidding lady? The boss doesn't want police anywhere near hear.'

'Sandy?'

'No.'

'Jerry?'

'Who?'

'Okay who are we talking about here?'

Reg and Mary looked at one another knowingly but said nothing.

Zoe didn't really need to know just yet, she was just holding their attention while she watched the screens behind them. The audience had managed to get out of the dining area and attempted to leave for their cars via the front doors, but as Zoe watched they were met by the vicious dogs.

One man had his leg severely bitten before he was dragged back inside, with the dog still attached until it was beaten senseless with a candlestick and then dispatched with a rather blunt axe from an ornamental suit of armour.

One man had not sought to leave though. He went and checked out each of the dead guards first, possibly in the hope of arming himself. No luck there, Zoe smiled as he headed upstairs, but on the landing he turned right.

As Zoe continued to watch the man went to a room and then she lost sight of him. There was no coverage of that room.

Seeing that Zoe appeared engrossed with the screens Reg thought this was his chance and made to jump at her. She seemed to shoot without looking and the double tap put him back to the floor. Mary screamed certain now that she would be next.

The man who had vanished from the CCTV quickly reappeared, armed with a pump-action shotgun. As he crossed the landing Zoe noticed a female guard on another screen who was down stairs, then her attention was drawn back to the man with the shotgun. He held a swipe card and a radio.

'Where is she now?' his voice came over Reg and Mary's radio's as well as the console and it was clear that he was heading for the control centre.

Zoe moved fast.

The lack of response was all the information the man thought he needed, and when he arrived at the control centre door and swiped the card reader, he flipped the handle down with his left hand, kicked the door open with his right foot then levelled the shotgun. He moved out from the cover of the door frame to target Shelley, but he didn't see her. She wasn't beside the door, and she wasn't behind it. He span wildly in frustration. She had vanished into thin air. He even thought to look up at the high ceiling.

Looking back down at the scene on the floor he noted the chest and head shots Reg had taken but his attention was drawn to the sight of

Mary writhing on the carpet gurgling as she raked at her neck. He leaned in for a closer look and realised what he was looking at was a plastic zip-lock tie. He seemed amused that she was unable to release the ratchet and reached for the protruding strip.

'Mary, Mary, what have I been wasting my money on you people for?' and with that question he yanked hard on the tie, ratcheting it as tight as it would go.

His enjoyment of Mary's confused and horrified expression, as she struggled through her final few seconds of strangulation, did not last up to her limb flailing end. He found himself dropping the shotgun and collapsing into his own hell instead.

Zoe had silently re-entered the control centre from a neighbouring room just as the man, who she now believed might be the boss, was distracted by Mary's predicament. With a hard slash of her knife Zoe hamstrung both of his legs. But even in his agony he tried to fight, twisting and trying to reach for his dropped weapon.

Zoe trod on his outstretched forearm and picked up his gun as his right hand grabbed her ankle. The shotgun blasted the flesh and much of the bone away from his trapped left hand, raising the pitch of his screaming and bringing additional expletives into play.

'Now…are you going to tell me who *you* work for?'

He didn't deny that he worked for someone higher, but then he might have been too busy with his pain management. Time would tell.

'How about the password to your computer system then?' she prompted. 'Or would you rather I put a stop your *wanking*?'

'Go fuck yourself!' he rasped through gritted teeth.

Zoe kicked him hard in the chest and pumped a fresh round into the chamber, and as his right arm went out to balance him she stepped over him and stood on that forearm. 'Oh have it your own way.' She blasted his remaining hand.

Blinking against the pain and blood loss, close to passing out, his screams dying to whimpers, he watched Zoe reach into her blouse.

'One for me,' she announced as if sharing treats, removing a USB4 stick from the centre rib of her bra where the underside of the cups met, proceeding to slide her hacker-program into a computer port to let it do its thing, 'and one for you.'

Zoe removed another zip-lock tie from her bra and the man knowing what this meant attempted to shuffle himself backwards on his bottom with his bloodied stumps, dragging his useless legs behind him, towards the still open door. Zoe came after him slowly, twanging the tie between her clenched fists, knowing there was no need to use it other than to threaten with.

'No worries, my device will soon have access to all of your system and I'll be able to sift through all of your dealings at my leisure,' she laughed.

In his attempt to avoid death, leaving a thick trail of blood behind him, the nameless boss almost made it all of the way out of the door before he lost consciousness and collapsed to bleed out fully where he dropped.

Slipping the plastic tie back into the channel in her bra as Zoe returned to the computer to check progress. She noted that the one remaining security guard was still searching around downstairs and kept looking through the windows. Since she was not using her radio Zoe couldn't be sure whether she was looking for her or someone else, or maybe considering where to hide or run to, since the dogs were still loose.

She would have heard the shots upstairs, and with no further radio support would surely have concluded Zoe's present whereabouts, as it did for her boss. Nevertheless, the guard made no attempt to come upstairs to confront her.

The stick had given Zoe system-managers access rights to the security and files, and quickly she checked out the building schematics and other data to plan her next move.

The group of guests still gathered in the foyer were frantic by this point. This evening's misery was not what they had paid for, and now they were beginning to argue amongst themselves as to what to do about getting away.

Some guests had left their car keys in their rooms but there was no great urge to go get them with that Shelley girl up there. Anyway, none actually felt they would fare any better than the man who *had* attempted to get to his car only to be met by the vicious dogs.

They all agreed this event had been appallingly mismanaged and would be demanding reimbursement.

Shots and screams had come from upstairs a while ago and there had since been no sign of security which begged the questions, had they all been killed now? And what was going to happen to *them*?

The guests had been annoyed that there was a phone signal blocker somewhere on the premises making any attempts to organise outside aid impossible. They also had no idea where it would be transmitting from, to switch it off.

They began suggesting and discussing other solutions to their dilemma. Someone suggested that they head for the kitchens and a possible back exit, as long as there were no dogs there. After a short discussion and agreement to stick together, some people armed themselves with whatever was at hand and they all headed away from the foyer. A short way down the corridor to the right, in search of the kitchens, they ran into a security guard and came to a halt, promptly demanding that she switch off the phone signal blocker.

She didn't respond immediately, watching the last of the guests pressing down the corridor towards her, urgently looking to her with hope as a figure of authority. 'Sorry folks. I don't know where that is, we don't all get the same security clearance.'

'What nonsense,' groaned one exasperated man, 'I trust you *can* at least get the dogs back into their kennels?'

'Sorry no.'

The guests moaned their disappointment.

'Only the dog handlers can do that. Those things would go for me just as they would any of you.'

'Well where are these bloody handlers?!' asked one angry man.

'That crazy woman shot them all sir.'

'Damn it!'

'And I believe she will have destroyed the communications centre too, so we can't call out from up there either.'

'Fuck!...Have you been up there to check?'

'No sir. That would be suicide.'

'You're armed, and it's what you are paid for,' said one woman crossly.

'Sorry, maybe it escaped your notice, but the four dog handlers were armed too,' the guards tone was one of sarcasm now.

'So what do you suggest we do to get out of here?'

'I have an idea.'

'Go on.'

'It involves bringing the dogs inside.'

'*Inside*? Are you mad?!'

'That way we can trap them and then get away. However, I am working on the assumption that each dog will first attempt to get back to their handler rather than look to attack. I could be wrong I don't have a better idea. If we go back to the hallway we can drag each handler's body through the foyer and into the storeroom. Then if everyone waits back inside the dining hall with the doors closed, I will attempt to open a front door hiding behind it and when the dogs run into the storeroom I'll lock them in, and...'

'Forgive me,' a cynical older woman interrupted. 'But my instincts tell me you will fail, and then what do we do? You'll get savaged and *we* will be trapped in the dining room.'

'Why don't we just continue on to the kitchen like we were doing,' a voice from the back suggested. 'Is there a back way out?'

'There is,' confirmed the guard. 'I already tried that, with a view to going for help, but the dogs came racing round the side of the building. Their hearing must be very good. I only just got back inside in time.'

'Can't you just shoot the *fuckers*?' someone pleaded.

'Oh...Okay.'

Brad Coulson was Ex-Navy Seal. He had been working the domestic security market freelancing in the USA a number of years before deciding to try the UK market. He had received a code red call-out from a new client in his area of the Northumberland borders half an hour ago, and now faced a high electric fence.

He had attempted to call the client on the landline a few minutes ago but there had been no response to open the gate never mind cutting the power to the fence. It must have been serious for him to be called out, but he now had to assume that a more serious scenario had taken place inside.

Crouching quietly listening and watching with his night vision goggles Brad could see the guard dogs were out and barking at the building, and he heard gunshots which suggested hostiles were inside.

Turning his head to one side then the other, looking along the fence from the cover of the trees it did not surprise him that there was trouble. The general quality of security service provision in the UK had actually gone down since the late teens. Its destabilising society had increased the demand faster than it could supply the required experienced personnel. This was why he had moved to the UK. This country had a way to go to catch up with US patrol and protection services, which meant plenty of opportunity for the likes of him with his skills.

Once he saw that the dogs had move round to the other side of the building Brad was over the electric fence in under a minute by climbing a tree trunk going out on a bough and dropping down to a paratrooper roll in the grass. He had told the client to cut the trees back but clearly had not been listened to. Nevertheless, it had made this evening's job a little easier for him.

Up and sprinting across the lawn, he kept scanning for trouble as he aimed for a drain pipe which would take him to the roof. He needed to get inside without drawing attention to his entry. The layout of the building and grounds were well remembered from his previous visits.

Up on the roof he located the skylight that he had a key for. Putting his night vision goggles into his backpack he then looked through the glass to check for any signs of life inside, but seeing nothing in the corridor below, he unlocked the keypad box. There should have been a low warning beep for the ten seconds delay on the main alarm for him to input the entry code but there was no sound. Tapping in the digits he considered the main security system may have been compromised.

This was confirmed when having entered the corridor and moved straight to the security control centre he saw a body in a pool of blood in the doorway even before he got to look inside.

'Coltsworth,' he whispered the name of the dead manager before looking into the dark room. The CCTV screens and computer monitors were all dead, as were two security guards.

Turning the lights on Brad checked the guards closer. The man had been killed by a double tap, so the killer or killers appeared to be professional. The woman had been strangled by a cord or something which had been removed. Brad looked back at Coltsworth and his injuries and decided the two guards had been shown mercy in comparison, which suggested that some personal motivation was involved here.

He tried to reboot the computer but it just brought up a *disc not found* error message. The system had been erased, or worse stripped. His client was not going to be happy about this. He needed to find out more if he could, then get this mess cleaned up. Moving out into the corridor, stepping over the body and turning right he headed for the landing by the main stairs. He heard nothing but the dogs barking round the back of the building. Either the intruders had detected his presence and were now keeping quiet, or they had already left having got what they came for. It seemed feasible that the attack could have been by a team of people representing the client's competition.

As he neared the stairs he saw a security guard looking out of the window. She caught his reflection in the window and turned. 'Coulson, thank God, I thought you weren't coming.'

'Where are the intruders?'

'I don't know…gone maybe.'

'How many?'

'I heard it was one of the entertainment.'

'Entertainment?'

'Yes you know, the girls that Sandy has tortured and killed for the guests.'

'Where are the guests now?'

'I…They…are all dead.'

'*All* dead? How many? Where?' he asked as he came down the steps.

'There must be a couple of dozen, dead in the corridor. It looks like they were trying to get to the kitchens.'

'Where were you when this was happening?'

'I was looking out for you like Coltsworth told me to…When I came to check things out after all the gunfire had finished they were all lying there dead.'

'This rogue *entertainment*… How did she manage to escape? She must have had inside help. Show me what happened.'

'I wasn't there when it happened, but I can take you to the dining room and stage to look for yourself.' She led him down the stairs, and across the foyer.

Brad noted the four dead guards at the bottom of the stairs and the dead dog. There were also the two guards to one side of the double doors to the dining room, and the one just inside. Heading across to the stage Brad saw Sandy and then her two dead assistants in one of the cages as he got onto the stage. He also noted a further two guards with their throats slit propped up against a stage door.

'One person did all this?'

'Yes.'

'All I can think is this person was a plant. Someone who had inside information at the very least, someone who knows how you operate. This sort of thing just doesn't happen by chance.'

'I don't know. It's all kind of *freaky*. It makes me question whether this isn't our comeuppance for being in this business.'

'You can't afford to get all moralistic in this profession. If *you* don't take the job someone else will. You are either in or you're out.' He suddenly drew his gun on the guard, but her reactions were very fast and there was no flicker of surprise on her face as she brought her own weapon to bear on him.

'How long have you known?' she asked.

'Since you turned on the stairs, and I saw your face.'

'Makes sense,' she nodded.

'I have been introduced to all the staff.'

'So why didn't you shoot me on the stairs?'

'I needed to find out what I could first, and I decided the best way to do that was play along.'

Zoe nodded again.

'So why haven't *you* shot me?' he asked.

'Likewise, I needed to see how much you knew and what your take was on all this.'

'*My take*? It's just a job, though it is for a particularly powerful client, and I do intend to honour my contractual agreement with her…So who do you work for?'

'I don't. It's not about the money…You see I enjoy the…' Zoe pulled the trigger.

Seeing Zoe's finger tense Brad was faster and dodged. Her round managed to clip his broad shoulder. He fired his own weapon as he rolled away.

Brads first round whistled past Zoe's neck as she ducked down. Her legs span towards Brad rather than away and his second round caught her in the left side as her torso twisted away to deliver a kick to his gun hand which knocked the weapon skittering off the stage. Brad wasted no time scrabbling after his lost weapon. He brought his boot up fast and hard into Zoe's groin.

Zoe's gun was lining up with Brad's head but with the combination of the round to the side and the blow between the legs she found herself falling forwards with insufficient control. Brad grabbed her wrist and twisted it aside. The weapon discharged uselessly into the floor as he punched her face.

Zoe turned her head to lessen the impact, using the same motion to reach behind her for her back-up weapon. It wasn't there. It must have fallen out when she ducked and twisted. In the time it took her brain to catch up and her head to turn and face Brad again he had twisted her wrist back on itself forcing her forearm round and down wrenching her muscles and joints as he pointed her weapon at her head.

Instead of pulling away or aside she struck with her head, past the gun, to crush Brad's nose with a vicious head-butt. Her gun fired into the ceiling leaving her left ear ringing. Then gun was being released as Brad screamed under the blinding pain of his nose plus the deep bite to the hand that gripped Zoe's gun hand. This woman did not fight fair.

Zoe was seeing her own stars. Brad was faster than most opponents. He delivered a stunning blow to the side of her head with his left fist. She fought to remain conscious, bringing the muzzle of her weapon to his eye socket and pulling the trigger. She couldn't believe it, she was out, and cursed herself for not checking that the spare magazine she had put in was full.

Brad's left hand gripped Zoe by the throat and began to crush with such force that it was debatable whether he would strangle her or simply break her neck.

Everything had come down to touch now as he was blinded by his own blood. He could feel Zoe's fingers at his own neck rather than her own and he almost laughed at her imminent defeat. She seemed to be capable of little more than trying to tickle him to death.

Then his throat was in pain from what felt like a garrotte, and hands and knees were pushing on his chest to break his grip on her throat. He squeezed and squeezed and then blacked out.

Coughing and spluttering, rubbing her bruised neck, Zoe rolled away.

'Fuck!' she croaked. 'Serves you right for playing games I suppose.'

Getting to her knees she rubbed her side. She knew she would be bruised there too, but was thankful for the bulletproof vest she had taken from the control centre.

Picking up her dropped gun which she found next to the box with the fan she moved back to Brad's still form, looked at the zip-lock tie which had bitten deep into his neck and fired a single round into his dying brain, taking no further chances.

Then with a release tool she also had hidden in her bra she pressed it into the ratchet head and released the tie from his neck, as she had from others. She wanted to be able to use these again and didn't want to leave them like a calling card. Nevertheless, she knew it was only a question of time before some overworked forensic team identified her from genetic material traces left behind in her many crime scenes. She just wanted to see how many more of the *bad guys* she could take down before her game was over.

People would not come to investigate this place for maybe a couple of days Zoe reckoned. Nevertheless, Zoe wanted to pay someone a visit a little later this Sunday morning, so got on with what needed doing.

First she turned Brad's body over and removed his back pack and looked through its contents. Then she frisked him for ID and took his watch. After that she went to the kitchens. Stepping around and over the dead kitchen staff Zoe looked through a number of draws until she found what she was looking for, zip-seal freezer bags. Her next task was to remove and bag separately all staff and guest's ID, keys, wallets and other valuables. She would be very busy over the next few days, making a series of exciting home visits.

Then she picked a guest room at random removed the uniform she had taken from the last guard she had killed and showered off the blood and grime she had accumulated in the last couple of hours.

Feeling refreshed, but eager to press on with her plans Zoe moved from room to room naked, till she found clothes that fit her in a guest wardrobe. Then it was time to pack up and leave.

With her own blood stained clothes wrapped in a bin bag now secure in a guest's Samsonite suitcase, along with all the possessions she had looted she soon stood at the front door. The looting always served two purposes, it could make the crime scene look like an organised robbery, but most important to Zoe it often provided information on future targets.

Opening the front doors she could see no dogs, but was not prepared to believe they had got bored and gone to sleep. She hurled the case crashing down the steps and whistled for good measure. The dogs came running and she ducked behind the open door. As the three dogs rushed in she stepped out and locked them inside.

They would have more than enough food in there till someone came to try and find out what went down here. She just hoped they didn't get put down for developing a taste for human meat.

Zoe had already decided how she intended to leave when she had removed a Lamborghini key fob from one of the female guests, and was soon driving away from the old hall having made sure to lock the front gates behind her.

The two bouncers watched through dead eyes where they had been left slumped in Jerry's office as Zoe stood in a puddle of salty water loading money from his safe into her pack.

Once the safe was emptied she closed its door then swung up the coral reef diorama cover. Then she went to the desk and removed her stick from the now hacked dead computer.

Coming round to the shelving and reaching behind a book on marine aquariums she pressed a button which raised the tank out of its pedestal back up in front of its diorama image. In the glass she looked at the faint reflection of her bruised face. So much for her zero-injury policy, she would have to try and take more care in future.

However, for now she was done playing shark bait, she had bigger fish to fry with her rather extensive contact list of do-badders. At least she had come out of this better off than her victims.

Jerry's battered form floated face down in his aquarium like a turf war message. 'Just thought I'd help you feed the fish Jerry,' Zoe quipped. 'Now I'm off to help Kirk feed the birds.'

**Other titles by
Kevin H. Hilton**

Breakfast's in Bed

Dark Net

Imogen Powers Trilogy:

Possession

Afterlife

Singularity

Printed in Great Britain
by Amazon